Unforgivable

BLUE SAFFIRE

Perceptive Illusions Publishing
Bayshore, New York

Copyright © 2026 by Blue Saffire.

All rights reserved. No part of this publication may be reproduced, distributed or transmitted in any form or by any means, including photocopying, recording, or other electronic or mechanical methods, without the prior written permission of the publisher, except in the case of brief quotations embodied in critical reviews and certain other noncommercial uses permitted by copyright law. For permission requests, write to the publisher, addressed "Attention: Permissions Coordinator," at the address below.

Blue Saffire/Perceptive Illusions Publishing Inc.
PO BOX 5253
Bayshore, NY 11706
www.BlueSaffire.com

Publisher's Note: This is a work of fiction. Names, characters, places, and incidents are a product of the author's imagination. Locales and public names are sometimes used for atmospheric purposes. Any resemblance to actual people, living or dead, or to businesses, companies, events, institutions, or locales is completely coincidental.

Ordering Information:
Quantity sales. Special discounts are available on quantity purchases by corporations, associations, and others. For details, contact the "Special Sales Department" at the address above.

Unforgivable/ Blue Saffire. -- 1st ed.
ISBN 978-1-941924-41-9

True love is never forgotten. However, betrayal changes everything.

–BLUE SAFFIRE

PREFACE

Let It Burn

Rico

"Fuck," I mutter as shots fire, alerting everyone to our presence. I had hoped we could at least get off the grounds before we or the fire were noticed. We've only made it to the back door we need to exit through.

I rush out the doorway and dart by the pool to find cover behind the thick Roman pillars in the backyard. My cousins Eduardo and Aldo are hot on my heels. Eduardo brings up the rear as he covers us. Then the two take the lead and rush up ahead as they continue to return fire.

Pop Pop Pop.

I duck behind the wall with Oni in my arms as shots continue to ring out in our direction. Two bullets hit the pillar above our heads and debris falls down around us. I look down at her gorgeous brown face as she lies unconscious, and murderous rage fills me.

"What have they done to you, baby?"

I'm going to get her out of here. I need to get her to safety. I can't lose her now, not again.

Not after all I've done. All of this is for her; everything I've done has been for her. I glance up as my cousin Eduardo calls my name.

He was the last out of the house they had Oni held hostage in. These fuckers thought they could take what belongs to me—over my dead fucking body.

Anyone who dares to touch what belongs to Federico Gallo Jr. learns their lesson. I'm the last motherfucker you want to fuck with. I don't have the conscience to think twice.

Especially when it comes to this woman in my arms. I'm insane for Oni, always have been. Ruthless is who I was before her. Utter destruction is who I am now.

"I have you covered. Let's go," Eduardo yells over the gunfire.

Quickly, I glance behind me and see the mansion burning down. Baring my teeth, I work my jaw. For what they've done, I hope those fuckers burn with it.

I'm just getting started when it comes to my wrath. When the dust settles, everyone will understand the message I plan to send. They will all pay.

"Hold on, baby. I'm going to get you home," I mutter as I turn back to Oni and kiss her temple.

More shots sound, causing me to look up. Eduardo jerks back as he takes a hit to the shoulder. I grind my teeth as his brother Aldo appears, guns blazing. My other cousin catches the guy in the head who shot Eduardo.

"I've got you. Come on," Aldo growls.

I reposition Oni in my arms and make my move. I make it to Aldo, who's helping a bleeding Eduardo as I'm hit in the leg. I stumble forward but tighten my hold on Oni.

"Fuck, man. You're hit," Aldo says as he turns to me.

Way to state the obvious. I want to growl the words at him, but I know he's just worried about me and Oni. My cousins are putting their lives on the line for the woman I love. I could never repay them for that.

"I'm fine. Get him in the car. We need to be on the move. We're running out of time," I bite out.

He grunts and helps Eduardo into the front passenger seat, then opens the back door for me as I let off a few shots of my own. "I'll drive. Get in," he commands. I take out two more guys before turning my focus back to getting into the vehicle.

A bullet whizzes by my head and shatters the window of the open back door. I wave Aldo off as he tries to move to help me. He starts to round the vehicle to follow my orders.

I go to climb into the back seat of the SUV with Oni in my embrace. Suddenly, I fall forward and begin to lose focus as I'm hit again. I've managed to cradle my body around hers.

"Son of a bitch," Aldo bellows.

I can hear him moving around to get me in the vehicle and close the door behind me. My back burns something awful. However, I grind my teeth against the pain and try to focus on Oni.

I groan as I push up off her and look her body over. She's covered in blood, but I think it's all mine. She's still unconscious.

If the motherfucker who did this isn't already dead, I'm going to treat his ass to an acid embalming while he's still breathing. Those responsible will pay. I already have a list.

Pain rocks through me and I have to fall back into the seat. No matter how hard I try, I'm losing consciousness.

Shit, this can't be happening. I have her back. I'm almost at the top. One more play and there's nothing else in my way.

How can I, Rico Gallo, lose now? I've fought too hard to have her. We've been through too much.

For years, something or another has tried to keep us apart. This was my final straw. I went to war for her, and this is my result? It can't be.

Everything begins to flash before my eyes. The first time I saw her. Our first kiss.

The moment I knew I loved her and would do anything to have her in my life. The ultimatum I was given to try to take her from me. The way she fought for me like no one else would.

Oni deserves to be by my side. No one else. There isn't a person in this world who has loved me more than she has. This is the reason they want to take her from me.

I'm stronger with her. There was a time that if you told me that, I would have told you to *get the fuck outta here*. I'm my own man.

However, truth is … she makes me a better man. I begin to hear her voice in my head. Something tells me that ain't good. I can't open my lids at this point.

"Rico, do you love me?" she says.

"Yes, baby. You know I do. I have loved you since the first time I laid eyes on you," I reply.

"Then prove it."

"Prove it how, my angel?"

"You don't get to leave me. They don't get to win."

My job was to get to my woman. Get her out of that hellhole. Then get her home where she can heal, and I can love her.

How the fuck did I fail? I had one job, one job only. Don't die.

Oni

I feel like I'm floating underwater. Although I feel like I'm lying on soft clouds, my body aches. My head is pounding, and I can't find the energy to open my eyes.

I get the feeling when I do, I'm not going to be safe. Bad things are waiting. I've been holding on for so long.

That much I know. I've been waiting on something or someone. What or who, I can't remember.

Frustrated, I try to remember what's going on. Where am I and why haven't they come yet—whoever they are? I try to push at the surface of my consciousness one more time.

I'm a fighter. I can't give up. I have reasons to survive.

What those reasons are, I can't figure out through this fog. However, I know I have something important to survive for.

Survive. I'm a survivor. I've always had to survive, and I always find a way to.

I've got it out the mud before, right? Ugh, my thoughts are right there. He will come for me.

Who is he? Why don't I feel fully confident that he will? Something happened and he might not find me.

What happened? Think. You have to think.

Let's start with the basics. Yeah, that's a good idea. Who am I?

Oni Raven. Yes, that sounds right. I'm Oni Raven.

How old am I? Thirty? No, thirty-one.

Okay, good. I'm thirty-one, but sixteen is ringing in my mind as if it's important as well. I push that nagging thought back.

I know I'm thirty-one and that was the question. I want to stick to facts that can help me figure out what's happening to me now. *What happened to you, Oni?*

Hazel-gray eyes pop into my head. It's him. He's who I'm waiting for.

I grab ahold of those eyes and try to figure out who he is. I love the man those eyes belong to. I have for a very long time.

His face begins to become clearer as his dark hair fills my thoughts. I remember running my hands through those dark locks more times than I can count. I've seen it in many styles before.

Those fleshy lips. I've kissed those lips before. I know the way they feel and how they taste.

I love the voice that comes from them. It's warm and deep and brings me so much comfort. When he speaks, my entire body tingles.

What happened to take him away from me? He keeps me safe, so what has happened? Where is Rico?

Rico! Oh my God. His name is Rico, and he always protects me. He has been my protector since the first time we met.

I try to remember how we met, but my head begins to hurt more. I try to reach out for the memories and push past the pain. I have something to tell him, something he needs to know, but first I need to remember who he is to me and why we've been apart.

That feels really important. Rico is a safe place for me … I think. Or I could be wrong?

I'm hurt and he's not here. Why? I want him here. I need him here.

Why can't I remember? I try harder even as my head hurts. Finally, I grasp a small memory.

"I've found you, bitch. This time, nothing will save you. You have nowhere else to run. With you out of the way, I will finally get what I deserve.

"Knock her out. Fucking nuisance. What does he see in her?"

I was kidnapped, but where was Rico? Where were my men? I am Oni Raven.

Oni Raven is that bitch. I'm that deal, so how am I here? Where is my man?

Another memory comes as the other fades. I grab ahold of it and force my focus on it. Maybe this one will be another clue.

I'm standing in a room with Rico. He's holding me close as he nuzzles my neck. I savor the feel of his beard against my skin.

"I only want to see you happy, Oni. I wish you would talk to me and tell me what's going on. Is it my family? Has someone done something to you?

"No, Rico. I'm fine," I murmured.

He pulled back and pinched my chin between his fingertips, lifting my gaze to his. Searching my eyes with his gorgeous hazel-gray ones, he inhaled deeply. Guilt filled me, but I didn't say a word.

"You would tell me if someone was fucking with you, right?"

"Yes. I would, but I would handle it myself if they were. I'm fine, Rico. I promise no one is bothering me."

He brushed his thumb against my lip. I held my breath as he leaned in to kiss me. The moment his lips crushed mine, I felt like everything would be okay.

He pulled me into his body and held me tightly as he devoured my mouth. I released a moan and pushed my fingers into his hair. My love for him spread through my veins.

"I love you, Oni. Nothing can tear us apart. I will always protect you. I will always find you. There will never be a day that I don't love you. You are mine," he breathed against my lips.

Yes, Rico is safe. He will come for me. All I have to do is hold out for him.

Suddenly, the fog is broken as I hear voices. I'm not alone. Others are in the room with me.

I note the scent of cologne. I know the fragrance right away, but can't place where I know it from. I check my body to see if I can fight back if I need to.

"She's still not awake?" someone says.

I try to grasp ahold of the voice. It feels familiar. I push harder to burst through the fog that's holding me back. Pain explodes in my head, but I'm determined to stay focused on the voices in the room.

"No, I don't know what to tell her when she does." Another familiar voice fills the room.

"Rico would want us to tell her the truth. Nothing less."

CHAPTER ONE

Thief in the Night

Oni

Have you ever known you shouldn't be doing something, but you do it anyway? That's me. It's how I always get my butt into trouble.

Brooklyn, New York, is no longer a safe place for me. I'm not able to call it home anymore.

Twenty-seven hours on a bus. A whole day and three hours. A one-way trip to get me away from all the drama and keep me out of a jail cell.

Twenty-seven long, boring, stinking hours that I will never forget. That's how long it took to get me to where I know no one and no one knows me. Because of my uncle, I can now live with a little less fear.

Or at least that was the plan. I'm sticky, I'm hungry, and I want to go to sleep, but my one weakness is staring me in the face. The reason I'm on the run in the first place.

Incredible. This has to be a sickness. I have to be insane.

I'm running for my life, and I still don't know how to say no. If I had walked away in New York, I would still be there. Why am I like this?

Jail time is the least of my worries back in New York. I'm not stupid in the slightest, which is why my mom is so angry with me. I have the potential to do so much more with my life, but I haven't been able to let this vice go.

Fuck, all I need is for them to find me because I'm too stupid to walk away. I can't do it. My mother has risked so much to help me. I have to walk away this time.

I chew on my lip as I circle the sleek black Lamborghini.

"I should just walk away, but I can't. This baby is too sweet. She's taunting me to take her," I mumble to myself.

They're still out there, I know that. They always will be. That's why I'm going to walk away.

"Who am I kidding?" I huff.

I'll never be the good one who puts common sense first. I have to scratch this itch. It's my own daddy's doing.

Sure, we seemed like a really nice, well-off family on the outside, but how does everyone think we got that way? The police just always looked the other way. My uncle and my dad used to run shit back in New York, then my dad was taken away from me and everything changed. My uncle moved here to Miami, and my mother and I were alone.

She was happy to get me away from that life, thinking I would never steal another car. That was a pipe dream. It's ingrained in me.

I've been stealing cars since I was nine. That's right, nine, with pigtails and Chucks on. Daddy was always so proud when I could pop a lock and hot-wire a car in record time.

I was faster than any of his boys. I was thirteen when I graduated to the high-end stuff. That's when things got out of control. I love a piece of expensive heavy metal between my legs.

Too bad the last piece of metal I stole was worth more than just the sticker price with its inconspicuous cargo and lethal owner.

"Fuck it," I mutter.

I look around and get ready to get to work. I'll just spin the block and park it somewhere once I'm done. I don't know anyone here to take it to a chop shop.

I pop the door open and go to climb in, but someone pushes the door closed from behind me. I go to turn to fight, but freeze when I come face to face with the last person I thought I would see here in Miami.

"They said you wouldn't be able to resist. I had hoped they were wrong. Hello, Oni. Do you know who I am?"

"Y … yes," I stutter. "You're Rico Gallo."

"Do you know how stupid I would look if you stole another of my cars filled with product? In fact, I'm starting to feel like a target. Are you targeting me, Oni?"

"No," I say and swallow hard.

Shit, I didn't even know he was in Miami. How was I supposed to know this was his car? I didn't know the first time.

"Your uncle knows my father. He was trying to smooth things over for you. My interest was piqued when I found out who you were. I watched the surveillance tape of you stealing my truck a million times.

"You're good. Really good. However, I don't think you use this much," he says and taps his fingers to my temple.

I close my eyes and groan. This was stupid and too good to be true. I should've known it was a test.

I open my eyes as he pushes my hoodie back from my head. He takes a sharp inhale of air as he looks down into my face. He stands quietly watching me for a few beats. I fidget with my sleeves, wondering if he plans to kill me.

"You're … wow … not what I expected."

"Were you expecting a boy?" I find my confidence and snarl.

"No, I knew you were a sixteen-year-old girl. That's why you're still breathing, sweetheart. I had no idea you were a gorgeous sixteen-year-old girl. That's all."

"What now?" I breathe.

"I have a proposition for you. Since I got the car and most of the product back in New York, I don't see why I have to punish you. Your uncle also agreed to compensate me for my troubles as long as I don't hurt you."

"Proposition?"

"Yes, Oni. I want you to come work for my family for the summer. Your uncle has agreed. I will keep you out of jail and alive as long as you're working for me. You will stay at my estate and do as I say, but you have to say yes now."

"Yes," I whisper.

"Good, get in. You're driving."

Rico

"You can make a left up here and jump on the highway," I command as she drives.

This girl is fucking gorgeous. I wasn't expecting her pretty face hidden beneath that hood. Those eyes, her lips, the deep, dark complexion of her skin.

I have to shift in my seat as I grow hard from her scent filling the Lambo. Her uncle knew she wouldn't be able to resist stealing it. I set her up.

I had been intrigued by her from the moment she dared to steal the first car. The Trackhawk was filled with almost two million in coke. I'll admit, she caught me slipping.

I had this chick in Brooklyn I'd been trying to take down for a few months. While I was up in my spare apartment pounding her out, this little thing was stealing my truck. She did that shit so fast I was impressed.

I wasn't lying. I watched the video a million times in awe. She has skills.

"Why are you doing this?" she speaks up as we float down the road.

She's an excellent driver as well. Not many people impress me, but Oni Raven is doing one hell of a job. I turn to stare at the side of her face.

"I see something in you." I shrug. "It seemed like a waste to kill you. I have better uses for your talents. You're smart on top of it all."

"You sure about that? I have stolen from the mob twice now. I'm feeling all kinds of stupid at the moment."

"We all make mistakes, sweetheart. What matters is how we learn from them."

"Uncle Claude is foul for this. He set me up," she pouts.

"I set you up. Your uncle just gave me a warning and some info on how."

"Why are you here? I mean, in Miami?"

"I'm spending the summers here. You and I will travel back and forth to New York over the next few months," I reply.

"When you say I have to do as you say, what does that mean?" she says softly.

"It means you won't steal anything I don't tell you to. You will be where I tell you, when I tell you and you will stay out of anything I tell you to stay out of."

"That's it?"

"Yeah, what were you thinking?"

"I don't know. I've never killed anyone or buried a body. So I'm just asking," she murmurs.

I laugh and reach to brush her braids from her face. She turns to glance at me. I'm punched in the gut by her beauty as she does.

"Also, I'm still a virgin, so I'm putting my foot down when it comes to you trying to pass me around or something. That's a no-fly zone."

I don't know why her words trigger something possessive in me. I'm nineteen. I shouldn't be this fucking hard for her. I'm normally focused on business. Sure, I love a good lay, but I don't allow women to distract me.

"You don't have to worry about that. If anyone touches you, I'll kill them. Your virtue will remain intact until you choose to have it otherwise. That's not my style."

The car falls silent as I program the GPS to have something to do with my thoughts and hands. My fingers are itching to rest on one of her shapely thighs. However, I won't break my promise.

No one will touch her if she doesn't want them to. I'm still deciding if I want her to want me to. I look her over—she's in a simple hoodie with jeans and a pair of high-top Air Force Ones.

When I'd walked up on her as she tried to steal my car, I noted that she had a cute little ass on her. I can't help wondering what's hiding under that hoodie. She'd probably be smoking hot in a dress.

In fact, I know she would. I'll be sure to find out at some point during this summer. I take a glance at the floor between my legs at her little backpack.

"Is that all you brought down with you?" I say, nodding at the backpack.

She glances in my direction quickly. Then she shrugs. "I didn't have much time to think about what to take while rushing out of town to keep from getting my head blown off."

"Fair enough. We'll go shopping in the morning."

"How? I don't have any money."

"I'll take care of it. You're not working for me for free, Oni. I will be sending money to your mother and taking care of you. Anything you need, let me know. I'll handle it."

"Forgive me if this all seems a bit unreal. Just a week ago, I was shitting bricks as I found your load in that truck. Now you're being all nice to me and offering to take care of me and all my needs.

"Be honest, am I driving to my death? You have a cement truck waiting to cover me up, or some hogs ready to eat my body or something?"

I roar with laughter. She's fucking adorable. One thing is for sure. I'll be entertained this summer.

"He laughs. At least we're not in the desert. I'd know for sure he's planning to off me then," she mutters under her breath.

"For the last time, I don't plan to kill you. You're my employee. Are you hungry?"

"God, I'm starving. I thought you'd never ask," she breathes.

I chuckle and shake my head. We'll have to work on her telling me what she needs. She should've told me she was hungry sooner.

"Make a U-turn up here. We'll go get something to eat before we get to the house."

She busts a U-turn before I finish speaking. I groan and throw my head back as the flashing lights and sirens come on behind us. I can feel her panic before she speaks.

"Fuck … fuck, fuck, fuck," she says, freaking out.

"I need you to calm down and relax. I've got this," I coach.

I wasn't joking about having product in this car. I need her to play it cool and allow me to handle this. She looks at me with wide eyes.

"Dude, I don't have a license. I'm Black and driving a more than two-hundred-thousand-dollar car. You've got to be fucking kidding me," she hisses.

"Just calm your ass down," I bite out as she pulls over.

"Rico," she drags out.

"Hush and follow my lead. I've got you. I've always got you, Oni."

CHAPTER TWO

Rico to the Rescue

Oni

What the fuck? Is he kidding me? How am I supposed to stay calm?

My heart is racing as I watch the officer climb out of his vehicle and make his way toward us. I grip the steering wheel tighter and bounce my knee while debating whether or not to take off. I can outrun this guy in this car, I know I can.

My palms are sweating, and my mouth is suddenly dry. I've never been caught for stealing a car. I've kept out of a jail cell and don't plan to end up in one now.

"I'm gonna run," I murmur.

Rico places his warm palm on my thigh and gives it a squeeze. "Calm. Down," he bites out.

I bite my lip and try to ignore how his touch has my body tingling all over. I don't have time for boys. The last thing I need is to fall for the son of a crime boss. Rico is next in line, from what I've heard about him.

I'm sure he's not interested in me. I think he has me by a few years. He's probably like twenty or something.

I've only been on two dates in my life. One of which I probably shouldn't count because he was my best friend, and we went to the movies together all the time.

The only reason I count it is because he tried to kiss me, taking me by surprise. Mason is handsome and every girl's dream back home. I guess I'm just too close. I know all the things about Mason he doesn't want anyone else to know.

I'm starting to think I'm a magnet for dangerous guys. Who am I kidding? This guy isn't thinking about me.

I shake my stupid thoughts off and roll the window down as the officer taps at it. Shit, I should have run. The sour look on this guy's face tells me I should have taken off and gotten my behind the heck out of here.

"License and registration," he commands.

"Good evening, officer. How you doing?" Rico croons as he leans across me.

The scent of his cologne hits me and makes my mouth water. It's been lingering in the air since we got into the car, but now it's so strong I can taste it. He gives my thigh another squeeze as I begin to squirm.

"License and registration," the officer repeats.

"I'm sorry, officer. My girlfriend doesn't have her license. Here's my information. She's driving because I twisted my ankle while we were at mini golf. Shit's embarrassing.

"The house wasn't that far away, so I didn't think we would run into any trouble. She got hungry at the last second and I thought I'd grab her something to eat from a drive-through or something.

"She came a long way to spend the weekend with me and so far, it's turning into shit, bro. I'm so sorry, baby." He says the last part to me and kisses my temple.

My cheeks heat and I turn to him. Instead of pulling back, he ghosts his face against mine, breathing me in as he holds his information out to the cop. I feel like I'm falling into his gaze.

Rico isn't just handsome. He's gorgeous. His Italian heritage adds to his good looks. Those eyes.

They are gray, but his irises are surrounded by a light brown and the outside of the gray is circled by a dark blue. His dark lashes are so long and full, emphasizing how gorgeous his eyes are. He licks his lips, drawing my attention to his mouth.

Gah, his lips are sexy. They look fleshy and have the sexiest lip lines I've ever seen on a guy. I bite my lip as I stare at his.

He smiles and kisses the tip of my nose. I thought my heart was racing before, but it's ready to burst from my chest now. I almost forget all about the officer standing right outside my door until he speaks and pulls me from the trance I'm in.

"Oh, Mr. Gallo. I didn't recognize you. Let your father know Officer Andy said hello. You two be safe. Get some ice on that ankle."

"Thank you, Officer Andy, will do," Rico says.

"This is a nice car, sweetheart. Drive carefully. Have a good night," he says as he hands Rico back his documents.

"Oh my God," I breathe and sag in my seat.

I wait for the cop to get back into his car, then turn to Rico with my mouth hanging open. He's sitting there with a smug grin on his lips. I toss my thumb over my shoulder.

"What the fuck was that?"

He winks at me. "I told you I had it. Come on. Let me get you fed. I have some shit I need to do tonight once I get you to the house."

"Hot date?" I tease before I can stop myself.

My face begins to burn. I want to palm my forehead. Way to put my foot in my mouth.

"Jealous?"

His eyes light up as he looks me over. I squirm in my seat, feeling flustered. Not wanting to answer him, I turn and start the car to take off.

Rico roars with laughter beside me. I'm glad he's so amused. I'm starting to wonder if this was such a great idea.

But what other option did I have?

He reaches to brush my braids from my face and tuck them behind my ear. I shiver a bit, causing him to chuckle, making me feel stupid. I need to get my shit together.

I'm here for the summer to pay my debts and stay alive. Nothing more, nothing less. I'm not a silly girl.

I have one weakness: cars. I'm not about to add a second. Catching feelings for Rico Gallo is out of the question.

"Stop overthinking, Oni. I'm here for business. Pleasure is the last thing on my mind. I have to keep focused. If I want to sit at the top, I have to set myself apart and prove to my uncle I'm the one."

"Your uncle?"

"Yeah, I want more than my father's capo position. I want to be Don."

Rico

"Do you mind if I ask you a question?" Oni says as she wipes gravy from her mouth.

I got us some pasta from my favorite spot. Since my family owns the place, I was able to walk right in and collect our order before heading home to come out here by the pool to sit and eat. Oni is sitting cross-legged with her plate in her lap.

I shrug my shoulders as I chew my food then clean my teeth with my tongue. She tilts her head and stares at me. I can't help feeling like she sees through me.

"Yeah, what's up?"

"You said you want to be don, right?" she whispers.

I smile and nod my head. I don't miss that she understands this isn't something to go around yelling about. I'm liking this chick the more I'm around her.

That's probably why I'm sitting here with her, instead of making sure that car is unloaded. My guys will get it done. They all know the consequences if they don't.

"Yeah, you got it."

"What's the difference?"

"As Capo, I will only run things in my father's New York territory. As Don, I get it all. Italy, New York, Miami, Vegas. I'd sit at the top and run shit. None of this small-time shit to prove myself."

"Okay, I think I get it. Capo, we're stuck in New York. Don, we-own-the-world-type shit," she says.

I can see the wheels turning in her head. I'm not going to lie. I love hearing her include herself in the equation.

"Something like that." I nod.

"Okay, how do we get you the world? I've always wanted to go to Italy. Maybe I can come back next summer too." She looks around and smiles. "This place is nice. It's been so long since I've lived like this."

I lean in and reach to wipe the gravy she missed with her napkin. Her lips part as she looks back at me with wide eyes. I pull my finger back and stick it into my mouth.

"It's simple. I run the product I've been put in charge of and keep the businesses on my books earning until my twenty-first birthday, and then I get a promotion. My uncle doesn't have sons of his own, so he's going to choose between me and one of my cousins.

"I'm in the lead so far, but I'm also the oldest. Al, and Fredo haven't turned eighteen yet. Ed just did. I have a head start, so I'm making the best of that," I explain.

"How old are you?"

"Nineteen, but I've been running point since I turned eighteen. My uncle is grooming me. Has been since I could walk and talk."

"Do your cousins want it?"

I shrug. "Not Aldo or Eduardo. Fredo, now that's another story."

I'm not in the mood to get into that, so I change the subject. My family can be complicated at times. One minute, you think you know where you and everyone else stand. Then, in the blink of an eye, it all changes.

I've learned to keep my head down and bring in my earnings. As long as my uncle gets his points, he doesn't give me shit. I prefer it that way.

"Let me ask you a question."

"Okay, shoot," she says over a mouthful of garlic bread.

She's cute while she eats. I could watch her like this all night. I did a lot of digging to find out more about this girl. My father was as impressed and intrigued as I was. When her father and uncle came up, my pop knew of them.

That's how I got permission to spare her and collect my debt some way other than in blood. Oni lucked out because we run a chop shop that runs parallel with our pharmaceutical business. We scrape the VINs on the more expensive cars that can fetch us a nice price. Then load them with product before they're shipped out.

Some cars have sat right in auctions as our distributors bid to pick up their work. The system works for us. It's not often that someone outbids one of our distros.

It's happened once or twice, and the party has been dealt with. Most auction houses know our cars and will ignore bids on purpose to avoid problems.

I'm about to use Oni to take that business to the next level. I've got it all set up. She's the final piece.

"You mentioned not living like this anymore. What happened?"

She puts her plate aside and slumps her shoulders. A sad look comes to her face. I have an idea what went down, but I want to hear it from her lips.

I need to know if Oni is as tough as I think. If she is, this is going to be a lucrative relationship for us both. I don't bring many in close, but when I do, it means I see something in the individual.

"My dad was locked up for some BS. All our things were seized. He never made it out.

"My mom didn't want my uncle's help or whatever. After my dad was killed, he left and moved down here. He sends me money, but I can't tell my mom or use it for anything nice enough to get her attention.

"I couldn't even let her know I had the money for my ticket here. I had to let her use her last bit to ship me out. I'm going to pay her back," she says.

"You don't have to worry about that. I'll take care of it."

"Yeah, about that. I know you said you would be sending her money, but my mom wants nothing to do with your world. I doubt she will take it."

"You let me worry about that. She'll be straight. I take care of my own," I reply.

"How long will I be one of you? What happens to me after this summer? What if I still owe when the summer is up?"

I allow my gaze to search her face. Reaching to finger a few braids from her face, I then drag my finger down the side of her cheek.

"I think you will be one of us for a long time, Oni. If you prove your loyalty to the family, you will have a place here long after the summer ends. For now, we'll take it a day at a time."

I think about leaning in to take her lips, but remind myself not to mix business with pleasure. I need Oni. If I'm going to impress my uncle this summer, I need her to do it.

I have plans. Big plans for Oni Raven and none of them involve having her in my bed or my arms.

"Come on, I'll take you to your room."

CHAPTER THREE

Living a Dream

Rico

"This will be your room," I say as I open the door for Oni to walk in.

I chose one of the rooms down the hall from mine. I keep telling myself I want to be able to keep an eye on her, nothing else. She's safer close to me.

"Thanks. I wasn't expecting all of this," she says, moving farther into the room.

"Why not? Did you think I was going to stick you in a broom closet or place you in front of a fireplace?"

She shrugs. "I didn't know what to expect. Certainly wasn't expecting a queen-size bed and all this."

Anything for my girl almost slips from my lips. I'm not even sure where the words come from. I've been enjoying my time with her, but things can never go anywhere between us.

She's a fucking kid. In life, in my world, in age compared to me. I know I had to grow up faster than most, but I would still be three years older than her if I had been raised like a normal guy.

I lean into the doorjamb of the room with my arms crossed over my chest as I watch her. She's spinning around as she takes it all in with her backpack held tightly to her chest. This time, I'm really getting a chance to take her in.

She has to be about five-five to my six-three. She'd probably fit right into my arms perfectly. I push off the doorjamb, wanting to find out. As I move toward her, I start to release the first four buttons on my dress shirt.

She freezes and looks up at me. Her big brown eyes are so pretty with their oval shape. She has long, natural lashes that bring your attention to the shape and reddish-brown hue of her gaze.

I drop my eyes to her lips. They are so full and plush-looking. I want to devour them right here on the spot. I wonder if she knows how pretty she is.

"I should probably get in a shower and some sleep," she says softly.

I clear my throat. "Everything you need will be right through there. If you can't find something, my room is the one with the double doors right at the end of the hall."

"Okay, thanks," she says and licks her lips.

I reach to cup her face, searching her eyes. I wonder if she's ever been kissed. Do I have it in me to have a taste and forget her after tonight?

Fuck it.

I lean in to find out. Her lips are taunting me to take them. I'm a breath away from sealing the deal when my phone rings, halting me.

I bite out a curse as she pulls away and spins for the bathroom I pointed out. I guess that's for the best. Bringing my phone to my ear, I snarl into it.

"What?"

"We have a problem. You're not going to like it."

"Go on," I snap and turn to leave the room.

I hate when people take something that should be simple and turn it into some shit I need to clean up. Everyone knows I don't have tolerance for bullshit. I have to be ruthless to get to where I want to go.

Especially since I'm nineteen running a crew. Most of my guys are around my age, but I have a few men my father gave me who have been with him for years. I use them to deal with the younger guys.

They help me keep them in check. So far, it works for me. I haven't had any pushback.

For one, no one wants to deal with my pop or my uncle. You fuck with me, you die. Second, I keep my guys happy.

Everyone in my crew earns well. There's no need for bullshit when the bag is nice, and mouths are fed. We keep our shit clean.

If you have a need, you come to me, and I fix it. Simple as that, so when someone fucks up, I take it personal. I put my neck on the line for each and every member of my crew.

Fucking up means (a) you don't respect that or (b) you don't care. I have zero tolerance for those who don't care, and everyone better remember to respect me or face the consequences. This is a family.

Family comes first. If you can allow your family to go down out of selfishness, you ain't shit and never will be. From what Mario is saying in my ear right now, I have a member in my crew who ain't shit, which means he has to go.

Placing my phone between my shoulder and my ear, I jog down the stairs while rolling the sleeves of my dress shirt up to my elbows.

"Push the drop back to tomorrow night. We can't afford to blow the operation. I want you to personally replace the bags first thing in the morning," I bark out orders as I move.

"And what should I do with our friend?"

"I'm on my way out back. Have him waiting for me," I say and end the call.

The drugs in the car were meant for the Raphael crew. They run a strip club here in Miami. Twice a month, one of my guys drops a duffel bag off to one of the dancers. She then walks that bag right into the club. When she leaves at the end of her shift, she leaves with an identical duffel filled with cash.

My guy goes to see her again to pick up the cash. It has to be the same bag every time. The bags have to match. Some asshole fucked up the duffel bag the coke was loaded into.

I can't have my guy show up with a random bag for our girl. Now Mario will have to get a new bag into the club and replace the one we have to make a perfect match. All avoidable bullshit.

I run a hand through my hair. I was about to fuck up. This mess stopped me from fucking everything up. I didn't recruit Oni to get in her pants.

Tomorrow will be different. I'm her boss and she's an employee with a debt to pay. Nothing more, nothing less.

Get your fucking head in the game, Rico.

Oni

I think he was going to kiss me. If not for his phone ringing, he would have kissed me. I can't help feeling a little disappointed.

However, I know it's for the best. Rico oozes danger. I'd be getting myself into so much trouble falling for him. I need to focus on clearing my debt and regaining my freedom.

Now that he's not here, I can think clearly. I know I don't need to get any more involved in his world than I already am. My mom has so many regrets.

I allowed myself to get caught up earlier. Now, as I lie here staring up at the ceiling, I know this has to be one summer and one summer only. I punch the bed in frustration.

"Why can't I stop thinking about him?" I huff into the dark room.

I blow out a breath and sit up. Maybe I should take a walk to clear my head. Or I could go sit out by the pool. It was gorgeous out there.

I slide from the bed in my T-shirt and panties. Since I only plan to dip my toes in the pool for a bit, I don't bother to put anything else on. I creep out of my room and look down the hall.

I wonder if Rico is sleeping. Chewing on my lip, I think about going to knock on his door. He did say I could come to him if I needed anything.

I poke my lip out as I catch myself having silly thoughts again. Turning, I head for the stairs Rico brought me up. The house seems to be so still.

I keep going until I get to the double doors that head out to the backyard. I pad toward the pool, but something catches my attention. There's a shed-like structure down the stairs, off to the left of the pool.

It catches my attention because it's completely dark out here except for the landscape lights, the pool lights, and the light coming from the structure. I turn and head for the stairs. They lead down to the flat grassy lawn below and a path winds toward the shed.

It's bigger than what it looked like from above. Making it to the front of the shed, I peek through the crack in the entrance door. My mouth falls open as Rico comes into view, shirtless.

Sweat drips down his back as he stands towering over the guy who's on his knees, cowering away. I had a feeling there was a sculpted body under that dress shirt and those slacks.

"You know, at first I thought you were just a careless fuck." Rico looks down at the guy, seething. "But nah, you're a fucking cowardly idiot. You were going to let your little brother take the fall for the bullshit you orchestrated.

"As if I don't already take care of your family. As if you all want for anything. As if I'm not paying for your sister to go to school.

"Anything you've come to me for, I've done for you. Maybe that's my fucking problem. I'm too good to you guys.

"Is that it, Mario? Am I too good to my guys? Is that why this fuck is shitting in my face?"

"Maybe, boss."

I glance further into the room and find a handsome guy with a scar on the right side of his face. A slash right down the center of his right eye. It doesn't take away from his handsome face. It adds something to it.

Rico circles the guy on the ground, and his face comes into view. His dark hair is messy, falling into those gorgeous eyes. My gaze drops to his chiseled chest.

Damn.

He pushes his hair out of his face with one hand as he grabs the guy by his hair and tugs his head back with the other. The dark look on Rico's face is enough to strike fear in me. However, I'm frozen. I can't look away.

"What should I do with you, Jonny? Should I make you watch me kill your brother first, or should I kill you now and be done with your family forever?"

"No, please. This was all me. Ma needs your help.

"Anna still has two more years of school. Don't take that from her because I fucked up. You're right, you have been good to us.

"I got greedy. When Andy came to me with the offer, I took it and dragged Pauly into it with me."

"I had so much respect for your pop," Rico says as he releases Jonny's hair. "Too bad he wasn't around to raise you better. Because of him, I won't cut off your family. Mario, bring Pauly in."

Mario straightens and goes to another door inside. He brings in a younger-looking version of Jonny. His mouth is taped, and he looks like he's about to shit his pants.

Meanwhile, Rico has pulled a gun and is twisting on a silencer. The one Mario just dragged in begins to cry and tries to speak through the tape on his mouth. I should run from here, but I can't bring myself to not watch.

"Pauly, did I not tell you your loyalty should always be with me?"

Pauly nods frantically. Rico tilts his head to the side and wipes his forearm across his face. Pauly is trembling at this point and Jonny is on his knees, crying.

"Then why would you intentionally help your brother in a plot to set me up?"

Pauly tries to reply through the tape once again.

"You know what? I don't care. It's loyalty or death. You chose."

"No, no, no, no," Jonny cries.

His cries fall on deaf ears as Rico pulls the trigger and Pauly's brains splatter all over the plastic that has just drawn my attention. Rico then turns his gun on Jonny, who's doubled over, sobbing.

"Why? Why? Pauly … Pauly … I'm so sorry. I'm so fucking sorry."

"Save that shit. You should have thought of who you were double-crossing, asshole. I'll take good care of your ma and sister, you fuck."

With that, he pulls the trigger again. I jump and get ready to turn and run. I don't make it a step before I hear my name called.

"Oni, get your ass in here."

CHAPTER FOUR

Let's Talk

Rico

This girl is digging her way deeper into my life. What I'm supposed to do is blow her brains out and let Mario dispose of her along with these two. However, I fuck up and do something I know is about to change both our lives forever.

"Oni, get your ass in here," I growl.

I look toward the door where I know she's been watching. I don't know what made me off these two in front of her. What does it say about me that my dick got hard taking their lives in front of her?

I swallow hard when she steps into the shed dressed only in a T-shirt, her brown legs bare and her nipples straining against the thin shirt. Why do her legs look so silky?

Damn, I was right. She has a great pair of fat tits. This girl is killing me.

I might as well turn this gun on myself now. She's going to be the death of me one day. I know it. She opens her mouth, and her words seal the deal.

"What do you need me to do? If my hands are dirty, I can't snitch, right? Do I need to roll him up tight, or can the plastic be loose?" she says.

"Fuck outta here. I'm not allowing you to get involved in this. Especially not dressed like that. Why the fuck are you even out here?"

"I couldn't sleep. I was going to sit by the pool for a bit, but then I saw the light on. Curiosity and the cat and all that shit," she murmurs.

I laugh and shake my head. "You're something else, you know that?"

"Seriously, do you have a painter's suit or something in here?" she asks as she looks around the shed. "I can do my part. Or I can dig. You want me to go throw on some jeans and boots?"

I step over Jonny's dead body and stalk over to her by the door, tucking my gun in the back of my pants as I go. She looks up at me with determination on her face. Reaching up, I run a finger along her hairline, down under her chin and pinch it between my fingertips.

"You think you're going to be next because of what you've seen?" I breathe into her face.

"Well, that should be your next move. You don't know me, and you owe me nothing. I'm a loose end. What's stopping you from taking me out?"

I search her face. She's mine, that's what's stopping me. I couldn't let her go now even if I wanted to.

I wink at her. "You're safe. I only kill the useless and disloyal. You, baby, intrigue me, and you're far from useless. Mario, clean this shit up," I call over my shoulder.

"Got it, boss. See you tomorrow."

"See you later. Oh, and pay our friend a visit. Let him know he failed, then send him on a trip."

"Already on it," Mario says.

"Come on," I say to Oni as I link my fingers with hers and tug her from the shed.

We make it up the path and back up the stairs. I need a shower and my bed. This has been a long-as-fuck-day. Fuck, it's been a long-as-fuck-two weeks.

Everything since this little chick stole my truck begins to crash down on me. Killing her would solve a lot, but that's no longer an option.

"So you couldn't sleep?" I say as we step back into the house.

"No, not really. I have a lot on my mind."

I chuckle. "Yeah, I bet. You want to come stay in my room? I'm going to shower and then we can talk until you pass out. I'll even carry you back to your room once you're asleep if you want."

"I don't know. Is that smart?"

"No, but our track record of smart shit hasn't been so good since we've met. Come on. Like you said, I don't know you. I want to change that.

"I know all the guys on my crew. I should know my new driver. You need my trust as much as I need yours," I say as we climb the stairs.

"Shouldn't I wait for you to finish your shower and then you can let me know and I'll come over?"

I look down at her and smile as she chews on her lower lip. I want to be the one nibbling on that plump flesh. That thought alone should cause me to abandon this idea.

"I have a sitting area in my bedroom. You can hang out there if it makes you more comfortable. We're just going to talk until you fall asleep, promise."

"*Well,*" she drags out. "I guess if you put it that way and since you promise."

I wrap my arm around her head and drag her into my room with me. Releasing her, I allow her to sit in one of the accent chairs and curl her legs under her. I feel like a perv as her little panties come into view, taunting me.

I force my attention to her cute little toes. They are painted a soft pink. I wonder if she's ever painted them white.

I roll my eyes at my thoughts and head into the bathroom to strip and climb into the shower. Shit, have I been slipping? I've been so focused on that chick out there and how to pull her into my circle.

Maybe this was a mistake. Why did I want her here so bad to begin with? Yeah, I have work for her, but what are my real intentions?

"I'm so fucked," I say as I lift my face toward the spray and allow the water to beat down on me and cascade down my body. I look down at my hard dick and wonder if that's the head I've been thinking with. I would have seen Jonny coming if I had my head in the game.

"Fuck, fuck, fuck. What am I going to do now?"

I finish my shower and step out to towel off. Wrapping a towel around my waist, I use the other one to dry my hair as I walk into the bedroom. I don't see her at first, so I walk a little closer to the sitting area only to find she's gone.

I shouldn't feel this disappointed. I truly only intended to talk. It was going to kill me, but that's all I planned to do.

"Fuck me," I mutter.

Oni

"What in the entire hell are you doing, Oni?" I hiss at myself.

I stand up to leave, then sit back down, bouncing my knee as I try to clear my head. His scent is all over this room. It smells expensive and clean.

"He's a killer. There's nothing clean about him," I speak the words aloud to remind myself.

I glance toward the bathroom as I listen to the shower running, wondering what I'm doing here. I think I might be in shock. Did I just witness a double homicide? I'm pretty sure I did.

"Duh," I hiss at my thoughts.

At this point, I'm in survival mode. Rico isn't going to simply allow me to walk away after what I saw tonight. How do I get myself into shit like this?

I'm sure this isn't what Uncle Claude had in mind when he agreed for me to work for Rico. Uncle Claude has a lot of explaining to do. This is some bullshit.

I gasp as it dawns on me, I've been so wrapped up in Rico, I haven't checked in with Mom or Uncle Claude. I left my phone in my room. I bite my lip and stare in the direction of the bathroom.

Jumping up, I then race to my room to grab my phone and make a few calls. I know it's late, but Mom and Uncle Claude are probably waiting to hear from me. Once in my room, I decide to call Mom first.

I need to hear her voice more than anything. I also want to make sure she's not freaking out, which I'm sure she is. This is the most trouble I've ever been in.

The line rings twice before she picks up. She was probably waiting by the phone, making me feel worse. If I had called my mom instead of being nosy, I might have avoided the huge pile of shit I stepped in.

"Oh, thank God. I didn't want to call you and distract you from paying attention to your surroundings, but I did plan to call you soon if you didn't check in. How are you, baby?

"How was the trip? How's your Uncle Claude?" Mom rattles off.

"I'm fine, Mom. The trip was long. I haven't seen Uncle Claude yet. He was busy. I'm getting settled in," I reply.

"I thought he was going to meet you at the bus station. Did you find the house okay?"

I stop pacing in front of the bed and slide down to the floor. I hate keeping the truth from my mom, but she would freak out if she knew about any of this. I hope Rico truly has a plan for sending her money discreetly.

"He sent a friend for me. I'm fine. I'm going to go to bed soon though, I'm beat."

"I'm sure you are. Baby, I'm so glad you're safe. Do me a favor and stay out of trouble.

"Let this be a clean start. You're so bright. You have your whole life ahead of you."

I feel so bad as I hear the sadness in her voice. I promised myself I'd stop bringing her heartache and here I am, living with the son of a crime boss. A killer and crime boss in the making.

I close my eyes and nod as if she can see me. I have no way out of this now, but I'm going to make it out on the other side and do something she can be proud of. The last thing I want is to break my mother's heart.

"I'm going to do my best, Mom."

"That's all I ask. Your uncle and I were talking about some private schools we think would be great for you. He said he would cover the cost of everything. You know how much I hate taking money from that man, but I feel like if I don't do this, I'm going to lose you," she chokes out.

"Mom, I promise it's going to be okay. Get some sleep. We'll talk about this later. For now, I'm safe and staying out of trouble. Okay?"

"Okay. I love you, Oni. I'd do anything to protect you."

"I love you too, Mom. Stop worrying about me."

"I will always worry about you. You're my baby."

"Good night, Mom."

"Good night, baby."

I hang up the phone and stare off into space. I have to do better. My joyrides are going to break my mom's heart.

My dad is gone. Stealing cars isn't going to bring him back. No matter how much I try to connect with him through the thrill.

I swipe at my tears and hop up from my place on the floor. Not sure if my uncle will answer a call, I shoot him a text.

Me: *We need to talk.*

Uncle Claude: *I will see you in the morning. All you had to do was walk away and not try to take the car.*

Uncle Claude: *You're just like your dad. It hurt like hell to see you couldn't leave it alone.*

Me: *You were there?*

Uncle Claude: *I'm always here. Don't let them get you into anything I can't get you out of. This was the only way. I love you, cub.*

More tears spill down my face as he uses the nickname my father used to call me. I wouldn't be here if I didn't try to steal that car. I'm my own worst enemy.

A mouse, I walked right into the trap. The cheese was too sweet for me to ignore. Now look at me.

Not just caught with my hand in the cookie jar. My hand is stuck and I'm sure I'm going to break it if I try to pull it out now.

Exhaustion sets in and I'm too angry with Rico and myself to head back to his room. I don't want to talk to him. Right now, I don't want to get to know anything else about him.

I don't know who to be more angry with. Me for taking the bait, or him for setting it. I ran all this way to land in a gilded cage.

"Great job, Oni."

I freeze when I hear movement outside my door. Holding my breath, I climb into bed and pretend to be asleep.

Please go away, please go away.

I chant the words in my head like a prayer, hoping they are heard. Maybe he's changed his mind and plans to kill me.

CHAPTER FIVE

Unwanted

Rico

I needed to put distance between me and Oni this morning. Last night I thought she might have taken off after the shock wore off. Once I realized she only returned to her own room, I decided to back off.

I don't want to come off as some creep. I really am interested in getting to know her like I know all my guys, but I have to admit I'd never invited one of them to lie in my bed to tell me about themselves. I went too far last night.

That's why I'm here at the gym trying to clear my head when I already have a home gym at the house. I had Mario set up a driver and someone to take Oni shopping for new clothes. Anything to keep us both busy.

This chick on the treadmill keeps eyeing me. She's cute, and from the look in her eyes, I'm sure she's down to fuck. If I'm in her, I can't be thinking about Oni.

At least that's my logic as I watch her stop her machine and come over to the weight bench I'm on. I've tapped a BBL or two. Nothing like the real thing, and after a while, it's not as attractive as you would think, in my opinion.

It's a lot of work to keep up and not all the girls with them are up for the task. This chick looks older as she gets closer. Older women are fun.

They have just enough experience to keep my attention, but I still have the ability to shock them and put them down for the night. However, something turns me off once this one is standing in front of me.

"Hi," she says.

"How you doing?" I nod.

"Oh, you have an accent. Jersey or New York?"

I scoff. The nerve. While I have a shit ton of family in Jersey, New York is where I was born and raised.

Brooklyn has been my stomping grounds for as long as I can remember.

"New York," I say as if it should have been obvious.

"Are you on vacation or do you live here now?"

My phone rings, grabbing my attention. I'm not mad about the interruption at all. I've lost interest and my thoughts were already turning back to Oni.

Fuck, I've got it bad. In three years, Oni is going to be a smoke show. She's already fire. Smart, pretty, talented, and ready to ride or die.

That shit last night turned me on so much. She was ready to bag a body for me. That's the type of woman you need in this life.

"Hello," I say into the phone as I pick up and walk away from the chick from the treadmill, leaving her with her mouth flapping.

As she calls *asshole* after me, I shrug it off and laugh. She's all but forgotten. I'm not one to fall all over some chick. I'm pretty sure I'm not the first guy to dismiss her so easily.

"Hey, are you mad at me?"

"Oni?"

"Yeah, my phone died. Mario let me use his."

"What makes you think I'm mad at you?"

I bite my tongue before I can call her baby or sweetheart. I wish she were here so I could look into her eyes. There's something in them that pulls you into her spell.

The determination, the wit, and the constant look of acknowledgment. As if she's absorbing everything and learning every second.

"I haven't seen you today. You sent me shopping with the silent bodyguard and … I didn't come back last night. I thought maybe I pissed you off," she says.

"And …"

"My uncle said he's coming to pick me up. You're sending me home."

"What?" I roar as I freeze in my tracks.

"Before my phone died, he sent me a text. You changed your mind? You don't want me to work for you anymore? Is it because of last night? I went to call my mom—"

"Oni, you're not going back. I didn't give any such order. I don't know what the fuck your uncle is talking about, but you better be in my house when I get back," I say harsher than I mean to.

"Oh, maybe I misunderstood. We're almost back to the house. Once I charge my phone, I can call Uncle Claude and find out what's going on."

"Do nothing. I will get to the bottom of this," I say and hang up.

I have a feeling I already know what's going on here. I'm not the only one who can see I have a young and beautiful girl under my roof. A girl who would be mine to choose.

My uncle and I get along for the most part. He's always been like my second dad. However, about two months ago, he informed me of an arranged marriage I have no intention of taking part in.

Oni's uncle made an agreement with me and my pop. The only way he would try to renege on that is if my uncle got involved. Oni is a threat to him.

Any woman I show interest in is a threat until I agree to this marriage. Well, my uncle can call on an army because I'm not agreeing to that shit, no matter what. It's a power play.

He doesn't even like the Abato family. Juliana Abato is a whiny, entitled bitch. One hour in a room with her and I was ready to blow my own brains out.

Apparently, we used to play together or something as kids. Now her father and my uncle think we're a match. If anything will keep me from being don, it will be this arrangement.

However, I never lose. I always get what I want. I'm not about to allow some stupid arranged marriage to get in my way.

"Hello, I'll get my niece out of your hair within the hour. I'm on my way," Claude Raven answers the phone.

"Why the hell would you do that? I told you I have a project I need her for. I have already been paid six million for a single contract. Are you trying to make me look bad?"

"No. What the hell is going on? I got a call this morning that I should pick her up and send her back home, that her debt has been taken care of," Claude says tightly.

"That call didn't come from me or anyone under me. I'm almost a hundred percent it didn't come from my pop either."

"What have you gotten my niece into? The call came from Emilio himself. My brother's baby girl is now on that man's radar, Rico. What the fuck?"

"I'll handle it. I promised you I'd take care of her, and I will," I bite out.

He curses and mutters away from the phone. I have respect for Claude, so I hold my temper. In all honesty, I should allow him to take her back home.

I can find another driver for this job, but I want her. The fucked-up part is, when I say that, I'm not sure if I just mean for the job anymore.

"I'll handle my uncle. Oni stays."

"Respectfully, Rico, your family may have to just bring the smoke. I don't know what kind of bullshit y'all are on, but Oni won't be in the middle."

Oni

"Thank you," I say with a tight smile as the chef places a bowl of fruit down next to my plate.

Now, in the light of day, this place is so bright. The sun is pouring in through the floor-to-ceiling windows that wrap the house. Sitting here has made me nostalgic for the times when I used to sit with Daddy in our big house before everything went to shit.

I don't know why I was so disappointed to find out Rico wants to send me back. I was taken aback by the text from Uncle Claude. I woke this morning with a plan for how to make this all work for me.

After making a call back home and asking some vague questions, I was able to figure some things out as I mapped a course of action. This doesn't have to be all bad.

I was even a bit excited to get my new wardrobe. I can't say I was surprised when Mario took me to the high-end shops. From the looks of Rico's guys, they all dress to impress. Why should I be any different?

However, from his tone on the phone, I have this sinking feeling in the pit of my stomach. Things are about to change again. It feels like my life has shifted at least five times since I've been here. Each decision, each action, changes the course of my fate.

I should be happy. I'm getting out and I'm going home. Maybe I can actually spend the summer with my uncle like I planned. All my plans have fallen apart, and I will need to figure out what I'm going to do after the summer ends, but it looks like I'm about to take a turn off this dangerous road.

At least that's what I believe until I hear the sound of tires screeching in front of the house. After Mario and I returned from shopping with all my bags, he left me here, saying he had some business to handle for Rico. I was told to stay put.

Since then, I've been sitting here picking at the sandwich the chef made for me. It's not that the food isn't good—my stomach has just been in knots about what's going on. The alarm announces the front door has opened, and movement starts to pick up all around me. Even the chef looks a bit nervous.

"Where is she?" Rico bellows through the house.

I jump in my seat and turn just in time to see him storm into the kitchen like a madman. I stand and wipe my sweaty palms on my new wide-legged slacks. Reaching up, I touch my braids that I pulled up into a bun.

I shift from foot to foot, thinking I should have gone with a more sophisticated top, not this crisscross crop top that bares my stomach. Rico eats me up with his eyes. That heated stare makes me both nervous and curious about what he's thinking.

His fists are balled up at his sides, and his nostrils are flaring. He looks angrier than he was last night in that shed as he killed those two men. I can't help wringing my hands as I stand with my mouth hanging open.

"This is why I'm about to start a war," he mutters to himself.

"Huh?" I say.

I knit my brows in confusion. This guy makes my head spin. Even if he were attracted to me, he's so out of my league.

"Nothing. Your uncle wants to see you and make sure you're okay. We're going to do this on my father's property."

"Okay," I say.

"Oni, this is your chance to show me your loyalty. You're returning here with me, no matter what; it's your job to make sure that happens."

"What? What are you talking about?"

"Your uncle is ready to go to war with my family for you. That wasn't how this was supposed to play out. This was a friendly merger. If he pulls out now, not only do I look weak, but he's asking for the Gallo wrath.

"That's not what my father or I want. I want you here. I need you here, but I'm not going to tolerate the disrespect. I feel where your uncle is coming from.

"I would have the same reaction. I need him to chill so I can fix the real problem. Do you understand?" he explains.

"Yeah, I get it. You need me to calm my uncle down so I can stay."

"Good girl. Come here," he says.

Slowly, I move to where he's standing. Looking up into his eyes, I watch as he begins to calm himself down. My head is reeling.

I learned last night what happens to the disloyal. However, who is Rico to me? My uncle is my blood.

Should I really choose him over Uncle Claude? As I think about it, I may need to in order to survive. I know too much not to side with Rico.

He could decide to kill me and my uncle. Uncle Claude didn't ask for this. He's just trying to protect me.

I'm the one who stole the truck. If I hadn't, those drugs wouldn't have been lost. I wasn't thinking.

When I found them in the truck, I took a picture of the plates and took off. I didn't think of someone finding the vehicle and taking some of the product. I'm sure they had planned to go back for the rest, but I had already called Uncle Claude to fix my mistake.

I'm lucky they didn't take it all. I would probably be in a much different situation. Rico pinches my chin between his fingers. I come out of my thoughts and focus on his face.

"This is how you earn my trust, Oni."

"I get it. I understand."

He kisses my forehead. "Good, you look nice. Did you get everything you need?"

"I think so."

"Don't hesitate to let me know if you need anything else. I'll take care of it. Let's go. Pop is waiting."

CHAPTER SIX

Lethal Negotiations

Rico

"Stop fidgeting. First rule of the game, you never let anyone see you squirm," I say as I glance over at Oni in the passenger seat.

She's been yanking at that seat belt and wiggling in her seat since I drove off from the house. I need to know she can handle herself in a room with bosses. I get the feeling I'm right about this girl.

She releases a long breath but stops the fidgeting. She looks fucking fantastic. The beige outfit looks great on her. Classy but still cute and age-appropriate.

I mean, she doesn't look like one of my pop's old side pieces. The top is tasteful if you ask me. The way it's tailored draws your attention away from her bare midriff.

"Don't be nervous. My pop is on our side. He's going to smooth things over," I say out loud, more for myself than for her.

If my father wasn't counting on this deal to happen, I might have had to kiss my girl goodbye to keep the peace. However, he stands to gain quite a bit from the setup I have going on. Even with the kick up to Uncle Emilio, Pop will clear a few million.

When I called him to tell him what has been going on with our driver and how his brother is trying to stick his nose in our business, he decided to step in. That's huge. My father doesn't normally get into Uncle Emilio's business, and he never bails me out.

He will give me advice and guidance, but my mistakes are my own. I learned that early on, even though I've never looked for a handout or for special treatment. I've been my own man from the start, but I know when I need to take a step back.

"Rico?"

"What's up?"

"There's something you're not telling me. You want my trust, but where is yours?"

"What are you talking about?" I try to laugh her off.

"Don't do that. Remember, I've been outside. I may not know everything, especially when it comes to your world, but I'm not stupid. You're holding something back."

I glance over at her quickly, then turn my attention back to the road as I think her words through. I don't owe this girl anything. She's the one with the debt to pay. So why am I questioning myself and what I should share?

Should I tell her I'm supposed to marry someone else? No, because that shit's not happening. Do I tell her that my uncle will most likely show his face at this meeting because he wants her gone? Hell nah, she'll run if she knows.

Italians can be like a pit with a bone. My uncle is going to become a problem before I can even get my plan into play. Granted, my plans are changing right as I sit here with her, but I can't lose her before I make my next move.

I sigh. "In this business, blind trust is needed. Know that everything I do is to protect my crew. You guys watch my back, I cover yours.

"Right now, what you need to know is that your uncle is a problem for me. When he stops huffing and puffing, we can get to work. Your first job will earn you half a million, but we can't get to that if your uncle starts a war or takes you back to New York," I reply.

"What?" she gasps. "A half a million?"

"Minus a hundred grand for your first payment on your debt," I say and turn to wink at her with a smile.

"You should've led with that. I'm no gold digger, but I have dreams and aspirations that money will go a long way to obtain."

"It's not gold digging when you work for it. Besides, I don't want to buy your loyalty, Oni. I want you to give it to me."

I want to kick myself for how dirty that came out. From the view out of the corner of my eye, her chest begins to heave, and I know my words hit their mark just as they were said. I chide myself.

My uncle can't pick up on any of this. Oni needs to come off as one of the guys. A driver with a set of skills I plan to put to use.

I pull into the gates at my father's estate. He's been here for a few days. Because of the deals I have coming in, he'll be in Miami for the summer as well. I'm running point, but my father has all law enforcement around here in his pocket—I need that to pull this off.

He'll be the one telling them when to turn a blind eye. I've dotted all my *i*'s and crossed all my *t*'s. Oni dropped into my lap at the right time. This works best with her.

As I pull up to the house, I notice Uncle Emilio's Rolls-Royce. Just as I thought, I'm going to be forced to prove myself today. Oni needs to play her part to keep her uncle out of the middle of this.

I'm not forcing her to choose me. I'm getting her to protect her uncle, who only wants to protect her. When I find out who's been telling my uncle my fucking business, they're dead.

That's my next order of business after I calm this storm. What the fuck is going on in my camp? Clearly, I need to step my shit up.

I park and look over at Oni. She's perfect for the job. A little makeup and we'll be able to play up her age. No one will suspect the young woman on my arm of anything I have coming.

"Come on. I have so much to teach you and a ton of money to make," I say before I get out to open her door.

She gives me a bright smile. I have to fight not to lean in and finally taste those lips. I'm in so much trouble.

Oni

This house is so much bigger than the one Rico took me to last night. Its size alone makes me feel like I'm in over my head. I haven't missed the fact that Rico is keeping his distance from me.

I'm not sure what that's about, but I roll with it and keep my head held high. I have a task to do. I'm going to do it so I can get to my bag.

"Ah, you're here," a man who looks like an older version of Rico says as we walk into the sitting room.

My uncle is already seated in the room and there's another man who looks like Rico here as well. My uncle stands and pulls me into his arms. He hugs me tight and kisses the top of my head.

I give him a tight squeeze as if to apologize for all the trouble I've caused. He releases me, and the man who greeted us places his hands on my shoulders. I look up into his eyes and they're almost identical to Rico's, the same hazel-gray color.

"How you doing, sweetheart? I'm Federico Gallo Sr. It is nice to meet you, Oni. You have left quite the impression," the man says as he pulls me in to kiss both my cheeks.

The other man snorts and folds his arms across his chest. He hasn't moved from his seat to greet us. Instead, he sits while looking me up and down as if he smells something funky.

I don't know what his problem is or who the fuck he is, but I already don't like him. Rico moves to greet him, and for the first time, the man pulls his gaze from me as he stands and pulls Rico into a hug by the back of his head as he whispers into Rico's ear. Rico stiffens.

I swear I can see anger rolling off him, but he only steps back from the man and turns to me, lifting his hand to beckon me over with his fingers. There's no tenderness in the gesture, as I have come to know. I step over to him and lift my head.

"This is Oni Raven. Jack Raven's daughter. Oni, this is Emilio Gallo, my uncle."

"Nice to meet you, sir," I say politely.

Emilio looks me over once again. Something crosses his eyes so fast I barely catch it. He tilts his head as if in thought.

"You're such a little thing to cause so much trouble," Emilio finally says to me.

"I'm sorry. It wasn't my intention for any of the trouble I caused to happen. I only want to pay what I owe and be out of your hair."

"Quiet, Oni," Uncle Claude bites out and gives me a pointed look.

"If she's old enough to be a thief, she's old enough to negotiate for herself," Emilio says slyly.

"I think we are all getting ahead of ourselves. Come have a seat, Oni. Rico, sit next to me, *my* son."

I don't miss the emphasis Federico Sr. places on the word "my." Emilio pulls a sour face and watches us as we go to take our seats. I make sure to sit across from Federico Sr., away from Rico, but with a clear view of him, his uncle, and mine.

My gut tells me to observe. My dad used to tell me to be aware of the situations I find myself in. Know how to read a room to know what cards to play.

I definitely have a hand to play here. My uncle wants me safe. Rico wants my loyalty and a driver.

I'm not going to analyze what else is in this for him. For now, I believe Federico Sr. has an agenda too, but I'm not sure yet what it is. That leaves Emilio, who I'm not sure wants me around at all.

"Oni, you took something that didn't belong to you. As a result, it cost my family a considerable loss," Rico's dad starts.

"Considerable?" Emilio murmurs and shrugs. "I would have written it off. Which is why I'm questioning my nephew. Why bring this little thief into your circle? Which head are you thinking with, *nipote*?"

"Brother, I think you should watch the video. She's more than a thief. The girl is smart. I backed his decision to hire her.

"If you think the boy isn't thinking straight, she can come and stay with me for the summer. A pretty thing like her probably shouldn't be back at the house with the boys anyway. I hadn't known she was a looker. Rico couldn't have known that either. This was a business decision," Federico says.

I keep my gaze on Rico. He looks like steam is about to come out of his ears. His fists are clenched so tight his knuckles are white. He's bouncing his knee beneath his tightly fisted hand.

I give him a pointed look so he'll catch himself. He drops his gaze to his leg and stops the movement immediately, unfisting his hands and placing them palms flat on his thighs. He gives me a curt nod of thanks.

"Pretty she is. She could come stay with me if you must have her here," Emilio says, eyeing me.

Eww, gross. He's the oldest man here. I don't miss that Federico shoots his hand out to place on top of Rico's to keep him in his seat.

"Claude has come to me as a friend. I feel like she's my responsibility. I'm vouching for the girl. She stays with me," Federico says firmly.

"Cub, what do you want to do? I'll come up with the money. I've been working on it in case something went south. You don't have to work it off if you don't want to."

"That wasn't the deal," Rico bites out.

"You chose a car she couldn't resist. You used a joke to take advantage of her one weakness. That was my bad.

"I never should have said anything. I made that deal with you, not her. You're trying to bring a little girl into a grown man's game.

"My brother would be rolling in his grave to know I allowed this. Give me a month, I'll have your money."

"She will make me twice that in a month." Rico seethes.

"And I'll get to keep a portion of what I earn for him. With that, I can go to one of those schools Mommy keeps talking about. I'm fine, Uncle Claude. You've done enough for me," I say.

"*Oni*," Uncle Claude bites out.

"I'm not a little girl anymore. It's time I own up to my mistakes. You and Mommy can't keep digging me out of trouble. Let me make things right and get my life back in order. I can do this."

"Then it's settled. Oni stays and she will live here with me. I will protect her like she's my own daughter."

Uncle Claude bites out a curse under his breath. Emilio narrows his eyes at me as if he's trying to see through me. Rico … Rico is glaring at me, and I have no idea why.

"I'll take her back to the house to pack her things," Rico says coldly.

Ut-oh. I think I fucked up.

CHAPTER SEVEN

You're Mine

Rico

"Can you please slow down? You're scaring me," Oni says from the passenger seat.

"*Fuck*," I roar and punch the steering wheel.

I know my father did what was right, but that wasn't how I wanted things to work out. Oni is supposed to be with me. Fuck, I sound like a spoiled brat in my own thoughts.

What's this girl doing to me? I press my foot on the brake pedal and take a calming breath. I need to think clearly and regroup. This isn't what I wanted, but it can still work.

"Why are you so mad at me? I'm staying in Miami, and my uncle isn't ready for war. Isn't that what you wanted?"

I tighten my grip on the steering wheel. I wanted to punch my uncle in his throat. Never in my life have I ever been so angry with him.

He took things too far. The bullshit he whispered in my ear still has my blood boiling. Oni isn't just a piece of ass because she's not the right skin color. I'm not subscribing to that bullshit.

Fuck him and that bullshit way of thinking. If he had called Oni a thief one more time, I was going to shoot him myself. I barely held in my rage during that meeting.

"I wanted you at the house with me. I didn't know my father was going to pull that shit," I snarl.

"Okay, but what difference does it make? Your place isn't that far away. Am I in danger with your dad?"

I roll my eyes. "My pop has enough whores to keep him entertained. He's no threat to you. He'll keep his word and treat you like a daughter."

"Then what's the problem?"

"*I don't know*," I bellow at the top of my lungs.

But that's just it. I do know. I don't want her away from me.

I can't deny how much I want her anymore. I'm starting to feel insane with my desire for her. It's not about sex.

Although I think she's hot as fuck, I want to know she's mine. I want to know she wants me as much as I want her. When we walk into a room, I want everyone to know she's with me and off-limits.

"Pull over," she yells back, breaking into my rambling thoughts.

"What?"

"Pull the fuck over."

"For what?"

I glance at her to see her lips are trembling. Is she about to cry? Fuck, what the hell am I doing?

"I'm already an emotional wreck trying to figure this all out. I don't need you yelling at me when all I'm doing is asking you a simple question. I want out of this car. I'll walk the rest of the way," she hurls at me.

I scoff. "You're not walking, Oni."

"Yeah, we'll see. Pull over now."

I grind my teeth and pull the car over to the side of the road. She hops out before I can put the car in park. I slam the car into park and hop out.

"Oni," I roar after her as she stomps away from the car. "Oni."

She doesn't stop or acknowledge that I'm calling her name.

"Damnit, Oni. Come back here," I bark.

She lifts her hand and gives me the finger as she continues to walk away. I tighten my jaw and slam the door shut as I take off after her. I don't have time for this shit. I've wasted enough time bullshitting in the last two days.

I eat up the distance between us in a few short strides with my long legs. She looks over her shoulder and tries to take off running when she sees I'm hot on her heels. I shake my head and quickly grab her.

"Put me down," she growls as I wrap my arms around her and throw her over my shoulder.

Oh my God, she smells so fucking good. As she wiggles in my hold, her scent surrounds me. I want to turn my head and bite her cute ass.

This is the shit she has running through my head. I'm turning into a pussy for her, and still, I don't want to be free of the hold she has on me.

She punches my back as I walk back toward the car. I tighten my hold when she almost slips. If she were anyone else, I would toss her ass down on the ground and tell her to figure her shit out. However, this is Oni.

I hurt her feelings and I'm not okay with that. Once I get her back to the car, I place her on her feet and press her into the vehicle with my body. I'm hard as fuck and I know she can feel it.

"I'm sorry," I yell into her face. "You have me acting like a pubescent teen and my head is all fucked up over you."

"What?" she asks, her brows knit.

I cup the sides of her face and tilt her head back until our gazes lock. She looks back at me with a mix of emotions. I'm sure I have a similar expression.

"I want you. That's why I want you with me. I tried to fight it.

"I know I shouldn't, but I want you and it's fucking with my head. That's why it matters where you are. I want you with me. You belong with me," I breathe into her face.

"Oh."

"Yeah, oh." I give a short laugh. "You're driving me crazy, Oni. I'm going to kiss you."

"Okay," she whispers.

Before I can talk myself out of it, I crush her lips with mine. She moans into my mouth, and I lose it. I begin to devour her as she opens up for me.

I know right away I've fucked up. She's mine. I'm not letting her go. Oni Raven will be mine forever.

I will kill a motherfucker for touching her. There isn't anything I'm willing to let come between us. She can go stay with my pop. I'll be right there with her.

This girl is everything to me.

Oni

Oh shit, oh shit, oh shit. He's kissing me. Rico Gallo is kissing me.

I don't know whether to stop this or to pull him closer for more. He's a great kisser … I think. I have no point of reference. My first kiss is from a guy I know is a killer.

I think I was dropped on my head as a baby. That would explain some of my life choices. I should not be this excited and happy to be kissing him.

"Oni," he growls into my mouth and reaches to squeeze my butt in one hand.

I can feel him growing harder against me. His bulge has been pressed against me since he first pressed me against the car. I whimper into his mouth, desperately wanting more.

My phone rings, startling me and causing me to jump away from Rico. I reach up to touch my lips as I dig my phone from my pocket. That was … I don't know what to call it. Magic, delicious, breathtaking—those are just some of the words that come to mind as I stand staring into his eyes.

He's breathing hard as he stares into mine. Pulling a hand down his face, he then blows out a breath and purses his lips. I think we're both in shock at first.

Breaking eye contact, I look down at my phone to see it's Mason. I begin to chew on my lip, wondering if I should take the call. I didn't exactly tell him where I was taking off to or that I was taking off.

I could have asked Mason for his help, but I didn't want to involve him and his family. I know who the Sullivan family is, but I do my best not to get into Mason's or his family's business. This would have dragged me right into the middle of their world.

According to Emory—our other best friend and Mason's father's right-hand man's daughter—the Gallo and Sullivan families don't necessarily get along. I will not be the reason for them going to war. Mason has never told me where he ranks in his family, but Emory has told me it's up there.

My gut is telling me to keep him out of this as best I can. Mason and Emory are the only other people outside my uncle and my mom who know I took that truck back in New York. Trackhawks aren't even my thing.

Mason had dared me to take it. He and Emory took off after I got out to accept the dare. I had been on my way to our usual meet-up spot when I accidentally knocked open the hidden compartment, causing me to pull over.

"You going to answer that?" Rico asks and lifts a brow.

"I … uh … maybe later. It's just one of my friends."

He nods and searches my eyes. I don't realize I'm holding my breath until he reaches to tuck one of my braids behind my ear.

"Say something," he breathes while searching my gaze.

I don't know what to say. I mean, I have a million thoughts, but I can't say any of them out loud to him. As I think of how I have no one here to talk to about this, I start to wonder if this is the smartest thing to do in the first place.

There's the fact that I now work for him. Then I watched him kill two guys just last night. I know who he is and who he wants to become.

Heck, if I had friends here, I still wouldn't be able to talk to them about him. That's a huge red flag if I'm honest with myself. I know for a fact I can't call Emory or Mason to tell them about all this.

The smart thing to do would be to get in this car, go and get my things, and head back to his father's house. However, I think it's clear that I haven't done the smart thing in quite some time. Instead of saying something to line up with the smart thing to do, I blurt out the first dumb thing to come to mind.

"I always thought my first kiss would be from my boyfriend. I don't know why I let you do that."

He snorts and places his hands on my hips. "Because you feel this too," he says as I drop my hand to my side away from my lips. He reaches to run his thumb over my kiss-swollen lips. He then nods his head toward me. "It's a good thing I'm your boyfriend then, isn't it?"

"What?"

He moves in closer to me until I'm pinned against the car by his strong body. "You're mine, Oni. I think I knew that the first time I saw your face. This pull is undeniable."

I shake my head as if to clear it. I need to get my thoughts together and think straight. I can't start something with him. Not too long ago, I was terrified he was going to kill me.

I scramble for something logical to say, not allowing my hormones to lead me into any more trouble. This summer has just started, and I've been finding enough of it to fall into.

"But isn't that why your uncle wants me away from you?"

He shrugs. "I won't stay away from you because I don't want to," he replies before kissing me again.

I lift on my toes as I lock my fingers in the top of his hair and kiss him back. He groans and deepens the kiss as he wraps his arms around my waist. I know I should pull away and stop this, but I can't find it in me to do so.

I'm drawn to him too. As much as that small voice in the back of my head is telling me this is going to end badly for me, I can't help myself. Just as I thought, he's become another weakness.

He breaks the kiss and places his forehead to mine. "Let me get you to the house to pack your things. We'll set some ground rules before I take you back to Pop," he says.

"Ground rules?" I repeat and frown.

"Yeah, baby. I just put a target on your back. We're going to have to be careful about this. My uncle can't find out, and neither can my enemies. Especially after last night."

"Why do I feel like I've jumped into a rabbit hole even after reading the warning sign?" I groan and press my fingertips to my temples.

Rico laughs, then pulls me to him to open the passenger's side door for me to climb back into the car. I watch as he rounds the car with a grin on his lips. Why do I always choose to make my life harder?

I can hear my mother's voice in my head, warning me to stay away from boys like my father. I should be running from Rico like my butt has been set on fire. Oh God, I hope I never have daughters because I'm going to be in so much trouble for all the grief I just can't help causing my mom.

Rico climbs in behind the wheel and reaches to pinch my chin to turn my face toward him. He leans in and takes my lips for another kiss. This time it's like he's drinking from my mouth.

My heart is pounding so hard as it sinks in that he's kissing me and wants to be my boyfriend. Reality hits. I'm in way over my head.

"Relax," he says as he breaks the kiss and pecks my nose. "You're overthinking. I'm not going to rush you into doing anything you don't want. Your virginity is safe for at least two more summers."

CHAPTER EIGHT

Impressed

Rico

Oni's phone is working my last fucking nerve. It's been ringing nonstop, and she keeps sending it to voicemail. I don't want to be that guy. I've never had a girl to be jealous. I've never had time for that shit.

However, as I sit here leaning back on my elbows as I watch her pack her things—using the suitcases I gave her to make things easier than carrying all those shopping bags—I'm growing more and more frustrated with that damn phone. Who the hell keeps calling her? Is it some guy?

"Why don't you answer it?" I bite out as it rings again, not able to help myself.

She glances over at me and shrugs. "I'm not in the mood to talk."

"Should I be worried about some other guy calling my girl?" I tease.

Her cheeks take on a glow, and she drops her head. I narrow my eyes because something tells me I'm right. It is a guy calling. Why wouldn't it be? She's fucking gorgeous.

"It's only one of my best friends. Yes, he's a guy, but it's not like that between us," she says softly.

I reach out and tug her to me. She falls onto my lap with a little gasp. My gut is telling me I should dig into her friends and relationships more.

However, the thought makes me feel kind of crazy. If I'm dating a sixteen-year-old girl, I should be able to keep my shit together about her having friends. Besides, her friends are in New York. For the most part, she will be here with me.

"If that's the case, you can answer him the next time he calls. I'll give you some space. I need to pack my things anyway," I say as I look into her eyes.

I don't get the feeling she's lying to me. I'm very good at reading people when they lie. I'm just getting to know her, but I have this feeling she's being honest.

"Pack your things? You're leaving?"

I chuckle as her face becomes crestfallen. I peck her lips and smile. "No, I'm not leaving. I'm packing to come stay at Pop's. How can I get to know my girl when she's so far away?"

She breaks into a huge smile. I know I'm asking for trouble by telling her I'm her boyfriend, but when she smiles like that, it's all worth it. I plan to call her my girl as much as I can to see that smile on her face.

"I won't be that far away," she says shyly and it's adorable.

"I know you won't because I'll be staying in my old room at Pop's."

"Are you sure that's a great idea?"

"You let me worry about that. As long as we stick to the rules, we'll be fine."

Slowly, I brush my fingers across her cheek. I get ready to lean in and take her lips, but her phone starts to ring again. We both sigh heavily. Oni stands and goes to grab the device.

This new jealous part of me wants to sit here and ear hustle, but the part of me that wants to be rational and to give her some space to breathe forces me to get up and leave the room. I'm not about to be jealous of some snot-nosed kid all the way in New York.

After all, she did say I was her first kiss and she's not into him like that. Besides, she's mine now. I may need to keep that from my uncle for the time being, but I have my ways of letting everyone know she's off-limits.

I grin to myself as I walk into my bedroom closet and grab a duffel bag. I don't need much. My room back at Pop's still has a ton of my shit there.

Some of the guys might be annoyed that we'll be moving to my dad's, but they'll get over it. Pop has never given us shit about our partying or any of that. I just didn't feel right fucking and partying under his roof like I used to.

I think of Oni and groan. I really want that girl, but I've made her a promise that I won't touch her for at least two summers. I don't even want to think about what she'll look like two summers from now.

I'm really going to have to focus on business for the next two years to keep my mind off sleeping with my girl. I have every confidence in myself that I can do this. My phone rings as I step out of my closet with my duffel bag in hand.

I'm knocked right back into reality. The business I've been putting off today comes looking for me. I roll my eyes and answer the call from Mario.

"*Ciao*, tell me something good," I say into the phone.

"I can't. Not this time."

"Fuck, what's going on now?"

"I went to visit that friend of ours. Someone already sent him on that vacation. I don't like the way this looks, boss. Something ain't right."

I bare my teeth as my mind begins to race. Jonny said he was working for Andy Cusumano. Andy has been jealous since Uncle Emilio gave my dad the go-ahead to give me a crew.

Andy has always bragged that he would become made before any of the rest of us. I call bullshit because his father knew he had shit for brains. This only proves my point.

He went and got himself killed. He was a dead man either way, but it looks like he found someone other than me to piss off.

"What are you thinking?" I say to Mario.

"Everyone knows you don't tolerant disloyalty. Someone knew you would take out Jonny and Pauly. Then they finished off Andy before he could talk.

"I don't think this was a coincidence. I think someone is trying to fuck with business."

I nod my head as I think his words over. Mario has been my best friend since I could talk. I trust him with my life. He's wearing that scar on his face because of me.

I know he always has my back. If he has a feeling, I trust it. The more I think about it, the more it sounds like he might be onto something.

"Yeah, I hear you. Start shaking some trees and see what falls out, but be as quiet as you can. I don't want anyone thinking I'm losing control of my business or my crew."

"I've got you."

"One more thing."

"What's that?"

"We're moving to Pop's."

Oni

I chew on my lip as I watch Rico walk out of my room. I think he's a little pissed off about Mason calling, but this is new. I've known Mason almost all my life.

He's my friend and no threat to Rico at all. While I know Mason had feelings for me before, I also know I've told him I don't see him that way. I made that clear after he tried to kiss me. We've been cool and in the friend zone since.

"Hello," I say into the phone as I finally answer Mason's call.

My stomach twists in knots. Rico isn't the only reason for me not wanting to answer his call. All of this is becoming more complicated by the day.

"Oni, where the hell are you? I went by your place, and your mom said you went away and you're not coming back? What's going on?"

I frown. I should have known Mom was going to do her best to shut all the doors she could while I'm gone. I got the feeling the other night that she wasn't going to allow me to come back home. I'm going away to school in the fall if it's the last thing she does.

"Relax, Mase. I'm fine. I'm just taking a break from New York to get my head on straight. I needed to take a step back from everything," I reply.

"And you didn't think to tell me or Emory? Your own cousin doesn't know anything. What the hell?"

I roll my eyes. Where I'm not interested in Mason, my cousin has had a crush on him for forever. I'm sure she fell all over herself to tell him everything she knew.

Which is why I didn't tell her anything about where I was going or why. In fact, I told Megan nothing at all.

"Megan is too caught up in herself to worry about me. Besides, I needed to do this. I didn't want to drag anyone else into my mess," I say, trying to keep the annoyance out of my voice.

"Mess? What mess?"

"Nothing. Forget I said anything," I murmur into the phone as I continue to empty my shopping bags into the suitcase Rico gave me.

Mason curses on the other end then sighs. "Just confirm one thing for me. You didn't show up that night after that thing.

"Please tell me you didn't run into any trouble. What happened to the whip? Did Larry take it off your hands?"

I drop the dress from my hands into the suitcase and turn to flop on the side of the bed. I think over what's been happening since he dared me to take that car. Glancing toward the door, I think of Rico.

My gut is telling me it's not such a good idea to tell him about the drugs, the truck, or Rico. If I tell him about one, he will have questions about the other. I should be pissed at him for daring me to take that car in the first place.

"I didn't get it. The owner showed up right after you guys took off. I went home," I lie.

"Fuck, I knew I should have waited until you were inside. I'm sorry, Oni. That shit was stupid.

"I don't know what I was thinking. You could have gotten into some real shit out there."

"Mason … did you know who that truck belonged to?"

"Huh? Did you know them? Did you see the owner's face?"

"Um, no. I only saw his back. I walked past him but didn't get a good look at his face."

"Oh, okay. So this isn't about any of that?"

My thoughts are spinning as I think fast. Mason is smart. If I'm not careful, he'll catch me in my lies. I don't want any tension between us.

"No, I told you, I needed to get away and get my head on straight. Mom was upset because I came in so late, and she flipped on me.

"It took forever to get home because I had to take the subway. It was bad. She had a bus ticket for me a few days later."

"That's why you weren't answering our calls. You were grounded?"

"Yeah, bro. You know Mom. You and Emory are too close to all the shit she wants me away from. She's terrified I'm going to fall in with your dad and all that."

"Fuck. Damn, Oni. This is all my fault. Where did she send you?"

"I'm in—"

"Shit, I have to go. I'll call you back."

"Mason, I won't be able to answer. I'll be in touch when the summer is over, and Mom cools down."

"Okay, I get it. Text me if you can. I'm going to miss you, babe."

I blow out a breath as he hangs up before I can reply. Dropping my phone on the bed, I rub my temples. If I could turn back time, I never would have gotten out of that car.

"You all good in here?"

I lift my gaze and find Rico standing in the doorway, looking sexy as sin in a pair of black shorts and a light-blue polo shirt. It's the most relaxed I've seen him since I've met him.

All thoughts of turning back time fade away. I inhale deeply. What were the chances of my accepting a dare to take his car?

Maybe this was meant to be. My heart begins to race as he moves into the room and stands before me. He reaches to pull me up from my seat and wraps his arms around me. I look up at him shyly and get caught in his gaze.

"What?" he says as he searches my face.

"Nothing."

He pinches my chin between his fingertips. "Come on. Let's go. I want to get you to Pop's so I can handle some calls and then I'm taking you out for our first date."

"That's not going to be against the rules?"

"No. We're going somewhere my uncle won't know anything about. I have some people I think you should meet."

CHAPTER NINE

Change the Plan

Rico

"Bro, why the fuck are we staying at Uncle Federico's?" my cousin groans into the phone.

"Stop whining like a little pussy. He's not worried about us. Nothing is going to change," I laugh.

I jog down the stairs from my room after unpacking my things. Eduardo and Aldo's plane just landed, and Aldo called to let me know they've arrived.

"I didn't come to Miami to hang with my fucking uncle. Why can't we stay at your place?"

"I'm having some work done," I lie.

I'm not able to tell him I'm using that as an excuse so my uncle doesn't get suspicious. If I allow him and his brother to stay at my place, it will look crazy. This is where I need to be, so everyone will be here with me.

"That shit couldn't wait? Fuck it. What are we doing tonight?"

"I have plans. You'll see when you get here. Now get off my phone. I have shit to do."

I pull the phone from my ear and hang up. I want Oni to meet my cousins. Eduardo and Aldo are more like brothers to me.

None of this shit has ever come between us. I hope that it never does. Our other cousin, now that's another story.

Time will tell there. Moving to the French doors that lead out to the pool from this room, I stop and stare out. Oni is sitting out by the pool with my younger cousin, Emilia.

I should have known Uncle Emilio would have her come to stay to have eyes on Oni. My pop probably agreed to make Oni feel more comfortable. Emilia just turned seventeen.

She's your typical Mafia princess. She can do no wrong in our family's eyes. Emilia doesn't take any shit, but she's a sweetheart under it all.

She'll make a great companion for Oni. They already seem to be hitting it off.

"How did I know you would return with her?" my pop says as he comes to my side.

"What, you don't want your only son under your roof? Come on, Pop. You know you miss me," I say and turn to him with a wide smile.

He slaps my cheek and grunts. "This face. If I didn't love you, I'd punch you right in it. What were you thinking?"

"What do you mean?"

"You know Emilio. You don't show him your hand. You never show a weakness." He points toward Oni. "She is a weakness."

"Pop—"

He holds a hand up and shakes his head. "Come, take a walk with me. We need to talk."

I sigh and follow him from the room. Shoving my hands into my pockets, I stroll beside him quietly. I knew this was coming.

"She's pretty. I lot prettier than I thought she would be. Your plan needs to be adjusted. There's no way you're walking into a room and she doesn't pull more attention than necessary," Pop starts.

I thought about this myself. I had planned to have Oni on my arm, but after my uncle's reaction, I'm second-guessing myself. Oni doesn't need to pull unwanted attention if she's going to disappear mid-engagement.

"What if she doesn't come in on my arm? Listen, I can arrive and give the signal when our targets are all in the room. Then she can get the list, load up, and arrive after.

"By the time anyone realizes their shit is missing, she'll be at the party with me, and no one will suspect her."

"That's a great idea, but there's one problem."

"What's that?"

"I've never been a fool. I know you've either claimed the girl or intend to. Anyone looking to push your buttons will see they can use her. I think it might be better if I'm the escort. I've been known to have a pretty young face on my arm," he says.

"Not this young," I bite out.

"Relax, I'm old enough to be her father. This is business."

He waves me off. "You see what I mean? Rico, either change the plan and involve me or find another hustle. You're the one looking to impress my brother. I have other jobs I can set in motion."

"Fine, I like the idea, but I don't think we should run the same game as many times as we planned. There needs to be one or two where neither of you shows your faces," I reply.

"Now you're thinking. I'll have Estell come by to fit the girl for a few gowns. Meanwhile, I promised her uncle she would be safe. I'm going to have her work as my assistant. I don't need you making me a grandfather and starting a war."

"Pop, really?"

"Like I said, she's pretty, gorgeous in fact. I bet you don't make it to the end of the summer without falling into her bed. I was young once too."

"It's not like that. She's sixteen. I'm nineteen. That ain't gonna happen."

He roars with laughter. "Whatever you say, son. Whatever you say."

He walks off, leaving me frowning after him as he continues to laugh like I told the world's funniest joke. I roll my eyes and turn to head out to the pool, where Oni and Emilia should be.

I pull my phone to shoot Mario a text. Now that we're changing the plan, we'll need to discuss a few things. I need to see him.

When I step out of the back of the house, laughter causes me to lift my head. I stop dead in my tracks as I find Oni and Emilia now in swimsuits. My mouth falls open as my gaze locks on Oni.

The little bikini she has on is going to get someone killed. The beige two-piece is showing off that sexy body and all that silky-looking brown skin. When she crosses her legs and places her arms behind her back, I can't help but wonder if she knows what she's doing to me.

"Fuck me. Come on," I huff.

Oni

"Oh my God. You don't have something else I can borrow? My ass is eating this thing," I say to Emilia and reach to pull the bikini bottoms out of my butt.

Emilia bursts into laughter. "You look hot. If I know my cousin, there will be tons of hot guys around here before the night is over."

That's the last thing I want to hear. Rico's head might explode if he sees me in this thing. He was pissed about a phone call.

He's not going to like this bikini one bit. I wouldn't even argue because I know it's inappropriate.

"About that …" I say and trail off, biting my lip.

"Don't tell me you already have a boyfriend back in New York. That's going to make this summer suck. Not only will you be no fun at all the parties I want to take you to, but you're probably going to spend all your time on the phone with him."

I snicker at her. I can't tell her about Rico. That would go against the rules he set back at his house.

Besides, Uncle Emilio is her dad. I'm not sure Rico would want her to know about us. Right as I get ready to tell her I don't have a boyfriend, Rico steps from the house.

"Look, there's Cousin Rico. Let's see what he thinks. He's always so focused on work. If you can get a reaction out of him, you might be right, and I'll find you something else."

"Or you could just give me something else now. I don't want to spend the day pulling this crap out of my butt cheeks."

Emilia bursts into laughter. "You're so funny. I thought this was going to be such a lame summer, but now you're here."

"Yay," I murmur and frown.

I like her, but this bathing suit has to go. My mom would kill me. This thing makes my boobs look huge and my ass is barely covered. I also look older in it.

Emilia laughs again as she throws her arms around my neck and hugs me. When she lets me go, I turn to look at Rico. He looks up from his phone and his eyes lock on me.

I know right away this bikini is a bad idea. Lust fills his eyes as he stands, taking me in from head to toe. I cross my thighs and reach to clasp my hands behind me as if that will cover my ass even though he can't see behind me from where he stands.

"Rico, come here. Have you met Oni? Your dad said she's his new assistant. She'll be here for the summer.

"She's so cool. She's from New York too. I think you guys will get along."

I bite my lip as Rico saunters over. His face becomes expressionless. I try my best to mirror him and have no reaction to his presence.

If he can sell this, so can I. However, when he stops before me, I'm not sure I can do it. He smells so good, and my body wants to lean into him.

"How much did he give you?" Rico says as he looks Emilia in the eyes.

"He promised five hundred a day and Demarco comes off the list," Emilia says, dropping her smile and her voice.

Rico snorts and rocks his jaw. I watch as a dark cloud comes over his face. I'm not sure what they're talking about, but he's pissed.

He looks at me and rolls his gaze over me, nodding to himself. I feel like I'm missing something here, but I remain silent and frozen in my spot.

"I'll give you fifteen hundred a day. If I have to, I'll take Demarco off the board myself. Fucker is too old to be trying to secure a marriage between the two of you anyway," Rico says.

"Deal."

Rico turns to me and grasps me by the back of my neck. I'm taken by surprise when he tugs me to him and pecks me on the lips. I look at Emilia and then back at him.

"I thought—"

"Your secret is safe with me. My father sent me here to spy on you guys, but Rico just made me a better offer. Besides, I like you and I really do want to be friends.

"My father doesn't allow me to hang out much. It will be good to have someone I can spend time with," Emilia explains.

"Oh."

This family is weird. I definitely need to keep my head on a swivel around them. I'm pulled from my thoughts as Rico glides his hand across my stomach, raising goose bumps.

I look up as he's examining me. Looking over my front and then my back. I lift a brow at him. He bites down on his lip and shakes his head.

"Nah, I'm not cool with this. You need to change," he says, looking me in the eyes.

"Oh, come on. She looks superhot. A body like that was made for that suit," Emilia whines.

"Yeah, if it were in her size, maybe. And that's a big maybe. My girl isn't sitting around like this. Not in this lifetime."

"Fine. I have a one-piece in my bag. What's the plan for tonight? Are Ed and Al still coming in?"

"They're already here. They should be pulling up soon. We're all heading out at eight. Oni here is going to have her first experience at The Garden."

"The Garden? What's that?"

"It's an underground club. I went for the first time last summer. It's cool." Emilia shrugs.

"I don't have my fake ID. I left it back in New York," I say.

Rico snorts. "You'll be with me. You don't need a fake ID."

I nod and lick my lips. He's been rubbing his thumb against my skin and it's driving me crazy. Loud voices and laughter begin to float from the house.

Rico releases me and taps my butt. "Go change. Now," he commands.

CHAPTER TEN

Meet the Family

Rico

"Look at this guy," Eduardo croons as he and Aldo walk out of the house with Mario.

I tear my gaze away from the side door Oni just walked through. I'm glad she didn't fight me on changing. That bikini was a problem.

Once my cousins know who she is, I doubt there will be any issue, but that doesn't mean I want her walking around here like that. There will be others around as the day goes on.

I didn't even know she had that type of body beneath her clothes. I knew she was stacked nicely, but not like that. My father was right.

Oni is a problem. She's fast becoming a weakness. Something I was raised never to have. If I'm not careful, I'm going to be caught out here with my balls in my hands.

I can't have that. I need to get this under control and fast—I don't need any distractions. Two more years and I'll be well on my way to my goal. As I have the thought, I wonder if this was a great idea in the first place.

"He looks like he thinks he owns the world or some shit. Can you believe this?" Aldo adds, bringing me from my thoughts.

I focus back on the newcomers and smile. It's been a while since we've had a chance to hang out. Eduardo and Aldo have been busy with high school.

"That's what I'm talking about," Eduardo says and shakes his head.

We clap hands and I tug him in by the back of his head. As we embrace, he claps me on the back. I release him and do the same with Aldo.

"It's good to see your ugly mugs. I was getting tired of all your bullshit excuses on why you couldn't come out," I say as I release Al and look between the two of them with a smile on my lips.

"Fuck you. Who are you calling ugly? We all know you need us to pull in the pussy. That's why you begged us to come out," Ed taunts.

"Fuck outa here. You wish."

"Emilia," Al sings. "To what do we owe the pleasure? Don't tell me the old man decided to let you out of your cage this summer."

Emilia flips him the bird but allows him to pull her into a hug. I shake my head at the two. They are close since they're the same age. Aldo treats her like his sister.

One phone call from her and he comes running, usually leaving Eduardo and me to clean up after them. Eduardo and I are a year apart.

We have always looked after the two. I think that's why they get into shit all the time. They know we'll have their backs no matter what.

"No, really. What's up? Are you going to get to hang for a bit?" he prods when she doesn't reply.

Emilia looks at me. I nod to let her know I trust them with this. She rolls her eyes as Aldo wraps an arm around her head and tugs her into him.

"Pop sent me to spy on Rico and his new little girlfriend. So I'll be where they are for the summer," she says.

"Girlfriend?" Ed says and looks at me with a raised brow.

"When did this happen?" Al asks.

"It's new and it's none of his business. She's off-limits, so don't go running your mouth about anything you learn about her or us."

"Well, where is she? I want to meet her," Al says.

"Why is Uncle Emilio so interested in her?" Ed asks.

"You'll see," Emilia says with a smug grin.

"Now my interest is piqued," Al says.

"Well, here she comes," Emilia says.

Oni comes back out of the house with a glass of ice tea in her hand. She's in a tank top and shorts this time. Not as revealing as the bikini, but she still looks sexy.

It's like she commands the space with her presence. I know she has all my attention. It seems like she has everyone else captivated as well.

I bite my lip and beckon her to me with the crook of my finger. She comes to me and stands right in front of me. I take the glass from her hand and take a sip of the cold-looking drink.

"Hey, go get your own," she fusses.

I laugh and tug her into me by the front of her tank top to take her lips. She grabs my shirt and lifts onto her toes as I devour her mouth and roll the ice cube in mine against her tongue. When I break the kiss, she looks up at me as if in a daze.

I tuck her under my arm and turn her to my cousins who are watching us with their mouths hanging open. It's my turn to have the smug grin.

"Aldo, Eduardo, I want you to meet Oni," I say, then place my hand on Oni's forehead to tip her head back and drop a kiss on her full lips.

"Nice," Al croons.

Oni's cheeks start to glow. She takes her glass back from me and downs the entire thing. I know I just put her on the spot, but I couldn't help myself. I had to kiss her.

This shit is going to be harder than I thought. For now, we're cool. Eduardo, Aldo, Mario, and Emilia have always been in my corner. I don't have to look over my shoulder around them.

I turn to look down into Oni's eyes and wink at her. "Oni, these are my cousins. I trust them both with my life. We can trust everyone out here right now," I reassure her.

Her entire body relaxes at my side. I look around me, and this feels right; these are the people I will have in my life while I rise to the top. I can feel it in my bones.

Oni

I'm filled with nervous energy. This is not what I signed up for. While Rico trusts his cousins and Mario, we're to act as if we're not a couple in front of everyone else.

I would be fine with that if we weren't going out tonight. We're going to an underground club. A place where there will be plenty of other guys. I'm not a fool and I've seen how possessive Rico can be. I feel like tonight is going to end in disaster.

"You look perfect," Emilia sings as she hands me a lip gloss to put on.

I look in the mirror and shake my head. Why am I allowing this girl to talk me into this shit? If Rico ends up placing both of us in the trunk of a car to drive us into a ditch, it's all her fault.

I swipe the gloss on and then look my reflection over. My braids are back down in a high-low style. I have on a jumpsuit that cuffs around the neck. Because the back and sides are out, I don't have a bra on.

That's just problem number one. I have on a thong and when I walk, I can feel my butt jiggling, so I know anyone looking hard enough will see it. That's problem number two.

"You had this all planned," I say to Emilia. "You went through my things and found this outfit, then you told Rico we would meet them there, knowing he would agree because we need to keep our distance. Are you really on our side?"

I narrow my eyes as I glare at her. I might end up breaking up with Rico because I'm going to kick his cousin's ass for setting me up. She gives me a mischievous smile and pops up on the counter to sit and look back at me.

"I love my cousins with all I am. Those three always have my back. I would go to the ends of the earth for them.

"Rico and the rest of us know you present something he's never had to deal with. You're a weakness. He either learns to deal with it now, or it will come back to burn him later. I'm only helping him to learn his limits." She shrugs.

I suck my teeth and roll my eyes. "Why me if I'm such a problem?"

"Because Rico has never looked at anyone the way he looks at you. You have to understand Rico has had his eyes set on my father's seat for as long as I can remember. Papa wants to give it to him, but he wants to know he's ready.

"My father has tried his hardest to trip Rico up with anything that would turn his head. He has never succeeded and then you show up and from what my father says, Rico turned his head.

"I don't know why you." She shrugs. "You're pretty and smart. Rico loves to have smart people around him.

"If you're a thinker, he either makes you a friend or treats you like an enemy. You know what happens to enemies. But you heard none of that from me."

"Why tell me any of this?"

"I told you. I like you. I think you're good for Rico. Besides, no one realizes how much I know. I'm to be seen and not heard, but you … I think you're here to change all that."

"I'm not too sure about that," I murmur.

"We'll see. Come on, Rico's going to have a fit if we take too long to arrive," she says and hops down off the counter.

"Oh, goody," I cheer under my breath.

This is going to be a long night. I just hope I make it back without witnessing a murder or being killed myself. Why do I get myself into these situations?

***

Mario is waiting outside the club for us. It's not at all what I was expecting. It's an old warehouse-looking building. A bunch of nice cars are parked outside like some type of car show. Cars I would normally case to take before the end of the night.

However, since my boyfriend is here and I'm trying to live a reformed life, I walk by the Lambos, Maseratis, and Aston Martins with appreciation. My palms itch, but I keep chanting in my head that I'm done with stealing cars.

"This is going to be an issue," Mario mutters and shakes his head as we get to his side.

He turns to the bouncer and gives a nod. We go to follow him in, but I take one last look over my shoulder at the cars and the crowd still outside the club, seeming to be having their own party. There is one guy who catches my attention as he sits on the hood of one of the cars, taking me in.

I shake off the eerie vibe that comes over me and head inside. The music is thumping as we enter the club. There are people everywhere. Mario takes Emilia's hand, and she reaches for mine.

I follow them through the crowd to a set of stairs that lead down to another level. The lighting changes as we enter what seems like a totally different party. We keep going until we get to the back where I see Rico, Aldo, and Eduardo sitting, surrounded by girls.

"What the fuck?" I whisper to myself.

I ball my fist at my side and get ready to turn to leave. Emilia tugs at my hand to stop me. She leans into my ear and tries to talk over the music.

"It's not what you think. Don't react like that. He's testing you too," she says.

I take in a deep breath and think her words over. For as long as I've known him, he's been testing me. If that's what this is, okay. It's go time. I'll show him just how I'll handle this.

CHAPTER ELEVEN

Drama

Rico

"Let's go," Ed calls as he downs a drink and grabs the girl closest to him to stand and dance with.

He doesn't even bother to take her down to the dance floor. I shake my head and roll my eyes for the millionth time and fight not to shove this chick's hand off me. I'm not interested in any of these girls who have surrounded us. I would have had them bounced right up out of here any other night.

Glancing at my watch, I work my jaw and frown. What the fuck is taking Emilia and Oni so long? I sent Mario out to wait for them thirty minutes ago.

"This place is lame tonight," the girl on my left says.

I grunt. She's right. It is. I've been ready to go.

I'm getting ready to say fuck it when the crowd parts and Mario comes into view, followed by Emilia. The chick on my right starts to whine about leaving and glides her hand up my arm. That's when Oni comes into view.

My mouth runs dry, and my pants tighten. How does this girl become more beautiful every time I see her? Disappointment hits when it looks like she's going to turn and walk away.

I was expecting a little more fire from my little car thief. However, Emilia stops her and whispers something that causes Oni's face to transform completely. She throws her shoulders back and lifts her head.

I'm in awe of how she commands the room around her. She looks like a model on the runway as she saunters over to the area we're sitting in and gracefully takes the seat farthest away from me.

I can't take my eyes off her, but she won't spare me a glance. Licking my lips, I take her in. Her nipples, pushing at the thin fabric of her outfit, grab my attention. When she crosses one thigh over the other, the clear heels on her cute little feet come into view.

"Should we get another round?" I call out, not taking my eyes off her.

"Yes," the one with her hands still on me says in an annoying, whiny voice.

"We'll take two frozen daiquiris," Emilia says from beside Oni with a smile.

"Actually, I'll take a Sex on the Beach. It can still be frozen," Oni says.

I work my jaw but nod for Mario to place the order for everyone. Pop would kick my ass for this, but I won't allow her to drink too much and no one's going to harm her.

I'm pissed as the guys who don't know any better now have their attention on my girl. The hungry looks they're giving her have me ready to pull my guns. Not a single one of them will ever have her on a beach or anywhere else.

However, I add it to the list of places I plan to have her once I claim her fully. I take a calming breath and pull it together. I can't lose my shit tonight.

"Maybe after this round, we can head out. There's this party not far from here, or we can hang at your place," the handsy chick says in my ear.

I pluck her hand out of my lap before she reaches what she's looking for. It's not for her. I'm hard for the one who won't look at me.

"I don't think so," I reply, still not looking away from Oni.

Our drinks come and Oni starts to suck down the large fruity drink. I know she feels my eyes on her. I lift my glass of water to my lips and keep my eyes narrowed.

I never drink when I'm out like this. I always have water in my glass. Let everyone think I'm getting shit-faced. I always learn who's willing to try me.

"Come dance with me," Emilia stands and says to Oni.

Oni finishes her drink and nods. I follow them with my gaze as I sit back and place my arms over the back of the sofa I'm lounging on. Redman's "Let's Get Dirty" bumps through the speakers as they make it onto the dance floor.

I'm not surprised when Oni starts to roll and snake her body to the beat. All that New York attitude comes out. I'm not going to lie, Oni is the baddest one on the dance floor.

When she turns her back to me and throws her arms in the air as she sways her body and rocks her hips, I nearly lose it. That cute ass of hers is jiggling in that thin excuse for a romper.

I can't tear my eyes away from her back as her bare skin starts to glisten with sweat. Images of taking her from behind while holding her tits and pounding into her fill my head. I'd fist those braids in my hand while getting so deep inside her she would feel me for weeks.

I shift in my seat and clear my throat. That's not going to happen anytime soon. As if reading my thoughts, she turns with her arms still in the air and bends her knees as she rocks her hips like she's riding me. She drops low and winds her hips as she comes back up to her full height.

Her little ass is trying to kill me or make me kill that little pussy. I nod my head to the beat as I remain transfixed by my girl. She locks eyes with me and keeps moving that sexy body.

When she turns and pops her ass, I'm done. My restraint breaks and I'm on my feet. I'm headed straight for her until the two girls who have been sitting with us run in front of me, blocking my way.

They start to wiggle in front of me, annoying the shit out of me. Oni looks at me and frowns. Then, some guy walks up and starts to dance with her.

All I see is red. When he places his hands on her hips, I can't see straight. I lose all focus.

"I think the fuck not. Fuck outa here," I growl, and shove past the two annoyances.

Oni

With all these bodies crowded together, it's hot in here. Sweat is dripping down my back and between my boobs. The music is bumping, and that drink is definitely hitting.

I sway and do a little two-step. I'm feeling nice. There was a lot of alcohol in that drink.

I'm not even thinking about Rico and his little friends. The guy who's dancing on me is starting to get grabby and I'm not with that. I continue to dance and start to throw my elbows to give him a hint to back off. I even dance away to get closer to Emilia, who's rocking her hips and lost in the music.

"Okay, girl," I sing.

Emilia bops her head and smiles at me. I grab her hand and rock from side to side with her. That's when this dude comes up on me again. I turn to tell him to back off, but Rico has placed himself between us and he's glaring the guy down.

Rico pushes me behind him. I now have a full view of his broad back, so I don't know if the guy has backed off or not. Not wanting to dance with either of them, I go to walk off. My arm is grabbed, and I'm tugged back.

"Get your hand the fuck off her," Rico snarls.

I go to yank away, but the guy ignores Rico and tugs me to him. Rico wraps his arm around my waist and tugs me into his chest. In the next motion, he pulls a gun and points it at the guy's face.

It all happens so fast. The guy is looking into the barrel of Rico's gun with a grin on his lips. That's when, out of the corner of my eye, I see another guy I know isn't with us pulling a gun.

Without thinking, I reach for Rico's other gun and pull it from its holster. Lightning fast, I aim at the guy aiming at Rico. Rico tightens his arm around me, but I hold fast.

"You don't want to do that. Drop that shit before I drop you," I say.

Rico kisses my forehead. "I think you should listen to her," he says as he releases me and takes his gun from my hand to aim them both himself.

He backs away from me to have both guys in his view as his arms are spread out. Aldo comes and grabs me, tugging me out of the way. Mario creeps up behind the guy I had been aiming at and places his gun at the guy's head.

"Looks like they're not vetting who gets in here anymore. Not everyone should have such privileges. Whatever, you two are done," Rico growls.

"Come on. He's got this," Aldo says in my ear as he tries to shove me to leave. Ed has Emilia, but my focus is still on Rico. "Come on, Bonnie. Clyde can handle this."

I look at Aldo and purse my lips. I wasn't trying to be Bonnie and Clyde. That guy was going to hurt Rico if I didn't act fast.

We get outside the club, and my heart is racing. The guys rush us into our car and Eduardo jumps into the driver's seat. I look around wildly as he pulls off, leaving Rico and Mario behind.

"They'll be right behind us. Stop worrying," Ed says.

"Oh shit, you pulled a gun on that guy. That was so badass. You and Rico looked made for each other. That was crazy," Emilia says.

"I don't know what I was thinking. I saw him going to pull the gun and I reacted."

"Did you even know how to use it?" Al asks.

"No," I whisper.

Aldo and Emilia burst into laughter. My cheeks heat and I feel so stupid for my actions. Here I go, still making bad decisions.

"Wait until I tell Rico this one," Eduardo grumbles. "You don't pull a gun unless you're ready to use it."

"I wasn't thinking that far ahead. I just didn't want that guy to shoot Rico."

"She's definitely a ride or die," Emilia sings.

"Crazy as he is for sure," Ed mumbles and shakes his head.

"I like you. You just earned my respect," Aldo says.

We get to the house and Eduardo parks the car. I climb out after Emilia and get ready to head inside and go to bed. However, I only make it a few steps before I'm grabbed around the waist and thrown over a shoulder.

The next thing I know, I'm being carried into the house as I bounce on said shoulder. I know it's Rico because of his cologne and the gun holster on his shoulders. His suit jacket is gone now.

I grasp his dress shirt and hold on as he moves through the house. It's all I can do to keep from falling onto my head. I'm starting to get a little queasy as we finally reach our destination.

He allows my body to slide down his front until I'm back on my feet. I look up at him as he steadies me with his hands on my waist.

"What were you thinking?" he whisper-yells.

"I … you. I reacted. He was going to shoot you," I say as I look at him pleadingly.

In hindsight, I already feel stupid. I could have hurt someone or something, or worse. I could have gotten us hurt.

Instead of yelling at me, Rico cups my face and crushes my lips with his. I whimper into his mouth and lock my fingers into his hair. He groans and wraps his arms around me tightly.

"You're making it hard for me not to—" He cuts off the words he was going to say against my lips.

I swallow hard and look into his eyes. In this moment, I feel like our connection deepens. If I wanted to turn away from him, I missed my last chance. This is it.

This is where I belong. There is no turning back. I can see it in his eyes. I'm his.

CHAPTER TWELVE

Want You to Stay

Rico

My phone is going crazy in my pocket. I should check it, but the only thing that matters to me is Oni. I need to know she's okay.

She pulled a gun to cover me. She pulled a fucking gun. I'm still trying to wrap my head around what happened tonight.

I was ready to blow that asshole's head off for putting his hands on her. He was in my spot, touching my girl, and had the nerve to disrespect me. Me … Rico Gallo.

"I'm sorry," Oni whispers, pulling me from my spiraling thoughts.

I shake my head. "This was on me. I've been allowing too much slack around here. You've been opening my eyes to a lot since you took that truck."

I run The Garden as an underground investment. I don't run around announcing it belongs to me, but if you're in the know, you know. That motherfucker knows.

Or should I say he knew. I took care of him and his friend. I also fired every one of the guys who were working security tonight.

That dude shouldn't have gotten in with that gun. My guys and I went in through the back door, where we're not searched. There was no reason for him to have had that gun in my place.

He had to pay someone to overlook it. Since that gun almost became a direct problem for me, it's a problem for everyone.

In a matter of minutes, I sorted all that shit out and took off after my girl. She pulled my gun, ready to have my back. I had to get to her and make sure she was all right.

I guess that's why they're blowing my phone up now. Just like that, I dropped everything for some girl. I almost told her that I'm falling in love with her.

I stopped myself before I did. It's been what? Two seconds. In those two seconds, she has shown me that she's down for me. I have soldiers in my crew who haven't shown as much loyalty as she has in the less than two days she's known me.

I search her face, wondering why. Does she feel this connection the way I do? Is it crazy that I'm falling for her?

"Stay the night with me," I say as I search her gaze.

Her eyes grow wide, and her chest begins to heave. This is the innocence I expect from her. This is the girl I thought I would meet when I went to trap her.

However, that's not who she is. There's so much more to her. I want to get to know every nuance of Oni Raven. I will learn everything that makes her tick.

"Won't your father be upset?"

I shake my head. "I'll get you out before he notices. I just need you with me. I'm not going to try anything you don't want. I want you in my arms."

She chews on her lip as she looks back at me. I don't realize I'm holding my breath until she reaches for my face. She lifts on her toes and kisses me.

I take over the kiss and consume her. I know without a doubt I'm falling hard for this girl. Tonight was an epic fail on my part.

But Oni? She held her ground and showed me she can handle being in my world.

"What about what I do want?"

"Oni," I growl in warning as I grab her hips.

I take her lips as I back her toward my bed. I shouldn't have brought her in here in the first place. Now that she's here, I want nothing more than to lay her down and feast on her.

I lost my virginity at fifteen to a girl who was nineteen. Yet I don't want that for Oni. I want her first time to be special. Something she'll always remember fondly.

She doesn't deserve to be fucked like a savage and tossed aside the next day. That's who I've become. I make sure they never want to forget me and then I'm gone.

"Rico," she whimpers as I kiss my way down her neck.

"I'm only going to hold you tonight. Sometimes it's not the right time for the things we want. I want you bad, but I need you more."

"What does that mean?"

It means I know where I want to go. I know who I need to be to get there. I'm losing more of myself with each day.

Oni is a breath of fresh air. She's what I didn't know I needed. However, I don't have the words to tell her all of that. So I swallow my thoughts down and tell her what I can say.

"You will understand one day. I'll get you one of my shirts. You can hop into bed while I shower," I reply.

She purses her lips and looks as if she's going to protest. After a beat, she sighs and nods. I close my eyes as she smiles then glides her small hands down my chest.

"Okay," she whispers.

I take a breath and open my eyes. "Oni?"

"Yes?"

"When I get out of the shower, you better be here. Don't run from me again. I just watched you stand in the middle of a gunfight.

"I'm not okay. I need you here," I say, then kiss her nose.

I turn to find her a shirt and gather my thoughts. I fucked up. Tonight, I was supposed to show I could be indifferent to Oni.

Instead, I showed I will kill you for breathing in her direction. I have to spin this and keep her safe. Right now, my head is too fucked up for me to see how.

Losing her isn't an option. I should send her home. I should walk away. I know all the things I should do, but those are all the things I will not.

"Fuck," I hiss and punch the closet wall.

Oni

"Here," Rico says as he hands me a T-shirt to change into.

"Thank you."

I take it and hold it to my chest as he turns and heads to the bathroom. I don't release a breath until he shuts the door behind him. Releasing a sigh, I go to sit on the edge of the bed and start to take my shoes off.

They drop to the floor with a deafening thud. It's then I realize how hard I'm breathing. I'm going to spend the night in his room. In the bed with him.

"What are you doing, Oni?" I hiss at myself.

Megan lost her virginity last year. We're a year apart, me being the oldest. I will never forget the look of regret on her face.

Would I regret going all the way with Rico? Something tells me I wouldn't. I chew on my lip as I stare at the bathroom door.

His words come back to me, and I shiver. *When I get out of the shower, you better be here. Don't run from me again. I just watched you stand in the middle of a gunfight. I'm not okay. I need you here.*

I understand how he feels. I want to be here with him too. Pulling up my big-girl panties, I stand and reach for the clasp on the back of my jumpsuit. It falls to my waist, and I cover my bare breasts.

I then reach for the side zipper and release it. The jumper falls to the floor, and I step from it. Quickly, I grab the T-shirt and pull it over my head.

The thing swallows me, falling well below my knees. I pick up my romper and shoes and take them over to the chair on the other side of the room.

As I set my things down, pictures on the desk grab my attention. I move to get a better look. A smile comes to my lips as I look at one that seems to be Rico, his cousins, and Mario as little kids.

Everyone has a smile on their face except for Rico. Even as a boy, he had a serious expression on his face. I wonder what he was thinking back then. Did he have so much on his shoulders even then?

The next picture is of Rico and a pretty, dark-haired woman. She's very pretty. Tall and thin, but not too thin. Rico has his arm around her shoulders and a genuine smile is on his face.

I get the feeling this is his mom. I'll have to ask him some other time. Suddenly, my body feels so heavy.

I stumble back over to the foot of the bed and climb onto it. The moment my head hits the pillow, my lids grow heavy. I snuggle into the pillow and release a yawn.

The bed dips and warmth hits my back. I open my eyes, confused for a moment. Then I feel soft lips against my skin.

"I didn't mean to wake you," Rico murmurs.

"I didn't know I fell asleep."

"Come on, let's get under the sheets."

I get up with him as he pulls the comforter back and then peels the sheet up for me to slide under. He climbs in behind me and wraps me in his arms again. I inhale his delicious scent as I lie stiff as a board.

Rico chuckles in my ear. "Relax, baby. I'm not about to pull anything."

I turn around to face him. He has a gorgeous smile on his face. Smiling back at him, I cup his cheek.

"Is that your mom in the picture on your desk?"

He seems to think for a second. Then recognition hits his gaze. He smiles and nods.

"Yeah, that's her. That was my sixteenth birthday. She surprised me with a trip to Italy right before that picture. It was just me and her," he says.

"You sound like she means a lot to you."

"She does. I think she will love you."

"Tell me about her."

"She's beautiful inside and out. Mama speaks her mind, but she's not quick to show she's angry. Oh, but you'll know when she does something so petty you have no doubt she's gunning for you.

"I guess you can say she's sweet until she's not. You know what I mean?"

I search his face and note that this is the most unguarded he's been with me. I move closer and snuggle into him. He places his chin on the top of my head and begins to rub my back.

"Yeah, I get it. I hope I get to meet her," I say softly.

"You will. Can you tell me something?"

"Yeah, what's up?"

"Can you shoot a gun?"

"No."

"Oni," he groans. "Really, baby?"

My heart skips a beat as he calls me the endearment for the second time. I lean in and kiss his bare chest. His hand on my back stills.

I move to press my lips to his, not wanting to talk about earlier tonight. He takes my lips and rolls me onto my back. I spread my legs to cradle him between my thighs.

He deepens the kiss and starts to grind his hips into me. I claw at his back, pulling a groan from deep in his throat. Pushing the T-shirt I'm wearing up, he palms my breast and begins to play with my nipple.

I whimper into his mouth and wrap my legs around him. My heart begins to race. My thong is getting wet.

He's growing harder as he grinds into me. No way. That can't be. All of that? No.

He breaks the kiss and looks down at me. "You are my greatest weakness. I don't want to tell you no."

"Please don't," I plead.

He stares at my lips with longing, then shakes his head as if to clear it. I see the lust in his eyes, but I feel the rejection coming. I sigh in disappointment.

"This once I have to. Good night, baby," he says and pecks my lips. Then he rolls onto his back.

CHAPTER THIRTEEN

Oops, Busted

Oni

I wake and my head is pounding. There's something poking me in my butt and something heavy is lying across my middle. I groan and open my eyes.

"*Mm,* what time is it?" Rico groans, reminding me I'm in his bed.

I gasp. "It's time for me to get out of here," I say.

He tightens his hold around me and nuzzles my neck. Whatever is poking me in the butt seems to jerk and jump against my cheeks. I wiggle a little and it happens again.

I gasp as my brain wakes and I realize what that is. Rico locks me tighter in his embrace. It feels like he's settling in to go back to sleep. I need to get out of here before his father finds me in his bed.

"Rico. You need to get up and sneak me back into my room."

"Just ten more minutes. You feel so good in my arms," he says sleepily.

"Dude, we need to get up now."

He rolls onto his back and huffs, throwing his arm across his face. I sit up and slip from the bed to head into the bathroom. My bladder feels like it's going to burst.

I sigh as I relieve myself. My head continues to pound. It feels like it has a pulse of its own.

I need to get to my room to take something to stop this torture. I hurry to finish and wash my hands so I can get back to my room. As I step up to the sink, I glance in the mirror.

I look a mess. Closing my eyes, I lean over the sink to splash some water over my face. When I straighten, I feel strong arms wrap around me.

I open my eyes to find Rico standing behind me. He leans in to nuzzle my neck. Once again, I feel him pressed into me.

"You still smell so good," he says. Then he points to the countertop where my phone is now sitting. He must have brought it in here. "Your phone was buzzing."

I reach for it and pick it up. It's a text message from Emilia asking where I am, Fredrico Sr. is looking for me. My head starts to thump more as I realize we might be caught.

"Your father is looking for me," I say to Rico.

"Relax, he doesn't know you spent the night. I'll get you to your room before he finds out you were here."

"Emilia says—"

"Oni, I've got you," he cuts me off. "Come on. Unless you're thinking about taking a shower with me first, I'll get you out of here now."

I turn in his embrace to see if he's serious. He gives me a mischievous smile. I frown at him and push at his shoulder.

"Come on. I don't want your father getting the wrong idea about me."

He chuckles lightly and takes my hand in his to lead me from the bathroom to collect my things. I grab my stuff, and he goes to the door to peek his head out. Once he sees it's clear, he waves for me to follow him out. He takes my hand again as he rushes us through the hall toward my room, which is on the other side of the house.

He stops when we get to the catwalk that crosses over to the side my room is on. Rico peeks out over the rail then looks back at me. He dips his head to peck my lips, then gestures with his head for me to go.

I clench my shoes and jumper to my chest, then race across. Nervous, I hold my breath until I reach my room and I'm secure behind the closed door. Releasing a deep breath, I head for the bathroom to shower and get ready for breakfast, where Emilia said her uncle will be waiting for me.

I make quick work of tying up my braids as I murmur to myself about not doing so last night. I can see they are already getting fuzzy.

I might have to take them out soon. I wonder if I can find someone to do my hair while I'm down here. I'll have to ask Uncle Claude if he can hook me up with someone one of his lady friends might know.

Once I'm showered, I race to find something to put on and get downstairs. After I'm dressed in a pair of leggings and a thin tank top, I shove on a pair of sneakers and dash out of the room with my phone in my hand.

When I get downstairs, I follow the voices that are floating through the main level. I enter the dining room to find everyone already seated. Mario is looking down at his phone as he scrolls through it.

Al and Ed are fussing among themselves. Emilia is talking to Fredrico Sr. while Rico is sitting lost in thought as he stares down at his empty plate.

Instead of taking the empty seat beside Rico, I go to sit beside Emilia. Rico gives me a scowl, but I ignore it. I don't think I should sit next to him, not after last night.

"Good morning, Oni. How did you sleep last night?" Fredrico Sr. asks.

"Fine, sir. Thank you."

"Um," he murmurs. "I'm going to have the staff change out your linens, as clearly your accommodations weren't to your liking—since you didn't sleep in your room but Rico's last night."

Aldo and Eduardo scoff and almost spit out their juice. Rico begins to choke on his. Emilia sits with a grin on her lips. I glare at her, thinking she ratted me out.

"Don't think Emilia told me. Rico, you have never been as slick as you think when trying to sneak girls in and out of your room. I've always known. This is just the first time I'm calling you on it."

Rico

I pound at my chest as I cough from my orange juice going down the wrong pipe. I wasn't expecting my father to blast me and Oni like that. I was never worried about him finding out, but I know Oni was.

She's adorable as her cheeks start to glow with embarrassment. She will look anywhere but at me. I can no longer hold back my laughter.

"Babe, it's not a big deal. Stop looking so guilty." I burst out into laughter.

Oni trains her gaze on me and glares flames in my direction. If looks could kill, she'd have me six feet under. With a grin, I stand and pick up my plate that's just been filled and my glass of juice.

I saunter around the table and stop next to Mario on Oni's right side. Giving him a nod, I wait for him to grab his plate and get up. Once he moves out of the way, I take his seat and put my things down.

"Now that's better," I croon and lean in to tip my head back and kiss the side of her neck.

"All I ask is that you two don't do anything under my roof that will make me have to lock horns with your uncle, Oni," Pop says.

"Oh my God, we didn't do more than sleep," Oni groans.

I roar with laughter and Pop does the same. Oni looks between the two of us with her mouth open.

"You're making a bigger deal out of this than is necessary. Chill out," I say through my laughter.

"Just let the floor swallow me. *Please.*"

"I'm loving this," Emilia says as she laughs on the other side of Oni.

Al and Ed are laughing so hard their faces are red. I wrap an arm around Oni's head and tug her to me, then kiss the top of it. Pop looks at us with amusement written all over his face.

"You can relax. *Mangiare*, the stylist will be here soon. She's going to make sure Oni has all the gowns she needs for the job," Pop says and begins to dig into the plate that was just placed in front of him.

I kiss Oni's temple before I go back to my food. Slowly, she starts on the plate that's been brought out for her. She even chews cute.

Placing my fork down, I sit back and watch her. From the way she's stabbing at her food, I know I'm in for it later. I grin to myself and shake my head.

***

Watching Oni has become my new favorite pastime. I wasn't expecting to sit in on her fitting, but I'm glad I did. She has modeled each dress she's tried on.

I'm happy to be here to point out to her that some of the options could hinder her from doing what the intended job is. She can't show up in a dirty or ripped dress, and she needs to move as swiftly as she did when she took that Trackhawk.

My phone buzzes with a text, grabbing my attention. Pulling the phone from my pocket, I check to see who the text is from. I roll my eyes as I see it's one of my guys in New York.

Antonio only texts me when there's a problem. When I call him back, I know he's going to tell me some shit to piss me off. Why in the hell is so much going on right now?

I never have this much shit going on. It's like someone is targeting me to make me look bad. Fredo isn't crazy enough to try me like this. My cousin and I don't see eye to eye, but he's not ready to challenge me.

However, I can't ignore that someone is coming for me. Mario was right. First, someone got Jonny and Pauly to betray me. Then, Cusumano turns up dead without having to answer to me first.

"How about this one?" Oni asks, causing me to lift my head from my phone.

When my gaze lands on her, my mouth falls open. She's in a white dress that fits her to perfection. It's not too long, not too short. It's perfect.

I sit back in my seat and beckon her to me with two fingers. As she comes to me, I take her in from head to toe. The silver heels on her feet are sexy and complement the dress.

She stops before me, and I grab her hand and tug her onto my lap. Placing a hand on her thigh, I give it a squeeze. She looks back at me as her chest heaves.

"Do you like this one?" she breathes.

I glide my hand up her inner thigh and lean in to take her lips. I want to peel this dress off her and spend the rest of the day getting to know everything about her.

"You're gorgeous. It's perfect. I owe you a date. Keep this one for that," I say against her lips.

"Are you sure?"

"Yes. She has plenty of others; this one isn't for the job—it's white. You wouldn't want to stain it or something. You should go with dark colors for the job. Nothing that could give away what you've done before entering the event."

"Okay, I'll keep that in mind."

"Good. Now come here, I can't get enough of kissing you. Your lips are so soft and feel so good."

I grasp the back of her neck and pull her into me for a passionate kiss. She wraps her arms around my neck as I deepen the kiss and devour her.

I groan as she pushes her fingers into my hair. Right as I get ready to lift her and position her to straddle my lap, someone clears their throat. I break the kiss and look over Oni's shoulder to find Estell and Emilia staring at us.

I shrug and smile back at them. Oni jumps up and rushes from my lap, leaving me feeling bereft. I shake my head and return to my thoughts of business.

Someone wants my attention. I'm going to find out who and give them all the focus I have. They are fucking with the wrong one.

CHAPTER FOURTEEN

First Job

Oni

I'm so nervous. Tonight is my first job. We've been training for it for a week and a half now. Rico also insisted I learn how to actually shoot a gun.

I've gotten a lot better at that. I'm not nervous about what I need to do. I'm nervous about failing. I don't want to disappoint Rico or his dad.

"You've got this," I murmur to my reflection then blow out a breath.

I smooth my hands over the gold bodycon dress I'm wearing and have to blink a few times to make sure I'm looking at myself. I look nothing like the sixteen-year-old girl who rode the bus here to Miami. I look like I'm in my twenties.

Emilia helped me take out my braids as we all thought they were too distinctive and risky. A Black girl with braids would be a dead giveaway. My hair is now in full, deep waves flowing down just below my shoulder blades.

A makeup artist came in to do my makeup, giving me a natural-looking glow. The red lipstick makes my lips pop with an ombre effect. My lashes make my eyes stand out as well.

"Hey, you. Uncle Freddy is looking for you," Emilia says as she pops her head into the room.

I nod at my reflection, then turn to face her. Her mouth pops open and she steps fully into the room.

"Holy shit. You look amazing. Rico is going to lose his shit."

I reach to tug at the hem of the dress. I'm starting to feel self-conscious. I'm not sure how Rico is going to react to this new look.

"Here goes nothing," I breathe out.

"You should totally be a model."

"Ha, I'm five-five. Who's letting me on their runaway?"

"There are more than runway models, Oni. Trust me, you would stay booked. I know a few people if you ever want to give it a shot," she says.

"I'll keep that in mind."

"What do you want to do?"

"You mean when I grow up?"

"Yeah, like, I know I'm going to be married off to be a trophy wife. I'm not going to get to follow any real dream, but what do you have planned? What do you want to be?"

I take a moment to think her question over. I haven't thought much about what I want for the future. I've been living day by day.

Talking to my mom in the last few days, I get that this is something she would like me to focus on. To make her happy, I am going to figure my shit out. This would be a good place to start.

"I don't know. I've never really thought about it."

"You're smart and beautiful. The sky is the limit. I think whatever you decide, you're going to be great."

I hug her around the waist and lean my head against her. "Aw, thank you."

"I mean it. The more I get to know you, the more I know you're a lot more than everyone thinks. You're going to shock the world, Oni Raven. You're going to be a force in a world that doesn't see you coming."

We stop outside Mr. Gallo's study and Emilia pulls me into a hug. I give her a squeeze. She's become such a good friend over the last week and a half.

"Well, I guess I'll see you at the party. He's waiting inside for you."

"Thanks," I say.

I move to knock on the study door before walking in. Mr. Gallo has been true to his word. When I'm not training for these jobs we're going to pull, he has taken me under his wing.

I know more about the Gallo business than I ever thought I would. Fredrico is a calculating man. I can see why Rico is the way he is.

They see things in a way others don't. I find myself feeling more like an apprentice than an assistant. Emilia is right, because I'm a girl, Fredrico's business connections speak freely in front of me like I'm not even there.

After meetings, Fredrico always asks what I have learned. It always reminds me of my dad and how he taught me to be observant. When I'm with Fredrico, I often think of my dad and miss him.

"Come in," Mr. Gallo calls from the other side of the door.

I open the door and poke my head inside. He's standing facing the window, looking out into the backyard. I move inside and close the door behind me.

He turns to face me, and his mouth falls open. I reach to touch my hair and then smooth my hands down the front of my dress. A little frown comes to my lips as I wonder if I look bad. Maybe I picked the wrong dress for the night.

He clears his throat. "How you doing, Oni?"

"I'm fine, just a little nervous."

"You look gorgeous, sweetheart. I wanted to talk to you before we head out."

"Thank you. What can I do for you?"

"It's what I can do for you. You don't have to do this tonight. We can go with our plan *B*."

"No, I want to do this."

"Why?"

I sigh and think of my talk with Emilia just moments ago. It all revolves around the same thing. My mom.

"If I only did one job, that would be enough to pay my own way to boarding school. My mom doesn't want me to come back to New York. Not to stay.

"But the schools she wants me to go to are so expensive. I don't want her to have that burden. I know she's going to do everything she can for me to have better, but that's not right. She shouldn't work herself like that.

"If I can do this, if I can earn the money, I can go to one of those schools and put distance between me and all the things that haven't been steering me in the right direction," I reply.

Fredrico stares at me for a moment. I stand trying not to fidget under his gaze. I appreciate him wanting to give me an out. However, I'm going to follow through for my future.

He opens his mouth to speak, but a knock comes at the door. I turn as the door opens. Rico steps into the room and we both freeze as we look at each other.

Man, he's killing that suit. The blowout his hair is in looks sharp, as if he has a fresh cut. Which he could because I haven't seen him since this morning.

"Are you fucking kidding me?" Rico breathes as he pulls a hand down his face.

Rico

I can't breathe. I mean, damn. My brain stops working for a moment.

"Are you fucking kidding me?" I manage to say as I find some air.

I instantly regret the words. Oni drops her head and looks away from me. Feeling like a dick, I move into the room and stand in front of her. I reach beneath her hair to grasp her neck.

She lifts her gaze to mine, and I lean in to take her lips. I can't help myself. I kiss her like it's the first and last time I ever will.

It isn't until she whimpers into my mouth that I release her and allow us both to catch our breath. I look down at her, searching her face. She's so beautiful and has no idea how gorgeous she truly is.

"I didn't think you could get more beautiful than you already were. It's going to kill me not to be by your side tonight. Promise me, when this is all over, you'll spend some time hanging out with me. Just me and you," I say as I gather my thoughts.

We spend a lot of time together, but not enough time alone. My cousins or Pop are always around. I don't think there's been a time when we haven't been surrounded. She hasn't spent the night with me again since being totally embarrassed by my dad.

I want to change that. Some time just for us. A moment for her to get to know how much I've fallen for her in such a short time.

"Promise."

"That's enough, youse two. Oni, I want to finish our talk later. Remember, you have options."

I look up at my father and give him a curious look. I had come in here to let him know the team is ready to go. I hadn't expected to find Oni in here with him.

"Everyone is in place. Ed is going to ride with Oni. He has a cape for you to cover your dress and the burner phone. I'll text when our targets arrive. You get the cars, get them into the truck, and Al will bring you to the party after. Any questions?"

"No, I think I've got it."

"Good. If anything feels off or you're not sure you can make a move without a problem, you walk. Don't try to be a hero, baby. You are more important to me."

"I'll be fine. I'll see you at the party."

I lean in and kiss her cheek. I'm regretting this more and more. I'm almost tempted to call it all off. When I pull away, she looks up at me and laughs.

"What?"

"You have lipstick all over your mouth."

She reaches up to wipe it away. I grin and pull out a spare handkerchief to hand to her so she can clean her hand. Pop walks over and claps me on the back.

"Oni, why don't you go find Eduardo. I need to have a few words with my son."

"Yes, sir," she says and turns to leave.

I reach to grab her arm to stop her. Swiftly, I lean in for one more kiss on her cheek. Then I lean into her ear to whisper.

"You're gorgeous. Be safe, baby. I've got you. I always do."

She looks up into my eyes and smiles, then gives me a nod. Releasing her, I allow her to leave and turn back to my pop.

"Are you sure about this? We can call it off," he says once Oni has left the room.

"They're waiting. Everything is set. The first half of the payment has been made. I think we've got this. I'm confident the team can pull this off. I trust everyone involved."

"Do you trust yourself not to expose her? Oni must look like my assistant as I have been establishing her over the last week and a half. You can't reveal how much she means to you, our organization, or this job. Are you ready for this?"

"I am. I told you, I've got this, Pop. I'm not going to endanger her or the business."

"Good, you should know Emilio plans to be there tonight."

"Fuck," I growl and ball my fists.

"He's not going to get in the way, but he will be watching you and Oni. I just think you should be careful. He's watching you more closely and you don't want to make any wrong moves."

"Thanks for the heads-up. Let's get this over with. The boys at the warehouse will have to work overnight to pull this off."

"My boys are ready at the docks as soon as it's done," he says.

"Sounds good."

***

Me: *Last target in the room. Go time.*
Oni: *Locked in. In progress.*

I nod at my phone then put it away and refocus on the room. These motherfuckers deserve what's about to happen. Each one of the targets has wronged me or my family in some way. Payback is a bitch.

It's not like they don't have insurance for the rides they're about to lose. Some will take longer to replace, but it is what it is. I'm getting top dollar for the whips and the product that will be shipped with them.

Once the VIN numbers are wiped, no one will ever know we took them. I'm killing two birds with one stone. If the cars are searched when they reach their destination, the product will be in hidden compartments that will be impossible to find.

The cars are so expensive and heading to individuals no one wants to piss off, so even if they're suspicious about what might be hidden in them, they're not going to take them apart to confirm their suspicions.

The product will be taken out and transported before delivery to the new owners—newly customized with fresh papers.

"There you are," Uncle Emilio croons. "I have someone I want you to meet."

I turn to my uncle, and my head nearly explodes. Why the fuck is she here? This is the last thing I need right now.

"Juliana Abato, this is my nephew—"

"No need for introductions. We've already met," I grind out.

"Good to see you again, Rico. I was so excited when your uncle invited me out for a few weeks. I'm looking forward to spending some time with you," Juliana says in that obnoxious voice of hers.

Just fucking great.

CHAPTER FIFTEEN

Playing Games

Oni

"You know, I didn't get it at first. Ten cars in less than five minutes," Aldo says as he drives me to the party, this time in a Rolls-Royce.

"I could have done better," I mutter.

I'm in the back seat, changing my sneakers out for my heels. I'm annoyed because I should have done it in four minutes. There was a guy lurking around car number three. He threw off my timing. Angelo, one of Rico's guys, was a bit slow too.

I'll have to talk to Rico about that. This is all about timing. If you can't keep up with me, you shouldn't be on the team.

I could have done the job faster by myself. I mumble under my breath as I shove my sneakers and the cape into a bag. I smooth my hands over my gold dress and check to make sure everything is in place.

"This is the second time you've impressed me. With you on his side, I don't think I stand a chance against Rico for don. He makes a fucking killer lieutenant, and he isn't even made yet. I have so much to learn from him," Aldo says in admiration.

"Are you thinking about challenging him for don?"

"If I said yes, would you shoot me in the back of the head now?" He chuckles.

"No. I'm just curious."

"Nah, I'm not really interested in that. I'd be fine with a capo position or just being made. Uncle Emilio can be crazy demanding.

"I've seen him get mad when someone fails him. He'd probably stress me the fuck out before I could get anywhere near being don. Nah, Rico is made for this. I'll have his back in any way I can though."

"What about Eduardo?"

"Same. I think the only one thinking about challenging Rico is Fredo. Which is crazy because he doesn't have the right temperament for any of it," he replies.

"What do you mean by that?"

"You have to meet him and then you'll get it. We're here. Break a leg or whatever," he says as we pull up in front of the estate.

The door is opened for me, and I step out. I feel a little weird arriving by myself. Fredrico said he'd stay within reach so I would see him once I arrived. I pull out my invitation as I get to the top of the steps, where the security guard is.

He looks me over hungrily and I have to force myself not to fidget. I lock down all my emotions and put on an expressionless mask. Thank God it only takes a few seconds for him to allow me to head inside.

I walk in and my mind is blown. This place is like a palace inside. I follow the red carpet that's leading everyone to the party.

When I step into the ballroom, I see Fredrico Sr. with a drink in his hand as he speaks with two other men. One of the men looks in my direction and smiles before saying something to Fredrico, causing him to turn and look toward where I stand.

He smiles and places his drink down on a passing tray, then starts to walk toward me. I keep moving to close the gap between us. When he reaches me, he leans in to kiss both my cheeks.

"You did very well. You have passed one test tonight. Another awaits."

"Huh?"

He looks over my shoulder, causing me to turn to see what he's looking at. When I turn, Rico and Uncle Emilio come into view. There is also some chick standing with them, smiling into Rico's face.

White-hot rage fills me when she places a hand on Rico's chest and leans into his ear. He looks past her at me and silently tells me not to react. I collect my feelings and shove them into a tight box.

I turn my gaze to Emilio and he's watching me closely. Ah, I get it. I roll my eyes and turn away from them.

"Why is he like this?"

Emilio has been a dick to me since the first time I met him. Okay, fine, I stole a car with his family's drugs in it, but he still doesn't know me or have to treat me like this. Fredrico gives me a smile and pats my arm.

"Showtime, bella. Don't let him see you sweat. You are being tried. I believe you will rise to the occasion," he whispers.

I feel Rico's presence behind me before I turn. My stomach sours because I know that girl is going to be with him when I turn around. However, I'm not about to be punked.

I paste on a smile and flip my hair before I turn to face our new arrivals. Emilio looks me over with an amused smile on his lips. Fredrico places a hand on my back, drawing me closer to him.

"My little thief, you clean up nicely. I almost didn't recognize you," Emilio croons with a smug smile.

"It's nice to see you again, Mr. Gallo," I reply with a smile.

"I'm glad you're here. I have someone you should meet. As Freddy's assistant, you should know his son's fiancée. Juliana, this is my brother's new assistant for the summer. I'm sure you two will see each other around the house."

His words are like a punch to the gut, but I don't allow my smile to fall. I don't even look at Rico. I turn to Juliana and hold out my hand. She takes my hand like it's something filthy she doesn't want to touch.

"Nice dress," she says, but the words drip with mean-girl vibes.

"Thank you." I turn to Fredrico, dismissing this skank. "Do you still want to introduce me to that real estate developer? We have that meeting with him on Tuesday."

He gives me a smile. "Yes, I do want you to meet Jim. Thanks for reminding me."

He holds his elbow out for me to take. I loop my arm through his and give a wave to Emilio before we step off, not sparing Rico a single glance. I can feel his eyes on me, but I refuse to acknowledge him.

"What the hell was that?" I ask when we're out of earshot.

"My brother playing his games."

"I hope that means you have another son."

"No, bella. I only have the one."

"Un-fucking-real." I seethe.

"You handled that well. I'm proud of you. You did good, kid," he replies and winks at me.

Rico

"Do you know why I'm so hard on you?" Uncle Emilio asks as we ride in the back of his car.

He demanded I ride with him so we could talk. This pissed me off because Juliana rode with Oni and Pop. This motherfucker had Pop offer Juliana the guesthouse on his property.

If he wouldn't catch me in a lie, I would move back to my place. I'm still tempted to. If I didn't know this was all part of his game, I would say fuck it and follow my first instinct.

This is the part of all this I hate. I want to be my own man, not someone's puppet. I'm not marrying Juliana. I don't give a fuck what he has to say.

"I have no idea. I think outside the box. I do everything you ask me to and then some. Behind my pop, I'm your highest earner," I answer.

"Yes, this is why. Fredrico could have easily taken my spot if he wanted to. He's not just feared, he's loved. My birthright is the only reason I am Don and not him. You are so much like your father, and you will fill my shoes with ease."

"But? I hear a but."

"But you have yet to show a weakness, which tells me when you have one, it will be great. I will not hand you my position to hand you your death. I want to make you strong, impenetrable. Not just here." He taps my head, then points to my chest.

"In here too. I've seen many men broken from the inside out. If you can break a man's heart, you can break his mind."

"So what are you saying? You want me to marry someone I don't love so I can't be broken?"

"This is not what I'm saying. The Abato family offers me an opportunity. A marriage between you and Juliana opens that door. I want their territory and contracts. It has little to do with you." He shrugs.

"You don't even trust them. Why would I marry her?"

"She's a pretty girl. No?"

I frown. "Not to me."

"Ah, no. You like the little *mulignan*. You think I don't have eyes?"

My nostrils flare as I ball my fists. I won't allow him to get a rise out of me. This is what he wants. I'm not going to play into his hands.

"Oni is one of my soldiers. That's it. She earns, I collect."

"Then Juliana shouldn't be a problem. You will entertain her for the next four weeks. Keep her happy. Make it seem like you are interested," he says slyly.

"Why should I bother? It's not like I'm going to agree to marry her. You need to stop calling her my fiancée."

"I don't *need* to do anything. If I wanted you engaged to her, you would be. Do as I say, Rico.

"You might be my first choice, but you are not my only option. You should know by now it's better to follow my lead than to think you know better than me. You have not gotten there yet," he says coldly.

I frown and purse my lips. I hear the threat in his words for what it is. For now, I bite my tongue. My time will come.

"Rico, stop thinking about how to outsmart me and clean up your mess in New York. Remember, I have eyes and ears everywhere. If I have to clean this up for you, you will be looking at another two years before I open the books for you."

I work my jaw. I thought I had my shit under lock. I've been dealing with things as they arise. It looks like I'm going to have to get a little more proactive.

"Yeah, I've got it," I say as the car comes to a stop in front of Pop's house.

I step out of the car and loosen my tie. Shrugging off my jacket, I toss it over my arm and jog into the house. I pull my phone and shoot off a text to Mario.

He needs to do me a favor. I also need to know where the bullshit is coming from. If I can't handle a little problem, I'll never be trusted with the shit I'm to move up to.

I'm not even thinking, I find myself walking right into Oni's bedroom. As I get inside, I can hear the shower running. I sigh and toss my suit jacket over the back of the chair in the room.

Finishing with the buttons on my dress shirt, I then tug it from my pants. I kick off my shoes, then pad over to the bed to sit on the foot of it.

I'm not leaving here until we have a clear understanding of what's going to happen around here for the next month. I know I'm asking a lot, but I need to play the game.

"Hello," I say into my phone as Mario calls.

"I was hoping you would answer. Yeah, no problem. I can look after Oni. What do you need me to do?"

"I need you to act like she's yours. Just until I can get that airhead out of here. I don't want her to find out anything about her. My gut is telling me to be wary of her, not just my uncle."

"You got it. I'll handle it. You sure she'll be okay with it?"

"I'm going to talk to her. It will be cool."

"Anything else?"

"Uncle Emilio mentioned my mess in New York. What do you know?"

"Nothing has been reported to me, but I can make the trip to drop in and check things out. I'll be back in the morning with a full report. Afternoon at the latest."

"I knew I could count on you."

"You can count on her too. She handled things like a pro. The deal is done on our end. Everything went smoothly. Like taking candy," he croons.

"Perfect, take care of the team when you get back. I'll set the next job up."

The bathroom door opens right as I hang up. I drop the phone on the bed and sit staring at Oni, wrapped in a towel, as she mutters to herself. She doesn't notice me right away, but when she does, the look on her face says a thousand words.

CHAPTER SIXTEEN

All Mine

Oni

I step out of the shower and wrap a towel around my body. I'm still grumbling to myself about that heifer who rode with us to the house. I know her from somewhere.

I hadn't recognized her at first because I dismissed her after that handshake and introduction. However, once we all climbed into the Rolls to head home, I got a good look at her. A better look than I wanted to be honest.

I know I know her from somewhere. I haven't figured it out yet. It's right there.

"Get your shit together, Oni," I growl at my reflection after I wipe the steam from the glass.

I snatch the shower cap from my head, leaving my scarf in place. This isn't me. I'm not about to date someone with a fiancée.

"He has me all fucked up. Is any of this shit worth all this? Crazy-ass uncle playing in my face.

"A boyfriend I can't show affection to. Nope, not a damn thing worth all this. I'm taking my Black ass back home.

"Fuck these people," I continue to rant as I walk out of the bathroom.

Feeling like I'm being watched, I lift my head and find Rico sitting on my bed. I fold my arms over my chest and glare at him.

"Get out," I snarl.

"Come here, baby."

I give him the finger. I'm not in the mood for this. It's been a long, draining night.

He snorts. "I know what this looks like, but it's not what you think. Come here, Oni."

"I'm tired and I'm going to bed. Please leave so I can get dressed and go to sleep."

Ignoring me, he stands and saunters over to me. I crane my neck to look up at him as he towers over me. He looks down into my eyes as he lifts his hand to my face.

Slowly, he runs his thumb across my lower lip. I jerk my head away, but he grasps the back of my neck and places his forehead to mine. He breathes me in as I fight to keep my lips from trembling.

"She means nothing to me. I never agreed to marry her or to an engagement for that matter. You are who I want," he says against my lips.

I push at his chest, trying to break his hold on me. However, his grip is too strong. I can only turn my face away.

"I'm done with all of this. The disrespect, the drama, and the bullshit. Y'all can play all these games among yourselves," I hiss.

"You're not listening to me."

I shove harder at his chest. "No. You're the one not listening to me. We're done, over, finished."

This time, when I give a good shove, my towel drops to my feet. I gasp and quickly cover my breasts and privates. Rico stands in shock. Then his eyes fill with lust.

"Do you really think I'm going to let someone else have what's mine? You are mine, Oni. I said she means nothing. I don't want her."

"Well, I don't want you. I belong to no one. Now get out."

Before I can fully get the words out, he has my face cupped between his palms as he devours my lips. I whimper into his mouth as he delivers a searing, demanding kiss. I wrap my arms around his neck as he deepens the kiss, wrapping his own around me.

In the next motion, he has my legs wrapped around him as he groans into my mouth. I'm so lost in the kiss, I don't realize we're moving until my back hits the bed. The weight of his big body on top of mine brings me back to reality.

"Rico," I whimper.

"I'm not going to take you tonight. I'm just going to show you who you belong to," he says in my ear.

Then he begins a trail of kisses down from my neck to my breast. I cry out when he takes my nipple into his mouth. He rolls the other one with his fingers as I wiggle beneath him.

My head is a mess as I go from being angry at him to wanting his touch all over. He reaches between my legs while he continues to suck and roll my nipples.

"Fuck, baby. Your body is so fucking sexy."

He begins to move lower down my body with soft kisses. I know I should stop him, but my body wants more. I want more.

Rico holds my thighs open with his palms as he stares at my core. I bite my lip, not sure what I'm supposed to do. He licks his lips, still staring as if he's deciding what he wants.

My pussy clenches and I feel my juices gush. I'm so wet. I want to close my legs and squeeze my thighs. However, Rico applies a little more pressure to keep them open.

"Such a pretty little pussy. My pretty little pussy," he groans.

He then dips his head and begins feasting on me. I fist the pillow beneath my head and buck my hips. My heart is pounding. Rico pins my hips to the bed and shoves his face deeper as he moans and hums.

"You taste so fucking good," he groans as I cry out his name.

My eyes roll into the back of my head as I thrash beneath him. He adds his fingers in, and my body takes flight. I begin to shake and convulse as I come for the first time in my life.

Rico chuckles darkly as he climbs back up my body and kisses me hard. My eyes grow wide as I taste myself on his lips. He breaks the kiss and looks into my eyes.

"All mine," he says with a smug grin.

"I'm not yours," I protest.

He moves his lips to my ear. "I licked it so now it's mine," he laughs and kisses me again.

Jerk.

CHAPTER SEVENTEEN

What Now?

Rico

I need to jump in the shower and rub one out, but I want to put Oni first. I want her to feel cared for after her first orgasm. As we lie here, and I hold her naked body against my chest, I can't keep the smile off my face.

She's perfect from head to toe. When that towel dropped, I lost my shit. The thought of losing her makes me crazy.

Staring up at the ceiling, I trace my fingertips across her soft skin. As my sanity kicks in, my thoughts tell me I probably should've let her leave. Give her two or three years to mature and figure out if I'm really what she wants.

I'm no ordinary guy. My life is far from normal. Oni has no idea what she's getting with me.

I'll kill anyone who tries to harm her, but some will still try. My uncle is right. Oni is my one weakness. If I have to have one, I wouldn't want it to be anyone or anything else.

"Rico?" Her soft voice reaches my ears and my smile grows.

I can only imagine hearing that voice every night for the rest of my life. Coming home to her will be no hardship. In fact, I know I will always look forward to it.

What the fuck are you talking about, man? How did this girl become a part of the plan? Do you hear yourself?

Fuck it. It is what it is. She's mine.

"Yeah, baby?"

"Why didn't you tell me about her?"

I frown, hating that she has to question me. I never wanted this to be an issue because it's never going to happen. I don't want to take the family by force, but I will if I have to.

That's what my uncle is asking for if he tries to force me to marry Juliana. Arranged marriages aren't uncommon, especially for power plays. However, I'm not that guy; no one's forcing me to marry anyone.

"I told you. I didn't agree to the arrangement. There was nothing to tell."

"But you're engaged?"

"No," I bite out. "Even if I didn't have you, I wasn't going to agree to that shit."

"So what now?"

I reach for her chin and tilt her head until I can look into her eyes. She looks at me with so many questions in her gaze.

"I play the game. The rules remain the same; we'll just have to be more careful. That's why Mario is going to play your boyfriend," I explain.

"What?"

I trace the side of her face with my fingertips. I'm not crazy about this idea, but I'll do whatever I have to to protect this girl. Oni has become a priority.

"I don't trust Juliana. I want to keep you off her radar. Mario will act like you're his. That way, he can keep an eye on you for me and keep Juliana out of our business."

I lean in to take her lips and roll her onto her back. Her mouth tastes so sweet. I almost go down on her again. However, I don't think I have that type of restraint.

Not with my dick this hard. I'm already horny as fuck and her soft body against mine isn't helping matters. If I eat her pussy again, I might lose my head and thrust right into her tight heat.

The worst part is, I don't think she would deny me or ask me to stop. The thought of her taking me only makes me harder. I have to shake my thoughts clear.

The war I had with myself the first time proved I'm stronger than I thought. Her moans, her soft skin, her sexy body, and the way she tastes were all a combination I wasn't expecting to hit me the way they did. Even now as I kiss her soft lips, I know I should've let her go before because there is no letting go now.

I don't just want Oni. I crave her. Four weeks of acting as if this isn't true will be my greatest test yet.

I break the kiss and look into her eyes. Pecking her cute little nose, I smile down at her. She returns the smile as she runs her hands up my back.

"Nothing can come between us. Remember, she means nothing. I need you to trust me. I want the world and you by my side while I take it.

"We play the game, Oni. We make it so I don't ever have to answer to anyone. Not about you or anything else," I breathe.

She looks down as if in thought. Then she lifts those beautiful eyes back to mine. I see the wheels turning.

"You have my trust and my loyalty, Rico. Don't take that for granted or make me regret it. You hurt me, you lose me."

Hearing her say I'll lose her pokes at the little sanity I have a grasp on. I pull her legs around my waist and capture her lips again. This time, I kiss her deeply as I grind my hips into her.

I'm on the verge of telling her I love her, and I'd never hurt her, but I stop myself. Instead, I keep grinding and sipping from her sexy mouth. I'm brought back to my senses when she begins to convulse around me again.

"Rico, please," she whimpers in my ear and it's almost my undoing.

I shiver and suck on her neck as she runs one hand through my hair and claws the other up my back. Not able to help myself, I flick my tongue out to lick her lips.

"When I finally take you, you won't have to hide your feelings for me in the morning. And you won't be able to. This is why we will wait.

"When I start fucking you, I'm not going to want to stop. I'll take you anytime and anywhere. You're not ready for that. Trust me."

She shivers beneath me and whispers. "Oh."

CHAPTER EIGHTEEN

Get Out My Face

Oni

"No, Mom. I'm fine. We were out last night. I attended a business event with Uncle Claude. I'm getting a late start this morning, that's all," I say as I finish getting dressed while talking to my mom on the phone.

She called this morning wanting to talk about my school options, but became concerned when I answered sounding like I had just woken up—which I had. I had just stepped out of the shower after sleeping in.

I hadn't planned to, but I didn't hear my alarm go off. Something tells me Rico cut it off sometime during the night. When I did wake, I had a text from Fredrico Sr.

Because of my good work last night, he gave me the morning off and said I could hang with Emilia and the others this afternoon instead of following him to his business meeting. I welcomed the reward.

I did earn it. Not only did I complete my assignment, but I dealt with all that other craziness as well. Grateful, I took the free time to get myself together. I sat in bed gathering my emotions before I jumped into the shower.

I couldn't leave this room with the smile I had on my face. Not if I planned to play things off. One look in the mirror and I could see the happiness in my eyes. It was written all over my face.

Rico didn't leave my room until early this morning. The kiss he left me with represented everything he made me feel last night. I thought I was going to lose my virginity last night, but Rico's words made sense after my hormones calmed down. It will be better to wait.

I wouldn't want to do something like that and then have to act like he means nothing to me. I don't think I could. It's going to be hard enough as it is.

"Okay, honey. I have to get back to work. I'd like it if you could call me back this evening. I really want to discuss your options. We need to get things in motion," Mom says, bringing me from my thoughts.

I smile. I'll be able to go to one of those schools and she's not going to have to pay for it. I have it covered.

All thanks to Rico. He's doing more for me than he knows. Giving my mom peace of mind is something I've always wanted to do. I can now, thanks to Rico.

It might not be the way Mom would want, but by the end of the summer, I'll be able to change my life for good. I can't help wondering how Rico will feel if I decide to leave the country for school.

I think I'm falling in love with him. I came close to telling him that, but I didn't want him to think I'm being silly. If Rico wants to take over the world, the last thing I need to be is a silly, clingy girlfriend.

I hang up with Mom and head downstairs to find something to eat. Breakfast has long passed, so I'll find some fruit or something so I don't have to bother the staff. I'm lost in thought as I hum to myself and look through the refrigerator.

I find some juice and a sandwich with my name on it. With a smile, I grab both and back out to close the door. Taking my sandwich and the juice to the counter, I then turn to grab a glass.

"Oh good, it's you. I need some things fetched from the store. Take notes to make sure you don't forget anything. Hurry up," this bitch Juliana says, snapping her fingers at me.

I spin in a circle, looking for who the fuck she thinks she's talking to. She can't be talking to me. I know she's not talking to me.

"Excuse me?" I hiss.

"You're Fredrico's assistant, no?"

"I'm his assistant. I'm not your dog or servant though. Talk to me like that again and I'll give you a permanent happy face," I deadpan.

"What did you say to me? Do you know who I am?"

"Do I look like I care?"

"Whoa, whoa," Mario croons as he rushes into the kitchen we're standing in the middle of. He wraps his arms around me and walks me back away from her.

I hadn't realized I'd been so close, ready to deal with her disrespect. Rico appears and his face clouds over with rage. He doesn't look in my direction.

"Relax. Don't allow her to bait you. She wants to get you punished. Rico hasn't been giving her the attention she wants," Mario whispers in my ear.

He then brushes his lips softly against my temple. I look up at him, surprised, then remember what Rico said last night. Quickly, I school my features and place my head against his chest.

"We have a problem here?" Rico asks.

"Who does she think she is speaking to me like that?" Juliana whines.

"What did you say to her? Oni stays quiet and does her job. We've never had an incident with her, so my father will have words with you when he returns."

"But ... you can't be serious. I'm to stay here for four weeks and be treated like this?"

"You don't have to stay here," I say coolly.

Rico and Mario snort a laugh. I look to Rico, and he winks at me.

"Listen, I have shit to do. I don't have time for this. Emilia is having some people over for a pool party. You guys should join her," Rico says dismissively.

He goes to walk away, but Juliana rushes after him, grabbing his arm to stop him. He turns and looks down at her hand; she draws it back quickly.

"But I thought we could spend some time together." She pouts. "Are you really too busy for your fiancée?"

"If I can, I'll join the party later. Right now, I don't have time for you."

A grin comes to my lips, and I have to fight not to laugh. The way her face shatters after she tried to throw that bullshit in my face is so satisfying. I want to give a slow clap to Rico as he turns to leave once again.

"Mario, let's go," Rico barks, causing Mario to release me immediately and follow after him.

I grab my sandwich and juice then leave Juliana sulking by herself as I go in search of Emilia.

Rico

"Shouldn't I be back there with Oni?" Mario says as we walk upstairs to the office I've set up for myself while we're here.

"You should, but I needed you to get your hands off my girl. Then I needed to warn you to be careful how well you play your part," I snarl, knowing I'm wrong even as the words come out of my mouth.

"Calm down, bro. I know who she belongs to. I was just selling the part. You know I mean no disrespect," Mario tells me.

I sigh and pinch the bridge of my nose. "Fuck."

"Should I head back down there?"

"Yeah, I'm sorry, man. All this shit is starting to get to me. Go make sure she's safe and stays out of trouble."

"It will all work out. I've already sent a message on your behalf in New York. You will get the right results. I have your back, man."

"I know. Thanks. You don't have to do any of this," I say and turn to continue to my office.

When I get there, I have a seat as my mind wanders to all the shit I've learned from Mario's report. There's no question someone is trying to set me up. My only questions now are who and why?

It might be time to shut the operation down. It's too risky with all this activity in the background. I rub my jaw in thought.

One more job ... I need to complete one more job. The others were bonuses. However, this one job will put the jewel in my crown.

I sit back in my chair and think over my options. I need to clean house. I can't trust everyone around me.

If I risk this final job, we'll be working with a skeleton crew. If this were my old crew, I might have been okay with that, but having Oni on the crew and now not knowing who I can trust changes everything. I grab my hair by the roots.

This is business, I shouldn't be making decisions based on a woman. Fuck, she's not even a woman yet.

"Pull it together, Rico. Handle your business," I breathe to myself.

Music blasts from the backyard, telling me that the party has started. I mumble under my breath. I'm not about to get any work done. Between my thoughts and that music blasting, I won't be able to focus at all.

"Fuck it."

I get up and head to my room to change into something else.

Mario

"He'll be out here in the next half hour, I promise," I whisper in Oni's ear as I stand with my arm around her shoulder.

She looks up at me, and I'm punched with the reason Rico is so taken by her. She's a beautiful girl. I would never violate the friendship I have with Rico. He's like my blood brother.

However, I have eyes and it's hard to miss how gorgeous the girl he's in love with is. Oh, my friend is in love, whether he's ready to admit it or not. Rico has never been interested in girls for more than a good fuck.

However, this girl has held his attention since she arrived. She's as smart as she is beautiful. I think she's good for him.

Rico is ambitious; he wants to make a great name for himself. I am here to make sure he does and to keep him and the love of his life safe while he does so.

"He has work to do. We probably won't see him until tonight," she replies, then shrugs. "It's cool. I'm in good company and it's not like I could hang out with him if he were here. I can feel her eyes on me."

I glance up and she's right, Juliana is staring daggers at her. I smirk, turning Oni so that my body is blocking hers. I then dip my head to bring our lips closer together.

"Rico might kill me for this, but I'll explain it to him later," I say as I hold her close.

Oni reaches up to cup my face. "Just keep your tongue to yourself and your hands above my ass."

"I can do that."

I close the distance and press my lips to hers. I'm not expecting the punch to my gut. I don't stick my tongue into her mouth, but I do nip her lip.

I break the kiss as soon as I feel myself growing hard. She places her head against my chest and sighs. Then she starts to giggle.

"What's so funny?"

"Before this summer, I'd never kissed a boy. Now I've kissed two."

"In all fairness, we're men."

"You know what I mean."

"I do. Friends? I don't want to confuse things. I know my kisses are magic."

She laughs. "You're now my new best friend. You'd do anything for him, so would I. I think he will need us to be close someday."

"You will be his queen. It will always be my job to watch out for you, so I guess you're right," I laugh.

I throw my arm back around her shoulder and turn to look at Juliana. She's no longer glaring at Oni. However, Rico is standing in the doorway, glaring at me with fire.

I clench my jaw and nod at him, telling him silently that I've only done my part. He nods back, but I know he's still pissed. I might have to go a few rounds with him later.

"Mario?" Oni says beside me.

"What's up?"

"Who's that guy? He was at the club that night. He gives me this eerie vibe. Do you know him?"

I follow her line of vision to see who she's talking about. There is a guy not far from Juliana who has his gaze trained on Oni. I don't know him, but I'll be watching him for the rest of the night.

She's right, there is something off about him. When he moves to whisper into Juliana's ear and she nods, I narrow my eyes at the two of them. I'm definitely going to keep an eye on him.

CHAPTER NINETEEN

My First

Oni

I look across the pool and find Rico talking to Ed, but his eyes are glued on me. I try not to smile, but I can't help myself. Rico looks handsome in a black polo, khaki shorts, and high-top Air Force Ones.

It's a good look on him. I watch as he licks his lips, then looks away to answer Al as he walks over and enters their conversation. My phone buzzes in my hand. I look at it to see a text from Rico.

Rico: *My office. Head up there in five. I'll be ten minutes behind you.*

I turn to Mario, who's been standing beside me, talking to Corey, one of Emilia's friends. I smile at Mario and nod my head to let him know I'm heading inside. Emilia stops me just before I get to the door to enter the house.

"Where are you going? I know you're not trying to skip out," she says.

"Calm down. I'm just going to the bathroom. I'll be back in a bit."

"Good, I have some friends I want you to meet."

"Cool, I'll be back. Save me a drink," I say, pointing to the one in her hand.

Her eyes look glossy, like she might need to slow down soon. She smiles and downs the rest of her drink while wiggling her brows at me. I laugh at her and shake my head.

I catch a glance of Rico and note that Juliana is all in his face. He keeps his face expressionless, but I can see his eyes scanning. Rolling my eyes, I head into the house.

Instead of going straight to Rico's office, I head into the bathroom first. I use it quickly and wash my hands. Looking in the mirror, I smile. This little white sundress is cute. It's a little short since we're having a pool party, but it's still tasteful. The swimsuit beneath is basic.

I smooth my hands over the dress and turn to head up to Rico's office. The house is quiet, but the party outside is jumping. The DJ has a thing for EDM. Not my jam, but I'm trying to go with the vibe.

Once up on the third floor, I step into Rico's office and look around. I inhale and take in a lungful of his scent that's all over the room. Closing my eyes, I remember last night and smile.

Suddenly, my mouth is covered, and I'm being shoved forward. I know right away this isn't Rico. The scent is wrong.

I bite the person's hand and run for the desk where I know Rico keeps a few guns. All I need is to get my hands on one. As I run, I'm pushed forward and fall onto the edge of the desk.

Pain shoots through me, causing me to whimper, but I don't give up my fight. I hold my side and stumble to the other side of the desk. As I push the desk chair out of the way, I'm grabbed by the back of my hair.

I look up, and to my surprise, it's the asshole from the club who was downstairs talking to Juliana. He looks down at me with evil in his eyes. Panic fills me and I go into fight mode.

I swing and catch him in the face. He growls and backhands me so hard I see stars. I fall back against the desk in a daze.

He grabs me and tosses me onto the desk. I keep fighting. He blocks most of my hits, but I get in a good one upside his head. I figure if I keep fighting, Rico will be here soon.

My heart is pounding so hard it feels like it's about to come out of my chest. He grabs my legs to keep me from kicking and steps between them. It dawns on me that this has just become the fight of my life.

I don't have time to wait for Rico to save me. I'm going to have to save myself. I calm down enough to think. He rips the front of my dress, causing me to scream out.

I punch him in his throat and begin to reach under the desk for the pistol I know Rico keeps there. Panic begins to rise again as my hand doesn't connect with the handle right away. Unfortunately for me, this asshole recovers and comes at me again.

He wraps his hands around my throat, but I keep reaching for the gun. He reaches between my legs and rips my swimsuit. Tears fill my eyes. This can't be happening to me.

I didn't even notice him following me in here. I think I'm going to be sick. With the hand not searching for the gun, I try to push him off.

My brain is in shock as I finally find the gun and grab it from under the desk. I release the safety, then lift it to his temple and pull the trigger all in one breath. The shot doesn't make more than a hissing sound as a silencer is on the end. I sit shaking as I stare down at the body on the floor.

"Oh my God," I choke out.

I look up at the mirror that hangs behind the desk. Snot bubbles are coming from my nose, and tears are streaming down my face. I can feel myself shutting down.

Just then, Rico and Mario burst through the door. Rico runs for me, freezing as he rounds the desk and finds the body on the floor. The rage that fills his face makes him look like a monster has taken over his body.

Mario is the first one to snap into action. He pries the gun from my hand, then rushes to lock the door. Rico tugs his shirt off and begins to pull it over my head.

They are talking, but I can't hear anything they're saying. My ears are ringing. Rico cups my head and pulls it into his chest. I inhale him deeply and begin to relax.

I just took my first life. Oh my God, I have a body on my jacket. Uncle Claude's words come back to me. *Don't let them get you into anything I can't get you out of.*

I did what I had to do.

Rico

"I'm excited to finally start planning for our future. The engagement party is going to be ah-mazing. Everyone who's anyone should be there. Don't you think so?" Juliana prattles on.

Meanwhile, I'm doing my best not to tell her to shut the fuck up. I lock gazes with Mario and notice the panic in his expression. I quickly shoot him a text.

Me: *What's wrong? I sent her inside. Relax.*

Mario: *That's not the problem. I lost sight of that asshole. The guy in the gray and white short sweatsuit.*

I look up and glance around the crowd. I don't see that guy either. When I noticed him earlier, I had wondered who had invited him.

"Where are you going?" Juliana whines as I start to walk off.

"I need to make a call," I toss over my shoulder and keep moving.

Something isn't sitting right with me. Oni went into the house to meet me upstairs. That cute little dress had my thoughts on last night.

I wanted to get a little time to hold her in my arms, maybe get a little taste if we have time. However, that guy is now out of sight as well. No one should have gone into the house, but Emilia has gone overboard with the number of people she's invited over.

"I had my eyes on him and then some guy intercepted me, asking me if I saw his girl or some shit and I lost him," Mario says as he runs to join me in the house.

"Oni was on her way to my office. Let's start with finding her. Then we can look for him. I want to make sure she's safe."

We jog up to the third floor without another word. As soon as we hit the landing, the sounds of a commotion can be heard coming from my office. I take off running without a single thought.

Just before we get to the door, a loud thump sounds, causing my heart to pound harder than I've ever felt. Mario and I burst through the door at the same time. The first thing I see is Oni's reflection in the mirror. Her tearstained face grips my heart, causing my feet to move me to her before I can take the entire room in.

I get around the desk, ready to draw her into my arms, but freeze as I see the body lying on the floor. We won't need to go searching for that asshole. He's lying on my office floor with his brains blown out.

Rage fills me. This motherfucker came into my father's home and violated what's mine. He forced my baby to take his life at only sixteen.

I may have made sure Oni could protect herself, but I never meant for something like this to be on her conscience so soon in her life. Maybe that's the problem: bringing her into this life opens doors like this. This is my fault.

"Baby, are you okay?" I turn to Oni and ask as the strange sound of her sobs draws my attention.

It's like she's trying not to make a sound, but the sound is still breaking through. I think she's in shock. Mario pries my gun from her hand, then rushes to lock the door.

I'm grateful to him as he snaps into action, calling for a cleaner and setting in motion the start of taking care of this mess. Seeing the front of Oni's dress torn and her naked breast exposed, I tear my shirt off and pull it over her head.

"Ashton Larkin," Mario says, tossing the dude's wallet on top of his lifeless chest.

"Irish? Who the fuck invited him here?"

I cup the back of Oni's head and pull her into my chest. She's still sobbing. I don't want to think about what happened before she dropped this piece of shit. I failed her.

I promised this wouldn't happen. I feel like such a fuckup. I didn't deserve her in the first place; now I really don't.

"No fucking clue, but I'm starting to have a lot of questions. I saw him talking to Juliana earlier. Oni said she saw him at the club that night. Neither one of us believes in coincidences.

"I wonder when your uncle invited Juliana out. He's playing a game, but what if he's being played as well?"

I snort and shake my head. "Bro, the eyes in the back of his head have eyes. If Juliana is up to something, he knows. *Fuck*, that would make so much sense.

"I'm going to kill him. New plan, I need you to find out what the Abatos have been up to in the last year. Who they've been connected to, who they owe, what they owe. See if any of that connects back to the shit you found in New York.

"I want to know if this is a me problem or a family problem. Then I want it shut down and everyone who allowed any part of it can be wiped off the map with the source. And I mean everyone," I snarl.

"I'm on it."

I look down and cup the sides of Oni's face. She looks up at me through tear-filled eyes as her lips tremble. My heart breaks a million times over.

"Oni, baby. I need to get you to a hospital. Someone needs to check you out," I say softly.

She shakes her head frantically. I open my mouth to convince her that this needs to be done. If not at a hospital, I need to bring someone in.

However, my mind is blown as she cuts me off. Holding her hand up, she takes a deep, calming breath. I watch as she goes from a sobbing, fragile, frightened bird to a phoenix right before my eyes.

"No. He didn't … he didn't get to hurt me. I need to stay here and help clean up my mess. Show me what you need me to do. Tell me what's next," she says.

"Oni, what the fuck?"

"If I fold now, if I can't handle this, I can't handle you. I'm okay."

I look at her with wide eyes. She's serious. It's like she's flipped a switched and turned the last fifteen minutes off.

I fucking love her.

CHAPTER TWENTY

Hard Decisions

Rico

"Son, here, take this," my father says as I pass him in the foyer.

I look down to find him handing me a leather notebook. I look back up at him and lift a brow. He gives me a smile and pats my cheek as I take the book from him.

"It belongs to Oni. She left it in my office the other day. You might want to take a peek. That is one special young woman."

I open the book to the page that has a ribbon in it. I'm taken by surprise as a sketch of me comes into view. It's so detailed I would think I was looking at a photograph of myself if I didn't know better.

"Wow," I breathe.

"Yes, wow."

I look up into my father's eyes, hearing his unspoken words. I have Oni here for the wrong talents. Once again, it sinks in that I don't deserve her.

I know this, but I also know I'm in love with her and it's going to be nearly impossible to let her go now. The look on her face from earlier comes back to me. The right thing would be to let her return to New York and forget about everything that's happened here.

She's capable of something this beautiful and yet I've turned her into a killer. I swallow hard and turn to walk away with my thoughts. Once I'm in my room, I change for bed and climb into it with the notebook to look through it.

Drawing after drawing takes my breath away. She's so skilled. How did I not know this about her?

I'm leafing through the pages when the door to my room opens. Lightning fast, I reach for my gun and flick off the safety as I aim at the door.

"It's me."

I release a sigh of relief and place the safety back on the gun. Placing the gun back where it belongs, I then move the notebook to my nightstand. Forcing a smile to my face, I wave her in.

"Come here, baby," I say as I open my arms.

Oni rushes over to me and straddles my lap. I envelope her in my arms as she sobs into my neck. I hold her tight and rub her back.

I had a feeling this was going to happen at some point. She handled everything like a champ earlier, but she's still an innocent sixteen-year-old girl. So much turmoil fills me.

The next words out of my mouth taste like shit. "I'm sending you back home. Your debt is clear. You don't ever have to worry about me or my family ever again."

She pulls away and looks me in the eyes. Big fat tears are gathering and spilling from hers. I cup her face and wipe them away with my thumbs.

"You're getting rid of me. You don't want me anymore?"

I crush my lips to hers, but don't deepen the kiss. I don't know that she's ready for that. I just want to show her I still want her, but this is the right thing to do.

"I still want you, baby. God, you don't know how much I care about you. I just feel like this is the right thing to do.

"You don't belong in the middle of any of this. If I love you, I should let you go."

She sits frozen as she searches my eyes. I think over my words and realize what I just said. A little smile comes to her trembling lips.

"You love me?"

"Yeah, baby. I do. I love you so much it's going to fucking kill me to let you go," I breathe against her lips.

"I love you too. I don't want to leave you. I promise I'm okay. I just needed to get this out of my system."

"Shh, we can talk about it in the morning."

I slide down until I'm lying on my back, and she is resting on my chest. Her soft body feels so right on top of mine, but I can't even get hard because I keep seeing images of her sitting on my desk with her dress and swimsuit torn.

I wish I could bring that motherfucker back to life so I could kill him again. Feeling like steam is coming out of my ears, I dial it back to focus on my girl.

"Oni?"

"Yeah?"

"What do you plan to do with your life? I mean, you can't steal cars forever."

"You're like the third person to ask me that. I don't know. I never thought about it."

"Have you thought about art school?"

She lifts her head and looks me in the face. "What would make you say that?"

"Pop gave me your sketchbook. You left it in his office or something. I have it here."

She turns to look at where I'm pointing. Shaking her head, she looks back at me. Sadness fills her eyes.

"I love art. I've been drawing for as long as I can remember, but I've always been told I couldn't make a living off it, so I never thought about art school."

"That's bullshit. There are a ton of ways to make money through art. My family alone has made a fortune in art dealing."

She scoffs. "You act as if I have the privilege you and your family have."

"You could. In fact, I'm going to talk to Pop and see what he can do. Talent like yours shouldn't go to waste."

"If you say so." She yawns and places her head back down on my chest.

My mind begins to spin with all the opportunities I plan to have opened up for her. I want Oni to have it all. This life isn't for her.

I'm going to make this right. If it's the last thing I do, I'm going to make this right.

Her little snores fill the room and bring a chuckle from my lips. I rub my hand down her back and close my own eyes. I can rest knowing she's safe in my arms tonight.

"I love you, Oni."

CHAPTER TWENTY-ONE

Uncle Emilio

Oni

I got a text this morning from Fredrico Sr., telling me to be ready to head out. Rico was already gone when I woke this morning, still in his bed. I didn't feel any way about that.

I know he gets up early to work out before he starts work for the day. I returned to my room to shower and dress. It was once I stepped out of the shower that I remembered Rico told me he loves me. I wasn't expecting that at all.

Although I've tried to deny it to myself, I know I've been falling for him as well. I couldn't help but say it back. I've been smiling so hard my face hurts.

"He loves me," I whisper as I get dressed in gray slacks and a red button-down.

Once I've passed a flat iron through my edges, I head down to breakfast and to wait for Fredrico Sr. I didn't think there was anything that could take the smile off my face. However, the moment I step into the kitchen and find Juliana standing in Rico's face while he sips from a mug, I scowl so deeply my soul feels irked with the gesture.

Juliana turns to look at me. Rico winks at me over her head as she glares right in my face. My scowl softens just a bit.

"What is she doing here? She's not coming with us, is she?" Juliana says.

"Good morning, Rico. Did someone say something?"

"Ugh, whatever. I'll be outside. Your uncle will deal with this situation, I'm sure," Juliana says and stomps off.

Ignoring her, I note the smile Rico has behind his mug. I continue to collect the breakfast that's been wrapped and left in the warmer with my name on it. I smile to myself as I find the food is still perfectly warm.

Humming, I uncover the pancakes and sausage and dive in. I'm extremely hungry for some reason. Closing my eyes, I moan as I chew.

Suddenly, I feel warmth against my back. I stiffen and drop my fork and knife. My heart is racing as Rico kisses the back of my head. I open my eyes.

"Are you okay?" Rico murmurs.

"Yeah, I'm fine."

"Fuck, I'm sorry. I wasn't thinking. I startled you, didn't I?"

He moves so he's standing beside me as he rests his backside against the island. I look into his face to find him looking back at me with concern in his eyes. I reach to place my hand against his stomach and shake my head.

"It's okay. The only way to move forward is to move through."

"I don't think it works that way, baby," he says with sad eyes.

"For this, it has to. I promise, I'll be fine."

He shakes his head. "You're amazing. I want to wrap you up and protect you, but you keep popping out of the box where you're supposed to be safe."

"I'm cool," I say around a forkful of food. "Do you know where your father is taking me?"

Rico groans. "We've been summoned. Uncle Emilio has asked that we all appear at his place this morning."

"Her included?" I ask, pointing in the direction Juliana went.

"Yup, her included." He gives a smirk and leans in to kiss my forehead. "Before you start to buck, I think this meeting will clear some things up."

"What makes you say that?"

"All of my uncle's games have a point to them. Everyone will learn from them, someone will pay the price for them, and someone will elevate from them. Never fails, that's how he works."

"Do you have any idea who is who this time?"

"After what I've learned this morning, I think I might." He shrugs.

"Ah, you are both here. Let's get moving. I have shit to do. I'm too old to be getting called to the principal's office," Fredrico Sr. grumbles as he claps his hands for us to get moving.

I try not to laugh at his last comment. However, I sober up as I get the feeling my actions at the pool party set some things in motion. I get the feeling that's what Rico just left out of what he said because there were holes in his words.

Something I'm learning to detect more easily the more I'm around him. With Rico, it's more of a *hear what I don't say* type of situation. There is a lot in what he doesn't say.

We walk out of the kitchen and find the cousins and Mario all waiting at the front of the house. We all climb into the awaiting cars. I get into the SUV with Emilia, Ed, and Al. Rico climbs into the car with his dad and Juliana.

As I stare out of the window, it keeps nagging at me that I know her from somewhere. The feeling is so much stronger today. It's like it's right there on the tip of my tongue.

I frown as she flips her hair and looks back at Rico. It's in the way she looks back up at him. Something clicks in my mind and my frown deepens.

A name comes to mind and recognition hits. I know exactly where I know her from. My mouth falls open as the memory comes to mind.

"This is rich," I mutter to myself.

"What's that?" Emilia says from beside me.

"Nothing. Hey, can I ask you a question?"

I remember her saying she knows things because people talk around her like she's not there. I get that a lot around here, so I'm hoping in this case she can shed a little light for me.

"Yeah, sure. What's up?"

"How long has the engagement been a thing?"

"Juliana's father came to my dad about a year ago with the proposition. It didn't seem like he was interested at first. Then something changed about two months before you arrived. It's totally weird if you ask me."

"What makes you say that?"

"Because my uncle hates the Abato family," Al answers for her.

Rico

"Any of that make sense to you?" Mario asks from the driver's seat.

I was surprised when my father asked him to drive as he climbed into the vehicle with us. I was expecting him to ride in his own car and take Juliana with him. Mario and I have things to discuss, but that won't happen with her in the back seat.

I was right not to trust her ass. She's lucky I haven't put a matching bullet into her head. She belongs with that motherfucker she brought into my pop's home.

"Nope. Not yet."

"Read it again. You will see what I did," he says with disguised heat.

I know him too well not to hear the true menacing tone beneath the words. I nod my head and open up the email he sent again. As I sit in the front passenger seat staring down at my phone, I reread everything Mario learned about the Abato family. I work to continue to keep my face expressionless.

"I'm enjoying Miami for the most part. I was happy to get the call from Mr. Gallo to come out," Juliana says in her annoying-ass voice.

"I'm sure you enjoyed yourself at the party yesterday. You young people kept me up past my bedtime," Pop says, not giving his true mood away.

He's not fooling me. I know he knows more is going on. He's as good at Uncle Emilio's games as he is. A glance in the rearview and I can partially see his face.

Yeah, he's onto the bullshit.

I snort to myself and shake my head. Then I return my focus to the phone before me. Something catches my attention, and my blood begins to boil.

Juliana has no idea I'm onto her and her family as she sits babbling to my father in the back of the car. I want to keep it that way. I have a million questions as I read this report Mario sent me this morning.

I'm seeing everything differently now. Pauly and Jonny, Andy Cusumano, the bullshit in New York. Everything.

If my uncle knows all this, why is Juliana here? What's his endgame? How do I fit into any of this?

My thoughts go to Oni. What have I gotten her in the middle of? The more I read, the more pissed I get.

We need to get to my uncle's so I can get some answers. Romeo Abato has been working with our enemies. He doesn't want this marriage between me and his daughter any more than I do.

"Juliana, is everything all right?" My father asks, causing me to look out the side-view mirror.

She has turned white as a sheet as she looks down at her phone. Good, it looks like she's been informed that her boy is dead and her plan failed. Oni killed that motherfucker in my father's house. There was no way I could keep that from him.

My father, knowing he shouldn't and probably couldn't keep the information from his brother, reported it to him. That's the reason for this little field trip.

I knew from the moment he requested Juliana's presence; he knew something more—the man always does. What Mario sent me only confirms my suspicions. However, I've yet to figure out what my uncle is up to this time.

What I do know is that asshole who attacked Oni works for Connor McFeely. McFeely is Finn Sullivan's right hand. The Sullivans have been after our New York territories since before I was born. It's no secret we don't fuck with them.

Those Irish fucks are a pain in the fucking ass. To work with them is like a slap in the face to a Gallo. Abato has some balls trying to arrange a marriage between me and his daughter when he's been dealing with those scumbags behind our backs.

"Oh, it's nothing. I'm fine."

"Are you sure? Your face just went white as a sheet. Did you have something for breakfast?" Pop presses.

"I did. If you'll excuse me. I just need to respond to a text," she mutters distractedly.

I want to burst out laughing. I told Mario sending those pictures to her was going to fuck with her head. I'm hoping it will cause her to show her hand.

I had them cropped so she could make out the dude with his brains blown out, but not recognize the location. I snort when I get a text from one of my guys back at the house, letting me know Juliana is texting the phone we found on that asshole and cloned before dumping the destroyed original with the body.

Oni's suggestion, by the way. He sends me a screenshot of the text she just sent to the dead asshole. This time, I can't hold my laughter in.

Juliana*:* *Why haven't you answered my calls? This isn't funny. What are these pictures? Where the fuck are you?*

"You're in a good mood this morning," Pop says to me.

"Nothing to be in a bad mood about. Business is good, I'm engaged. I see my promotion coming any day now.

"Who knows, Uncle Emilio could be calling us in to discuss the wedding or the promotion." I pause and rub my hands together. "This is all so exciting. Right, Juliana?"

"Uh, um. Yeah," she says, still sounding distracted.

I cut my eyes to Mario in the driver's seat. He's giving me the same look. I give a slight nod, causing him to pull his phone. At the next stoplight, he begins to type feverishly.

I shoot a text to Ed and Al, so they're on alert. We're not that far from my uncle's house now. However, I will feel better when we're all there.

My next text is to my uncle. He should know what's going on and what might be headed his way. However, before I can get the text off, a group text comes in from my pop. I stare down at my phone, wide-eyed.

Pop: *Floor it, Mario. Rico, look alive. Emilio, we are coming in hot. Be ready.*

I elbow Mario to get him to look at his phone. He looks down and then immediately steps on the gas.

CHAPTER TWENTY-TWO

Ambushed

Oni

I'm still reeling from Al's words as both his and Ed's phones ping. Al looks down at his and his eyes go wide. Quickly, he reaches for the bag between my and Emilia's feet.

I recognize the bag from training. It's the one where they keep the bulletproof vests and helmets. In training, the same bag sometimes had spare guns. Knowing what the bag carries, my curiosity is piqued, and my heart begins to race.

"This truck is bulletproof. As long as you're both inside, you're safe. Stay in the vehicle, Oni," Ed says pointedly.

"What's going on?" I ask.

Despite Ed's warning, Al still hands both me and Emilia a vest. I lick my lips and tug it on quickly. Emilia does the same. Ed is driving while tugging his on and fastening the straps.

"We might have incoming," Al answers my question as he gets his vest on.

He pulls two guns and checks the clips. I look down at my lap, to my bag. After yesterday, I decided I never want to be caught out there without my own gun. Al reaches to place the bag back on the floor between us. I note an extra helmet and gun still inside. There are also a few clips.

I look out of the windshield and see the car ahead of us is racing forward. Ed has begun to pick up the pace as well. He runs right through a red light to keep up with the car carrying Rico and his dad.

I grab onto the passenger handle above me. Everyone has fallen silent and it's like you can hear a pin drop. I'm holding my breath as we enter a residential area. There are large houses on either side of us, some hidden behind tall shrubs.

I finally take a breath as the car ahead turns on its blinker, indicating they're about to turn into one of the driveways on the left-hand side. Everyone in the car seems to relax. However, the moment is short-lived as a vehicle races around us and another appears ahead of the car Mario is driving.

As Mario goes to turn the car into the driveway ahead, the car that raced around us slams right into its side. The SUV that appeared out of nowhere slams into the other side at the front end. I sit in shock as Ed slams to a stop and starts to bark orders.

"You two get down and stay here."

He throws the truck in park as gunfire starts outside our vehicle. Ed throws on the helmet Al hands him and they both jump from the car. Heart and mind racing, I look around, not sure what I'm looking for.

Then my eyes land on the car Rico and his father are in. The gunfire has increased, but that's not what has my attention. Juliana has climbed out of the car and she's trying to crawl toward one of the cars with the guys firing at us.

My blood begins to boil. This bitch. I look back at the car Rico is in, and I see Mario has stumbled from the car with a bleeding head. However, I don't see Rico or his dad. My heart picks up and begins to beat double time.

"What are you doing?" Emilia hisses at me.

I hadn't noticed myself grabbing clips from the duffel bag to place in the slots in my vest. I also have the gun I noted earlier. I look into Emilia's eyes, and I see the fear and worry swarming along with her tears.

"I'm going to cover Rico and Fredrico. Something is wrong," I say.

"They told us to stay here."

"They also taught me how to help. I can sit here with you and be safe, or I can go out there and cover my man. You know me by now. What do you think I'm going to do?"

"Wait, I don't want to be here alone."

"Stay low. You're going to be fine," I say quickly and grab my gun from my bag to have a backup.

I tuck it into the back of my pants and place the spare helmet on my head. Taking a deep breath, I pop the door open and jump out.

I can hear my breathing in my own ears as I close the door behind me and move forward with my gun out. I've trained in one of these helmets, so it's not as distracting or jarring as it had been the first time I had to wear one. However, we train with blanks and paintballs.

I've just jumped into live action. These bullets are meant to kill. These guys are trying to hurt the people I care about.

I race forward, shooting as I go. I hit one guy, and he falls back. I don't have time to think about it, as I have to take out the next guy before I slide behind Rico's car. Mario is by the front, firing then ducking. I reach for the door where Fredrico is. It's completely smashed in, and I can't tug it open.

I look into the car and see he's lying across the seat. However, I can't tell if he's alive or not. I glance into the front, and I see Rico slumped forward against the dash.

I snap into action, needing to get around to the other side of the car. The problem is that's the side taking fire. Just then, a car races to the gate of the driveway we were going to turn into. Men hop out on the other side of the gate then rush to start firing at the assholes shooting at us.

I take this as my chance. I dart around the car and jump into the back seat, where Fredrico is. He groans and looks up at me. There's confusion written all over his face at first.

The helmets are black and gold, like the tattoos many of Rico's men have. I'm sure he knows I'm one of theirs, he's just not sure who.

"Oni?" he chokes out.

I nod as I check him over. His head is bleeding, but other than that, I don't think he's been hit. The back windshield blows out, causing me to jump and scream.

Looking into the front seat, I can see Rico still isn't moving. I go to kick into action, ready to climb into the front seat to help him, but gunfire outside the car pulls my attention.

I look up to find Emilia has gotten out of the SUV. She looks confused and scared out of her mind. That's when I see the asshole aiming at her.

I don't have time to think. I pull my gun and aim, but I'm out of bullets. Then I pull my spare, but it jams. There's no time for this.

I rush out of the car and run for Emilia. I pull a clip and try to reload as I get to her. At the last second, I reload and make it to her.

Jumping in front of Emilia, I turn and aim. I pull the trigger and catch the asshole between the eyes, but not before a burning sensation hits my shoulder.

"Oni, oh my God, Oni," Emilia screams as I fall into her.

We drop to the ground as pain sears through me. There's a ton of commotion happening around us, but I start to lose focus. *Oh, I'm hit.* I think to myself.

"Here, apply pressure. We need to get her to a hospital now," Mario calls out.

I want to cry out as someone presses into the pain. Shit, my mom is going to be so angry. Then everything goes black.

CHAPTER TWENTY-THREE

Going to Italy

Claude

I look Fredrico Gallo Sr. in the eyes as a storm rages within me. My niece was in a shootout and took a bullet for one of these motherfuckers. This is exactly what I was afraid of.

"I'm sending her back home," I say tightly.

"That wouldn't be wise," Emilio says as he appears out of nowhere. "This problem is coming from New York. Oni is in more danger there than here with us. Once they figure out what she means to Rico, this will be a problem."

I spin on him and glare. While I'm grateful to him and his men for getting Oni to the hospital safely, I know this man. This only happened because he allowed it. It's one of the reasons I hate fucking with him.

This wouldn't be the first time he could have prevented something concerning my family. He's lucky I haven't taken his head off. I'm close—the consequences be damned. I clench my fists as his words sink in.

"I'm not leaving her with you motherfuckers. You all have targets on your backs. She's not safe here."

"No, she's not. That's why she's going to Italy with my daughter," Emilio replies.

"What?" Fredrico and I say in unison.

"She will be going with Emilia to Italy. You did say she has a talent for the arts, didn't you? This is an opportunity for her. She will be raised as a Gallo from here on out."

"You motherfucker," I snarl as I lunge at him. However, Fredrico holds me back. "You planned all of this. We all just played into your hands like my brother did, you piece of shit."

Emilio fixes his cuffs as if I'm no threat, while his brother holds me off. I shove Fredrico and take a step back. I should have known. I should have seen this coming.

"You knew all about her, didn't you?"

"Honestly, not at first. I had washed my hands. Your brother got the girl. He started the family they wanted.

"I never thought I'd hear anything else about a Raven after your brother's death. I knew you were here, but you had walked away from ties to us. You've been no trouble to me, so I hadn't planned on being any trouble to you," Emilio says with a shrug.

"You're an asshole. You could have gotten him out of that mess. You let him die in that jail because you couldn't have what you wanted. Now you're fucking with his baby girl. Why?"

"I'm not the villain here. Believe it or not, I did all I could to get him out of there. I wanted to help Brenda the moment I found out what happened.

"She didn't want my help and wouldn't talk to me. I'm not helping Oni because of your sister-in-law. I'm setting my nephew on the right course before it all blows up in his face," Emilio growls back at me.

"What do you mean, Emilio?" Fredrico hisses.

Emilio rolls his eyes. "She is a sixteen-year-old girl. He is nineteen and being groomed to be Don. This is not the time for this distraction. She's going to Italy."

"He will follow," Fredrick growls.

"Not if he thinks she didn't make it."

"What?" Fredrico stumbles back. "You mean to destroy him. I will not allow this."

They begin to argue in Italian as I stand fuming. This motherfucker has lost his fucking mind. He thinks he's going to bark orders and we're all going to bow. Fuck that.

"The boy loves her. You're going to cause him to snap. I'm not lying to my son for you."

"Then you will go to Italy with her if I can't trust you to stay here and keep your mouth shut. You go home and run the business there. Those are your only options," Emilio bites out with finality.

Fredrico gives him an icy-cold glare. "You ruin everything you touch. Neither of them will forgive you. She's in love with him too. You know that, don't you?"

"Yes, I do. This is why I have made this decision."

"You fucking moron. Even if I went along with this, how will you keep her from running to him?"

"Watch how you talk to me, brother. You are more of a problem at the moment than I care to consider. Don't make me take how much into consideration."

"Are you threatening me?"

"I'm warning you. It would be easier to make you disappear for good than to have to explain to my nephew why you won't be in contact with him until I bring the girl back," Emilio bites out.

Fredrico paces away as he grumbles to himself. I'm still trying to wrap my mind around all of this. I don't want to send my niece back into danger, but can I really trust Emilio to keep her safe?

"My brother has told me that Brenda wants Oni to go away to school. My daughter attends an art academy in Italy. I have had plans for her to work for our art dealership when she comes of age until she marries.

"Since it was Emilia's life Oni saved when she took that bullet, I would like to offer her this opportunity. I am not trying to reenter Brenda's life or manipulate Oni into anything. She needs to be safe, and my nephew needs to be focused.

"I will deal with the fallout when the time comes. This is the best option. I will cover all the expenses. Oni won't ever have to steal another thing in her life.

"For saving my daughter's life, she will be treated like a Gallo princess. Your niece is smart. I will be the one to talk to her and offer her this option.

"She will take it, and she won't contact Rico until I allow it. Mark my words," Emilio says.

"You will not talk to her alone." Fredrico seethes.

"As you wish."

I pull a hand down my face. "Un-fucking-believable," I breathe. "If something else happens to her, I'm going to take your fucking head off."

"This was never on my or anyone else in my family's hands, so take your threats and drop them at Sullivan's door where they belong," Emilio snaps.

I rock back on my heels. So that's the real problem. Emilio may have gotten over Jack and Brenda, but he never got over Jack and Finn Sullivan. What does that have to do with Oni?

Oni

Pure fire is running through my shoulder. Slowly, I open my eyes and look around to figure out where I am. I blink a few times.

I'm in a dimly lit room. As I focus, a beeping sound catches my ear. I turn my head and realize I'm in a hospital room.

Swallowing hard, I try to remember what happened. Emilia … she got out of the truck. I groan and lift a hand to my head.

"Shit," I murmur.

My mouth feels so dry. How long have I been here? Is everyone else safe?

Rico was still unconscious when I got out of the back seat of the car to get to Emilia. I saw the moment one of the guys locked his focus on her and aimed. I've never been more fearful in my life.

I took him out as I raced for her, but I don't remember anything after that. My head is pounding as much as my shoulder is burning. My mom is going to kill me.

I'm in way over my head now. Uncle Claude is going to strangle me. Maybe Rico is right, it's time for me to go back home.

As soon as I have that thought, panic races through me. New York doesn't feel like home anymore. It feels more like a ticking time bomb waiting to go off the moment I return.

I try to think of why I have that feeling so strongly. I can't put my finger on the answer, but I know my feelings are valid. Trying harder, I push to grab onto the nagging thoughts hiding in the back of my mind.

"You're awake."

I look to the door to find Fredrico Sr. and Uncle Emilio standing in the doorway. It was Emilio who spoke. He is also the first to enter.

Fredrico comes and places a kiss on my cheek as he reaches for my hand and gives it a squeeze. I look into his eyes and note a sadness that's not normally there. My heart begins to race.

Did something happen to Rico? Is Emilia okay? Did something happen to one of the other guys?

I have so many questions running through my head. The machine starts beeping like crazy. Fredrico gives my hand another squeeze. Just then, Uncle Claude comes into the room.

"Relax, Oni. We just need to speak with you," Fredrico says.

"How are you feeling, cub?" Uncle Claude asks, also looking sad.

"I'm fine. I'd be better if you guys didn't come in here looking like someone died. What's going on?"

Emilio clears his throat, drawing my attention. I look to him as he sits calmly in the chair in the corner of the room.

"First, I want to thank you for what you did for my daughter. I wasn't expecting that. It's hard to catch me by surprise, but you have continued to do so since you arrived."

I go to fold my arms under my breasts, but the movement causes my shoulder to burn with a new ferocity. I wince and move the arm connected to the burning shoulder back to my side. However, I don't take my glare off Emilio.

"Emilia is my friend. I wasn't going to allow her to be hurt or worse. I did what needed to be done."

Emilio nods. "You have a lot of heart. My brother and Rico are right, you're very smart. Smart enough to make more of your life than stealing cars."

"You mean smart enough to stay away from your nephew before you have me killed or some shit," I bite out.

Emilio chuckles as he tilts his head and stares at me. "You have misunderstood me. I believe Rico has too. My intentions have always been to see how you both would handle pressure. Whether either of you was ready for what this world would bring your way.

"I knew my nephew was in love with you from the time you stepped into Fredrico's sitting room. Rico was trying too hard to make it seem as if you meant nothing. When I told him you could never be more than a bed toy, he almost lost it."

"You said what?" Uncle Claude growls.

Emilio waves him off. "I told him Oni was just a piece of ass. Nothing could ever come of him and some black girl," he says the words so nonchalantly and shrugs.

"Asshole," I say under my breath.

Fredrico has to restrain my uncle as he tries to lunge at Emilio. A part of me hopes Uncle Claude will knock Fredrico over to get to this asshole. The other part of me notices the bruise on Fredrico's face and bandage on his head and hopes he doesn't get hurt.

Unlike his brother, I like the old man. He has been nothing but nice to me. I sag in relief as my uncle regains control and begins to pace and mumble to himself.

"Can you get to your point?" I say dryly.

"You have become my nephew's one and only weakness. I know Rico. There is no getting rid of you. Only in death will he leave you alone—"

"So you do plan to kill me."

"If you would stop cutting me off, I could explain to you what my intentions are," he says in frustration.

"Okay, fine. Speak."

"Neither of youse are ready. Rico needs more time to rise into his role. You need to learn not to end up like this." He points to me in the bed.

"You are sixteen. There's plenty of time to get involved with Rico and become the woman he needs by his side. However, now isn't the time. You will both be dead within a year at this rate.

"Your own friends will be your undoing. I need you to take a step back from Rico because he doesn't know how to do it on his own. If you do as I say, you will want for nothing and when the time is right, you will be right back in his arms," Emilio says.

"Why should I trust you? How do I know you're not trying to get rid of me so you can marry Rico off to Juliana?"

"Juliana Abato isn't good enough for my nephew. She and her father are going to die like the filthy pigs they are. You can trust me because I'm sending you to my home with my brother and daughter."

I look to Fredrico curiously. He gives me a weak smile. I lick my dry lips and try to figure out what's not being said. I know better than to believe Emilio is doing this out of the kindness of his heart.

"What do you want in return?"

"The only thing I ask is that you don't contact Rico until I tell you it's allowed. That means absolutely no contact, Oni. None."

"What? What if he reaches out to me? Am I just supposed to ignore him and act like he doesn't exist?"

"Exactly. You can do things my way and give your mother a daughter to be proud of, or break my trust and lose it all—including my nephew and the security of my family. Trust me, you won't survive more than a month.

"Your mother and uncle will be left to bury you—or worse. You're going to drag them into your mess. Think about this carefully, Oni," he replies.

I think of my mom. All she wants is for me to be safe. I can't go back to her like this. It will break her heart.

I gasp. "Wait. He will only let go of me in death. You plan to tell him I died," I say. It's not a question; I know it's the truth.

I give this deeper thought. Could this be what's best? I don't want to be a distraction to Rico, and I don't want to be the cause of my uncle or mom getting hurt.

It would be selfish of me not to take this offer. I chew on my lip as I try to see how this could go south. The worse that could happen would be losing my mom or Uncle Claude. Rico might be angry, but that's a chance I'm willing to take for the safety of my family.

My heart aches just thinking about it. I love Rico, but look what's been happening to me since we've been together.

"Okay," I whisper.

CHAPTER TWENTY-FOUR

Destroyed

Rico

My entire body feels like I've been hit by a truck. My head has been throbbing, and this shit they have dripping into my arm isn't doing a damn thing for the pain. However, the pain in my chest is what's unbearable.

Something is wrong. Since I became conscious, no one will tell me anything about Oni. I need to know she's okay.

My father entered my room with his head bandaged and his face bruised, but he wouldn't look me in the eyes. That isn't like Pop. I know he's not telling me something.

"Good, you're up," Uncle Emilio says as he enters my hospital room.

"I've been in and out," I murmur.

"How are you feeling? You need anything?"

"Yeah, I need to know what's going on with Oni. Why is everyone avoiding giving me answers about her?"

He sighs and moves to sit in the chair. I follow him with my gaze as I swallow hard. There's a sinking feeling in the pit of my stomach.

My heart is pounding double time, causing the machine to beep faster. My uncle looks at the monitor and frowns then turns his eyes to me. I clench my fists as it's all I can do.

"Rico, I wanted to be the one to tell you. I will forever be grateful to Oni. Because of her, Emilia is still with us.

"I wasn't expecting what I witnessed with my own eyes. You were right, she was one of your soldiers. She had your back—"

"Was? Had? What are you saying?" I bark out a laugh because he has to be fucking joking. "Stop playing with me."

He clears his throat. "I'm sorry. She took a bullet for Emilia. She saved your cousin's life with her own."

My veins fill with ice. He can't be saying what I think he is. This shit isn't happening.

I shake my head because this can't be real. I don't believe it. Uncle Emilio stands and stumbles over to me.

Tears are soaking my face, but I don't care. She didn't deserve this. Why didn't I send her back home when I had the chance?

"I'm sorry, *nipote.* I'm so sorry."

I shrug my uncle off, not wanting him near me. He's as guilty as I am. Juliana was here because of him. Oni was nearly raped because of her and I'm pretty sure those motherfuckers ambushed us because of her.

"Don't touch me. Get away from me. She's gone because of you. She didn't deserve this," I bellow.

"In time, you will see this will only make you stronger."

"Are you fucking kidding me? Get out. Get the fuck out."

"Rico," he says firmly.

"What? I've done everything you have wanted from me since I was a little boy. For the first time, I had someone who made me happy.

"Something you didn't have a hand in. Now she's gone because of your bullshit. What is there left to say?

"I'm happy Emilia is alive, but I just lost everything. Is that what you want to hear from me? You didn't want me to have a weakness … now I have none."

"Rico, I want to be here for you."

"Don't worry about it. I just died with her. You will have your heartless soldier. Congratulations."

"This is fresh. Take some time. I will return later."

"Don't bother."

He frowns and leaves the room. When he's gone, I sink down in the bed and cover my face with my arms as I sob like a baby. I've never cried like this in my life.

I can't believe she's gone. I wanted so much more for her. This is all my fault.

"I'm so sorry, baby. I'm sorry. I was supposed to protect you. I'm sorry," I sob.

CHAPTER TWENTY-FIVE

Royal Screwup

Mason

"You find Oni yet?" my older brother asks as we sit waiting for my da to arrive for this meeting.

Something big is happening. I can feel it in my bones. Da never calls us in like this, not suddenly out of the blue.

I turn to Lorcan and glare. He wants Oni for himself. I've known this for a while.

If only he knew he stands less of a chance than I do. She will never be his. She's too smart for him.

Besides, she would never put up with his shit—the partying, the other girls, the drugs, the abuse. Oh yeah, I know about the abuse. The girls he beats black and blue for not doing what he wants.

My older brother is a spoiled child. The reason I know I will end up running the family, not him. Oni wouldn't tolerate his shit for two minutes.

Yet he's always worried about her whereabouts, like she's some property of his. I'm sort of glad she's gone. Maybe she'll stay away long enough for him to move on and forget about her.

"No, I haven't found her," I grumble.

"I might just have to step in and find her myself. Some best friend you are. Just tell the truth, you fucked up, and she ran off because of you, didn't she?" he taunts.

"Fuck you," I growl.

I don't want to tell him I think he's right. This is all my fault, and I know it deep down inside. Oni is out there somewhere. I don't know where and it's all my fault.

However, before I can open my mouth to retort, the door bursts open and my father storms in with a beet-red face. He marches over to Lorcan and knocks his feet from the table where he had them kicked up and crossed at the ankles like he owns the place. In the next breath, Da is roaring at the top of his lungs at Lorcan.

"What kind of moron are you? What don't you understand about discretion? What the fuck did you just do?"

I sit with my mouth hanging open, not knowing what my brother has done now. For Da to be this angry, he had to do something huge. I swear, if Lorcan wasn't his son, he probably would have blown his head off by now from the look on his face.

"What are you talking about?" Lorcan says with a frown.

Da hauls back and kicks him in the chest, knocking him out of his chair onto the floor. I take a deep inhale and try to hold in my laughter. This is not the time to draw attention to myself.

"You fucking eejit. What am I talking about? What am I talking about? You ambushed the Gallos, you cost us men, you. This was all you. Do you know how I know?

"I know because it smells like shit. Everything you touch turns to shit. You can't zip your fly right without catching your dick in the fucking zip."

This time I can't hold my laughter back. I throw a hand over my mouth as my shoulders shake. Da doesn't look away from

Lorcan, but my brother turns his glare on me as he still sits on the floor on top of his turned-over chair.

"How am I the idiot? I did something no one else in the family ever has. I got to three Gallos, not one but three. How am I the fuckup?"

"Because you got to three of them and every single one is still breathing. You did nothing but make trouble for me. The only one you took out was Rico's bed toy. What good does that do?" Da snarls.

Lorcan makes a sour face. I shake my head. He really did fuck this one up. He's a hothead; he never thinks things through.

"They had Juliana. The plan went south, and I had to do something to get her out of there," Lorcan says like a spoiled child.

Da roars and kicks him in the chest again. I reach to rub at the center of my own chest. That shit looks like it hurt.

From the puke that flies from Lorcan's mouth, I'm sure it did. He rolls onto his side and groans. Da is never physical like this with us. At least he hasn't been in a very long time.

"Whose door do you think Gallo will come to about his girl? Who do you think Emilio will want to answer for this? Do you think it will be the Abatos? No, you dumb fuck. That war will be coming straight to our door.

"I would rather one dead bitch over our entire family. That sounds more like the right move to me, Lorcan. Not some Italian cunt over all of ours. That's your fucking problem. Always worried about some fucking pussy instead of getting the job done.

"Why do you think we were using the Abato family? What don't you understand about this not having a single trace back to us? You were supposed to find a way in without it being linked back to this family."

Da pauses with his chest heaving. He then turns his gaze on me for the first time. I hold my breath, thinking I'm next to get my ass kicked.

My plans didn't go as planned either. There was the fuckup with Oni and I got word back that one of my guys got his head blown off.

As I realize these two just mentioned Juliana Abato, I believe I know how he got himself killed. Good thing he was from Connor's crew, trying to move over to mine or Lorcan's. With a little redirection, Da will count him as Lorcan's fuckup, not mine.

"At least I have one smart son. This information, you think it's enough to make it stick?"

I lick my suddenly dry lips. "It's a start in the right direction and can't be traced back to me. I tied up all the loose ends."

"That's my boy. Come, let's go for a drink."

I let out a relieved breath and nod. I still have one move in play. Someday, I'll find Oni, but for now, I need to focus on my family and business. I can't afford to be like Lorcan.

CHAPTER TWENTY-SIX

We Were Family

Oni

"Can I get you anything else?" the stewardess asks as I sit stewing in my seat.

I know I'm doing this for the safety of my mom and uncle, but something in the pit of my stomach is screaming something is wrong. Rico needs me as much as I need him. I don't know what's going to greet us at the end of all of this.

"No, thank you," I reply with a smile.

None of this is her fault. I'm not going to take my attitude out on her. She's just here to do her job like I am.

This summer has turned into a shit show. I wish I could rewind time and do so much of it over. I didn't even get to make all the money I was promised. I'm taking a big risk trusting Emilio's word.

At least my debt has been erased. Emilio gave his word to me and Uncle Claude that I'll never have to worry about that again.

I'll be honest, things have already started to change. Not all for the better, might I add.

The hardest part was the day I was moved out of the hospital. I felt like my heart was torn from my chest. As we exited the hospital, the cops were walking in.

I couldn't help the eerie feeling I got seeing them. I wanted to jump from the wheelchair and run after them to see where they were going. Were they looking for me or Rico?

Fredrico assured me everything would be okay. He helped me into Emilio's car, which would be transporting me to the house where everyone was waiting so we could get ready to leave. I was angry to learn Juliana got away. I wish I had gotten a chance to pop her head off her shoulders before I went down.

Now I'm just angry and sad. I knew Emilio would find a way to drive a wedge between us, but I didn't realize he would get me to go along with it. The man is always ten steps ahead of everyone.

I'm going along with this, but that doesn't mean I have to like it. Rico will have to understand that I did this for him. He wants the world, and I want it for him. I deserve an Oscar for the act I'm putting on to get through this.

Even Emilio seems impressed with how unbothered I am. Rico and I were the delusional ones in all of this, thinking we could hide anything from this man. In the past few days, I've come to see that more and more.

Our foolishness is why I'm on this plane headed to Italy. I have no one but myself to blame. It's a mistake I will never make again. Emilio is someone I will always keep an eye on from now on.

"You sure you don't want anything?" Emilio asks from across the aisle of the private jet.

Yup, the man ended up following us. I'm not sure what that's about, but Fredrico seems more than annoyed about something. The brothers have been at odds since the day they walked into my hospital room, and I was given the ultimatum.

"No, I'm fine," I reply.

"We had a big breakfast," Fredrico Sr. says.

True to his word, he's looking after me. Once we had a moment alone, he promised he would do everything in his power to look out for me and make sure I got back to Rico someday. He also promised I wouldn't be a sacrificed pawn in all of this.

We all know Emilio is moving pieces on the board according to his plan, not any of ours. Emilio grunts in response to his brother. I ignore them both and go back to the magazine I've been flipping through.

I flip the pages as hard as I want to flip Emilio. Emilia sits on the other side of her father, looking like a frightened bird. She's been this way since I got out of the hospital.

If she thanks me one more time for saving her life, I might take it myself. She's driving me crazy. Isn't this her world? Shouldn't she be used to all of this?

"You will learn a lot on this trip," Emilio says, breaking me from my thoughts. "You are Fredrico's assistant, no?

"You should know how the big boys do things. Stealing cars and trafficking are child's play.

"You should be honored. We haven't allowed Rico to learn any of what you are about to embark on. You pout now; you will thank me later."

I narrow my eyes at him, still not sure what his endgame is. I get he wants his nephew to toughen up, but my gut keeps telling me there's more to it. Fredrico snorts, drawing my attention to him.

He has a deep scowl on his face. I also get that he understands his brother more than I do. They are both holding cards Rico and I can't see.

At this point, I'm ready to be done with the whole family. Rico can have his empire. Emilio can have his precious nephew, and I can take my Black ass home.

Home. I don't have one of those anymore. If I go back, I'm putting everyone in danger. I've been trying to connect the dots there.

I believe the Sullivans had something to do with that shootout. I know where I know Juliana from, which tells me my gut feeling is right.

"Do you know why I respected and loved your father?" Emilio asks, halting my thoughts.

I jerk my head back in surprise. I knew Fredrico Sr. knew my dad. However, this is new news to me.

"What? You knew my father?"

"Yes, we were once the best of friends. I know your mother too. We were once family.

"Don't think my family is so weak we would have allowed you to get away with that stunt you pulled in New York otherwise. I would have killed you myself."

"You're not going to keep threatening me," I bite out.

He chuckles. "Relax, Oni. I'm not your enemy. I am only stating a fact."

"Same."

"You are so much like him. Your father always said what he thought too. That's why we got along.

"He wasn't afraid of me. If something needed to be said, he spoke up. Your father was an extremely smart man."

"I'm hearing a whole lot you haven't said. What are you getting at?"

"Your uncle and maybe even your mother will blame me for your father's death. The real blame should be with your friends back in New York," he says.

"This is the second time you've mentioned my friends. What don't I know?"

"The Sullivans are all trash. They respect no one and have no loyalty. You think you came across Rico by accident? I'm not the first to use you as a pawn. You were thrown to the wolves from day one, *cara*."

I gasp. "The dare. Mason knew that was Rico's truck?"

"Now you see. Some best friend. Everyone knows what the consequences are for taking from a Gallo."

"So you know Juliana is working for them, don't you?"

"I know a lot of things. I know the bastard you killed for trying to rape you was sent to Miami by your friend Mason, but he's from Connor McFeely's crew.

"I know Juliana is the one who told Larkin to attack you in my brother's home. I know that Sullivan is plotting to have my nephew arrested even now."

"What?"

"A drug charge that will be knocked down to a gun charge. None of it should stick, but it will. Rico will learn a tough lesson, but he will be better for it."

"You're going to allow him to go to jail? Then what is any of this for? Why am I leaving and allowing you to fake my death?"

"Because it will all harden him. And you … you are about to learn to be a true donna. Your father helped me get to where I am. If you can be half of what your father was to me, you will be the greatest prize my nephew has."

"But you're allowing him to go to jail. What if he doesn't make it back?" I nearly sob.

"He will. I will ensure it. I owe your father this.

"Sullivan got to him before I could get him out of that hellhole. You will not lose another man you love to prison or those Irish bastards. This I promise you. *Capisce*?"

I work my jaw as I allow all of this to sink in. The Sullivans are behind my father's death. On top of that, Mason did this. My own best friend.

I trusted him and he set me up. All of this started because of him and his family. I know Juliana because she was one of Lorcan's whores. I've seen her on her knees for him before.

As it all clicks together, one thing plays in my head.

They're all going to pay.

Rico

I'm numb. This is not how I thought things would end. I never saw it coming.

Oni is dead. She took a bullet for Emilia and now she's gone. I will never forgive myself for this.

I deserve to be here, locked behind these bars. She had her whole life before her, before me. Now she has nothing. There will never be another day for her.

I laughed in my uncle's face when he first told me. I thought he was playing one of his games. I didn't want to believe she was gone.

As I lay in that hospital bed, I prayed it was all a lie. If she had walked through that door, I would have let her go. I would have freed her from me if I had a second chance.

I would rather know she's somewhere safe from me, alive. Instead, she's gone, and I'm here. Uncle Emilio could have gotten me out of this shit. Fuck, my father should have gotten me out by now, but I know this is where I belong.

I'm broken. I have nothing left but anger. Mario comes to check on me, but I do nothing but stare into space while he's here, like now.

"Rico, did you hear me? What do you want me to do?"

I shrug. "I don't care."

"Bro, you can't give up like this. You know he's testing you."

"Testing me for what? I'm done. He doesn't give a shit about me. If either of them did, I wouldn't still be here."

"I told you, your father had an emergency in Italy. I don't know if he knows you're here. No one has been in touch with him."

"Yeah, well, my uncle knows. He wouldn't even get me out of here so I could go to her funeral. I should have been there.

"I owed it to her to be there. I should have buried her and had the chance to say goodbye. Instead, I'm in here over some bullshit."

"And all your enemies are out there. When you get out of here, they need to answer for Oni and all the other bullshit. Let me do my job.

"Tell me what you need done. All my life, I've been by your side. Since we were little, you wanted to be at the top.

"She wanted that for you. Make this shit happen in her memory. Lift your head, bro and take this shit."

I scoff. "He's punishing me for her. Do you really think he's going to promote me? Let alone hand me it all?"

"Yes, I think you're forgetting who he is. You see a punishment. I see a test.

"Hold your head up and tough this shit out. I've got your back. If he doesn't give it to you, we take it. For Oni."

I ball my fists on top of the table. He's right. I can't fail now.

Oni did everything she did in order to see me at the top. I vow in this moment I'll be Don. Because my girl believed in me without a doubt, I'm going to make it happen.

I nod. "Let the crew know nothing changes. They now answer to you, and you will report back to me. They keep shit clean like before.

"Find the rat and deal with it. When I get out of here, this shit will never happen again."

"What about Sullivan?"

"I'll deal with that shit when I get out." I pause and swallow hard. "They set her up. All of this started with them. Mason Sullivan will answer for his betrayal."

"I'll be back next week. I've got you, brother."

"Yeah, thanks."

CHAPTER TWENTY-SEVEN

Coming Home

Oni

Three years later …

"*Sembra buono,*" I say to Carmine as he hands me my earnings report.

"*Sì, sì. Emilio ne sarà molto contento. Ormai, da sei mesi di fila, sei la sua risorsa più redditizia.*"

I smile in satisfaction. I've actually been Emilio's top earner for seven months in a row. I just didn't say anything the first two months.

Emilio knew. He flew here himself to praise me for it. I'm about to turn nineteen and I already manage one of the most lucrative art operations in Italy.

Not to mention the other business dealings Emilio trusts me with. With Frederico by my side, I think I have surpassed all their expectations. I even have my own crew.

I run shit. Emilia has been my ears as I rise in power. There isn't anywhere here I can't go without people knowing who I am and who I'm connected to.

Emilio has stayed true to his word. You would think I was the man's second daughter. While sending me to private school with Emilia, he has allowed me to learn the business from Fredrico on the side.

The first two years, I focused on my schoolwork. This year has been all business. It's all I could do to stay focused on something other than Rico.

I miss him, but knowing this is all for him to become Don drives me day in and day out. That and the fact that I plan to make Mason pay for trying to have me killed, raped, and setting Rico up to go to jail.

There will be no peace for the Sullivans when I get back to New York. I've been waiting for the day to come when I can return. That day is here.

"Oni, we need to leave. Papa will have a fit if we miss our flight," Emilia whines as she walks into my office.

I only came in here to grab my tablet. Carmine caught me off guard with the reports. He was excited when I walked in.

"*Sì, sì. Devi andare. Mi dispiace. È una buona notizia. Vai pure,*" Carmine says.

"You don't have to apologize. It is good news. I will talk to you soon. *Ciao.*"

I grab my tablet and head out with Emilia. I can't help reaching up and touching my new pixie cut. I left it longer on the top, but the back and sides are really low.

It's a far cry from the braids I used to wear. This haircut matches my vibe these days. A lot has changed about me.

In some ways, the old Oni did die. I take a deep breath as I settle into the back of the car. I can only hope Rico will forgive me.

Emilia reaches over to cover my hand with hers. "It's going to be all right. He will be happy to see you. Love will make him forgive you; it's my father he'll hate."

"I hope you're right. He's been out for two years. I thought I would have been back with him by now."

"In those two years, he's been more focused and driven than ever. He's different, but so are you. I think now is the perfect time for your return."

"Why now? Do you know?"

She turns away from me and clears her throat. My stomach sinks. She knows, but she's not going to tell me and that's what scares the shit out of me.

"At least tell me if he's okay."

"He's fine, I guess. Always angry but fine. You will see."

Rico

I stumble into my Brooklyn apartment at five thirty in the morning. It's been a long night. I've been working harder to earn in the last six months.

Someone has been outearning my crew, but Uncle Emilio won't tell me who. I've been working double time to take my spot back.

"I need to figure this shit out," I mutter to myself.

I know it's not Fredo and his crew. He's been struggling and trying his best to figure things out. That's no surprise; I figured that was going to happen.

"If not Fredo, then who?" I muse as I loosen the buttons of my shirt.

Al and Ed have been working under me, learning the ropes and treading the line until they're ready to move up. My cousins are smart, but they're just not ready to take on their own crews.

All the older guys are complacent. Which leaves me to wonder who the fuck has been trying to outshine me. That shit is nagging at me.

Uncle Emilio is still up to his old tricks. Why make me aware that I'm coming in second if he's not going to tell me who's ahead of me? Why not at least give me a chance to know what they're doing to earn so I can outearn them or study their moves?

"Fuck him," I mutter to myself.

I haven't come in second since my father left. He's not back, so this can't be him. Besides, I took over most of his operations.

I'm too exhausted for this shit. I need a good night's sleep and a fifth of something strong. Something to knock me off my ass.

My phone rings, interrupting my thoughts. I pull it from my pocket and roll my eyes as I see it's Uncle Emilio. I already know what he's calling for.

I'm thinking about proposing to Salvator Romano's youngest daughter. It's not a love match. I will never fall in love again.

I want Romano's connections and his docks. Alyissa Romano is pretty enough; she'll make nice arm candy as a little Mafia princess, but that's where things will end. I don't fuck.

I would have to get hard for that. The only way I've been able to get hard in the last three years is if I picture *her*. I'm not willing to do that with another woman.

That shit makes me sick to my stomach, so I don't fuck. Not that I don't have plenty of ass thrown at me. I'm too broken to care or want to care.

If I were to marry Alyissa, she would have to accept the fact that there will be no sex. I'd keep her happy with gifts and shopping sprees. That would have to be good enough. Though I doubt that's what she'll want.

It's the biggest reason I haven't given her father a commitment. If not for that, I would have by now. Uncle Emilio hates the idea of me taking her for my wife.

I think that's what's driving me to want to do it more. I've almost convinced myself that it will be worth it and I'll be able to go through with it. After all, it was his choice that took the love of my life from me.

"God, I miss you so fucking much, baby."

I get to the bar in my home and grab a tumbler. As I go to grab a bottle, my phone rings again. This time it's from a number I don't know.

Given the hour, I don't ignore it this time. This could be business or a problem I need to handle. I answer and lift it to my ear.

"Don't hang up," Uncle Emilio says.

"*What?*" I roar into the phone.

"Lose the attitude. This is the call. A car is downstairs."

With that, he hangs up. I stand with my mouth hanging open. He's opening the books.

I'm getting the promotion. Finally, I'm a made man. I'm one step closer, baby. This is for you.

CHAPTER TWENTY-EIGHT

Alive & Well

Rico

I have to question the timing of it all. Why now? What's my uncle up to?

This would have been Oni's nineteenth birthday. Everyone knows I've crashed out on this day in the last three years. Why promote me, throw a party, and make a big deal out of this day?

My mother and father aren't around. Both traveling or whatever. This happening now makes me feel so alone.

This shit is pissing me off and I can't fucking breathe. Yet I've just been made, and I need to put on a smile for everyone. While I'm putting on an act for everyone else, I'm fucking dying inside.

That's why I'm in this bathroom stall trying not to lose my shit. My uncle didn't even have enough respect to be on time. I'm here holding on by a thread and he's nowhere in sight.

"What do you think is going on with the don? I thought he'd be here by now," a guy says outside the stall.

I'm not the only one who realizes the disrespect. I'm tired of this. Uncle Emilio has been riding me harder than ever in the last two years.

"*Marone*, word is tonight isn't about Rico. Well, it is, but it's not. He's giving the kid his flowers, but the real celebration is about his daughters. He's bringing them back home."

"Don't you mean daughter? He only has the one."

"Yeah, yeah, one by blood, but word is getting around fast about the other one."

I knit my brows. Emilia is my uncle's only daughter. These two must have had too much to drink. However, I lock in and listen.

"Other one?"

"*Marone*, you really don't pay attention, do you? You better get your head on straight. Gallo isn't fucking around about her. Word is, he'll blow your brains out himself over her."

"Who is she?"

"In the old country, they say she's more ruthless all on her own than the trinity put together."

I try not to scoff. He's referring to Uncle Emilio, my father, and me. This guy is talking shit. Ain't no fucking way.

"You're shitting me."

"Nope, not shitting you at all. My cousin back home says he had a run-in with her. One of his guys fucked something up and she handled him. Let's just say I'm happy to be on this side."

"You still haven't told me who she is."

"She's the one who took that bullet for the don's princess. Things are changing around here for sure. We're to bow down to a *mulignan*."

"If what you're saying is true, you better watch that shit. I've seen the Don bury men for less."

My head is buzzing as I stand in confusion. Oni took a bullet for Emilia, but she's dead. How … motherfucker.

I play that day in the hospital back in my head. My Uncle chose his words carefully. I was also too distraught to follow if he was lying to me or not. In hindsight, he gave all the tells that he was.

His wording was off, he wouldn't look at me, he tried to console me. If I wasn't so fucking destroyed, I would have picked up on all of it that day.

I storm out of the stall as rage rushes through my blood. This has my uncle written all over it. I never saw a body. I was in a jail cell before I could confirm a word he said.

"Hey, baby. Congratulations," Alyissa says as she appears in front of me.

"Not now," I bite out.

I move forward blindly. I need answers. So much is starting to make sense.

I haven't talked to Pop in three years, not for lack of trying. I figured he was pissed at me about Oni. I thought he blamed me for her death.

The two had become close. However, if she's alive. *Fuck.*

He knows. The old country. She's been right under my nose in Italy. That's where Pop has been.

Everything shifts in the ballroom. Everyone's attention turns to the door. I move to the empty dance floor and stand there, staring at the entrance.

In walks my father. He looks a little older, but still sharp. A smile comes to his face when his gaze lands on me.

He opens his arms and waves me to him. I go to embrace him, but I freeze when Uncle Emilio walks in with Emilia on one arm and none other than Oni on the other.

"Fuck outta here," I breathe.

She looks beautiful as she stands there, looking like she owns the room. There's something different about her. I swallow hard as I take her in.

She's a little taller, but not by much. It could be the red patent leather pointed-toe heels on her feet. Heels that are making her silky-looking legs look long and shapely.

She has cut all her hair off. The sides are short, but she still has full bangs that fall into her eyes. She's dressed in a black dress that's fitted with a sheer layer over top that bunches and angles in different places, bringing a sophistication and elegance to the look.

All that innocence is gone from her gorgeous face. Her eyes look sharper. There is also something about her presence that's more powerful than it once was.

Her lips are painted a bright red to match her shoes, making her full lips pop. Her gaze moves over the room as if she's searching for someone. When her eyes land on me, a huge smile comes to her lips.

I'm in motion before I can think of what I'm doing. My father forgotten, I move past him and straight for the love of my life. I wrap her in my embrace, cupping her head to my chest as I hold her tightly.

"Rico, we should talk," my uncle says.

"Fuck you."

"You best remember yourself."

"You lied to me. You told me she was dead. I have nothing to say to you."

I close my eyes and inhale deeply. Her scent does everything to calm me down. I begin to sway with her in my hold. She's real.

I can feel her heart beating against my chest. She's fucking alive. I tighten my hold.

"Rico," she whispers.

I pull away slightly to look down into her face. She cups my cheek and runs her finger over my facial hair. I must look so different to her.

Not able to wait a minute longer, I dip my head and press my lips to hers. I don't deepen the kiss, and I don't pull away, afraid she might vanish the moment I try to take too much or break the connection.

"Rico, what the fuck? Who is she?"

Reluctantly, I pull away to find Alyissa glaring at Oni. I'm hit hard with the feeling of déjà vu. I clench my jaw. I'm not about to do this shit again.

"This is my fiancée, Oni," I say as I give Oni's waist a squeeze.

She flips her long, waist-length, jet-black hair over her shoulder. "Your fiancée? What the fuck are you talking about?

"You were just talking to my father about proposing to me. Are you serious? What kind of game are you playing?"

"I'm not playing any games. Your father asked me to think about a merger between our families. I never committed to anything," I reply.

"You're going to pay for humiliating me, asshole."

With that, she storms off. Oni moves like she's going to go after her, but I grab her arm to stop her. She turns to me and some of the anger fades from her face as we lock eyes.

"Don't worry about her," I say.

"Fiancée?" she says and lifts a brow.

I wink at her and reach to brush her bangs out of her eyes. I still can't believe I'm looking at her in the flesh. I don't know what to feel.

"Oni?"

Turning toward the voice of Mario, I set eyes on him, Al, and Ed. However, Mario seems to be the only one surprised to see Oni. I shake my head.

He didn't know. As I muse on that, Oni runs into Mario's embrace. I take her in from behind.

Marone. My girl is all grown up. Her hips are more shapely, her ass is fatter, and she's filling out that dress like an Insta model. I move behind her and tug her into my front.

Not able to hold myself back, I press my lips to the butterfly tat on the back of her neck. It looks like she has a swarm of them rising up behind her ear and right into the corner of her hairline, just above her nape.

"What's going on?" Mario says in confusion.

"She's been in Italy. That asshole lied."

I can't take my hands off her. For the first time in three years, I'm growing hard. She has to feel me stabbing into her ass.

I probably should give her space, but I can't bring myself to. Mario's face lights up as he comes out of his shock. I think I can understand how he feels. I still haven't fully processed what's before me.

"Romano will be a problem," Uncle Emilio says in my ear as he claps me on my shoulder.

I shrug him off. I already know I'll have to deal with Romano and Alyissa. Trust me, I've learned from my mistakes.

Oni

It has felt weird to be back in New York. I've been in my new penthouse apartment in Manhattan since I arrived. A gift from Emilio himself, for my birthday.

However, the best gift I could have asked for is wrapped tightly around me. Rico hasn't let me out of his sight. I had planned to come home alone after the party.

This man wasn't having that. He insisted that we needed to spend the night together and talk. I don't think it's settled in that I had a part in disappearing.

I've been holding my breath waiting for it to. Once he figures it out, I don't know that he's going to be so clingy anymore. I don't want to lose him over this.

I smile as he tosses his jacket toward my couch. His gun holster is next. I guess he's making himself at home.

He presses a kiss to the back of my neck, still not releasing me from his hold. I melt into his embrace, savoring his strong arms around me.

"Can I get you something to dri—"

My words are cut off as he grasps my neck and turns me to face him. In the next breath, his lips are on mine. It's not like the kisses he's been giving me all night.

This one is desperate and all-consuming. He's practically eating my face. I moan into his mouth as I cling to his shirt.

"I want you so much," he groans as his hands are everywhere.

"Rico, don't you think we should talk?"

"I figured most of it out. I don't want to talk about it. Trust me, baby, I know my uncle.

"He told you some shit that sounded good at the time to get you to leave me. Then he made you my competition and brought you back home to rub it in my face. You're the earner who's been crushing my earnings," he growls as he pulls the zipper down on my dress.

He has most of it right, but I don't think Emilio intends to pit us against each other. I've been learning. What I now know will help Rico.

I'm home to be with him and help him to reach his goal. However, I get why he thinks his uncle is against him. I had no idea Rico was going to marry someone else.

I believe that was Emilio's real reason for bringing me home. I saw the way he looked at that bitch who threatened Rico. I had planned to handle her myself before Rico stopped me.

After pushing my dress to the floor, he backs me against the nearest wall. Pulling the cups of my bra down, he then lifts me onto his waist and starts a trail of kisses down my neck.

"Oh my God," I cry out as he pulls my nipple into his mouth.

His hair is so much longer than it used to be. Falling into his eyes and face now that it's come out of his neatly combed style. I push it out of his face.

He looks up at me as he continues to suck. Reaching between us, he shoves his hand into my panties. He groans as he finds my wet slit.

I throw my head back and whimper his name. Releasing my peak from between his lips, he captures my mouth once again. As he kisses me deeply, he begins to play with my pussy.

"Are you on birth control?" he asks tightly.

I nod my head as I can't find words to speak. He growls and tears my panties from my body. The fabric burns my skin with the gesture, but I can't focus on that.

He's setting my body on fire with his touch. Lifting me up, he then settles me on his shoulders and dives in to feast on me. I lock my hands in his hair and hold on tight.

"Fuck," I cry out.

"Mm," he hums, not missing a beat while feasting on me and removing his shirt.

Reaching up, he palms one of my breasts and squeezes it, then pinches and rolls my nipple between his fingertips. One of my shoes has come loose and is hanging off my foot, I'm sweating my hair out, and my back is cool from the wall behind me, but none of that matters as I start to come all over his face.

"Rico, yes, oh God, yes."

He takes a step back and allows me to slide down the wall as he releases his belt and shoves his pants down. Catching me before I slide too far down, he pulls my legs back around his waist and takes my lips in a searing kiss.

I scream into his mouth as he thrusts into me. He freezes and looks me in the face. He's so hard pulsing inside me.

"You … you waited for me?"

"Yes, I'm yours. I would never let anyone else touch me."

"Fuck, I didn't know, baby. Shit. I just fucked this up."

I cup his face. "It's okay. I need you too. Please don't stop."

He kisses me hard. "I love you so much. Where's your bedroom?"

"Down the hall."

He pulls out and scoops me into his arms bridal style to carry me to my room. My shoes fall off as he settles me in his hold. I wrap my arms around his neck.

He takes a moment to step out of his shoes and kick his pants aside, then moves up the hall. Once in my room, he gently places me on the bed, then climbs in with me. I moan and call his name as he climbs over me and takes my nipple into his mouth once again.

I'm ready this time when he pushes into my body. He groans around my breast as he pauses to allow me to adjust to him. I whimper and wiggle my hips. He lifts his head, letting my nipple pop free from his mouth.

"You're really here," he says as if in disbelief.

"I am."

I throw my head back as he lifts my legs over his forearms and moves deeper inside me. He's so thick and hard. It feels like he's coming out of my back.

"You feel so fucking good," he breathes. "Fuck, Oni. I thought I lost you forever.

"I've been drowning without you. Now you're here and I'm inside you. I'm never letting you go," he says and kisses me as he rocks in and out of my body.

"I've missed you so much. It was so hard to stay away," I breathe as I claw my nails down his back.

I'm so wet and he's hard as steel. The more he moves in and out of me, the better it feels. He's kissing me so deeply as if he's drinking from my mouth. My toes curl as he thrusts deeper.

"Fuck, this tight-ass pussy was so worth the wait. Do you feel how hard you have me? I haven't been hard for anyone since you left me."

He grabs the sheets by my head and really starts to drill into me. Nothing coming out of my mouth makes sense. He starts to lick and kiss my tat over my entrance wound and traces the path up my neck.

I don't think he misses one of the little butterflies that cover my skin. Reaching for his ass, I then dig my nails in. He groans in my ear, then nips it.

"You're so fucking sexy. Look at you taking this dick. You're mine, Oni. I'll kill for you. No one will ever take you from me ever again."

"I'm here. I'm not leaving. Oh God, Rico. I'm coming."

"Come, I feel that shit. Fuck yes, keep rocking just like this.

"Good girl. I love that shit. This pussy is insane.

"You're so wet. Happy birthday, baby. Come all you want."

I throw my head back on a silent scream as he rolls his body into mine. I start coming and I don't think I stop.

Rico keeps bringing my body more pleasure than I can stand. This has to be the best birthday gift ever. I'm finally home.

CHAPTER TWENTY-NINE

You've Changed

Rico

Between my uncle and Salvator Romano, my phone has been blowing up all morning. I'm not in the mood to talk to either of them, so I've been ignoring their calls. The woman in my arms is the only thing I'm worried about.

"What?" she giggles as I look down at her while rubbing my thumb against her hip.

"I'm just thinking about how much you've changed, but you're still the same."

"You've changed too. You're handsome with a beard. You look more dangerous," she says.

"Dangerous," I snort. "I've heard about you. Italy has to be happy you're gone," I tease.

"Whatever. I get shit done." She shrugs.

"I still don't know how I feel about that."

"Why? What's the problem?"

"You were innocent before you met me. Now look at your life. Uncle Emilio always wanted sons. You've become the other one."

I can see it in her eyes. Uncle Emilio has done with her what he has always done with me. I didn't comply, so he made another me.

"Innocent?" She scoffs. "I was a car thief when you met me. I stole your car. There was nothing innocent about me back then."

"You know what I mean." I reach to run my fingers through her bangs and push them out of her face. "I feel like I took your life away."

"I have a better one now. Uncle Emilio and your father are good to me."

"What about your mom? Does she know about all this?"

"She knows I went away to school and that I work for an art gallery."

I jerk my head back. "That's how you're doing it? He's letting you run the art operation. That's how you're outearning me."

She bursts into laughter. "Oh, you hate that, don't you? Yes, I run the art operation among other things.

"I've been killing it in the last seven months. I never thought of how mad that had to be making you. Poor baby, are you okay?" She purrs as she leans up to take my lips.

I take over the kiss quickly. She moans and wraps her arms around my neck. I tug her naked body into mine and devour her.

"We should get out of bed and find something to eat," I say as I break the kiss.

She chuckles. "You're not going to admit it."

"Yes, that shit was pissing me off." I shrug. "Now that I know it was you, I'm proud as fuck of you. It's not what I wanted for you, but I'm proud of you, baby."

"You're going to be Don. Your donna should be able to hold it down when you need her to. Emilio isn't as bad as you think he is."

"Don't," I bite out.

"You know we can't avoid the elephant in the room forever."

"*Oni,*" I drag out in warning.

"*Rico*," she says back.

"I thought you were dead. Not on vacation. Not at school.

"Not away training to be my other half. He told me you were dead. Do you have any idea what kind of pain I was in?

"I sat in a jail cell for a year because of him. I spent three years thinking I got the love of my life killed."

I begin to roar and have to pause to calm down. She's looking back at me with tears in her eyes. This is why I didn't want to go there.

I just got her back. I don't want to fight with her. I want to learn all the things that have changed with her and who she is now.

"None of that was his fault. Everything, and I mean everything, was Mason Sullivan's fault."

I blink a few times. I had no idea she knew about Mason's involvement. I had made the connection, but I didn't know how much she knew.

"I always wanted to know what the deal was with you two."

"Mason was my best friend. That's who had been calling me back then. He's the one who dared me to take your truck."

"What?"

"You don't know?"

"Fuck," I hiss and run a hand through my hair. "Now it all makes sense. When I got out, those motherfuckers had scattered. Uncle Emilio brushed it off and said some shit went down while I was inside.

"He wouldn't tell me what. After six months of asking and not getting anywhere when I tried digging, I dropped it. I decided if I couldn't find them and kill them, I would focus on being Don to honor your memory."

"What do you mean scattered? They're not here?"

I bristle as I see the disappointment on her face. I had no idea that asshole was her best friend. Does she want to see him now, after all he has done?

"A few of them went back to Ireland, from what I know. Others, Boston, some New Orleans." I shrug. "Why do you care?"

She looks up at me through her lashes. "Because I have hot slugs for them all. Mason, his dad, and Juliana Abato included."

"Okay, baby. I see we both have unfinished business. Tell me what you know. From the beginning."

CHAPTER THIRTY

Together Again

Oni

"No, that's fine. Those crates need to go out today."

"*Sì,* I will handle."

"*Grazie, Carmine. Fammi sapere se dovesse sorgere qualcos'altro.*"

"You are welcome. I will call if there is anything. I have everything under control.

"He wants to transition everything to your side. I will have it all done by month's end," he replies, switching to English.

He's getting better. His English was much more broken when I first got to Italy. We helped each other over the years.

Emilio had been pleasantly surprised to learn I could hold a complete conversation in Italian. Fredrico was so proud he wouldn't speak English to me for months.

"Great, talk soon. *Ciao.*"

"Listen to you. Watching you be a lady boss is sexy," Rico croons in my ear as he wraps his arms around me from behind.

"My work is never done. Just making sure nothing falls apart while I'm here. Are you finished?"

We've come to his place so he can pack a bag to stay at mine. I'll admit he's taking this a lot better than I thought he would. I can tell he's still angry with his uncle, but he seems to have forgiven me.

"I'm all set. Let's get out of here. I want to take you on a date. We have so much time to make up for."

"*Andiamo. Voglio sapere tutto sulla banda. Mi siete mancati tutti*," I say in Italian with a smile.

He groans. "I love hearing you speak Italian. I didn't think you could become more perfect. Now it's like you were made for me."

"I was. You will see."

He grasps the back of my neck and tugs me into him to capture my lips. I cling to his shirt as he devours my mouth. Sex with him was amazing last night.

I want him again, but my sore pussy and ass say I need a break. I think he did try to make up for the last three years in one night. I wasn't complaining at the time.

The passion and intensity of our lovemaking was mind-blowing. He nearly brought me to tears a few times. Not just because it was so good, but there were moments where I could feel his love and how hurt he had been without me.

I aim to fix that. I might be a bit bitter and angry that I won't get the revenge I came for, but I have Rico and that's all that truly matters to me.

"*Marone*. Let's get out of here before I take you again and we never leave.

"Don't worry, we'll make time to hang with the guys. I think they missed you too. It will be good to have things back to normal. I know they'll be glad I'm not biting their heads off for a while."

I smile and tuck into his side. When his suitcases come into view, I burst into laughter. Then I see the garment bags.

"Um, how long are you planning on staying with me?"

"Since our next stop is to pick out your engagement ring, I say we live together. This place is the bare minimum because I didn't give a shit, but your place is meant for a princess. It's where you belong."

"You do know that place is my birthday gift from your uncle, right?"

"I figured. Fuck him. It will probably piss him off that I'm there fucking you every night. Works for me either way," he croons.

I laugh and shake my head. He places his hand on my ass and leans to kiss my temple. I go to help him with his things, but he shakes his head.

"The guys will take care of it. Come on."

With a smile on my lips, I take his hand and follow him out of the apartment. I snort to myself. Bare minimum.

Back in the day, this place wouldn't have been an option for me and my mom. Boy, have I come a long way. I wonder what my mother will say now. That's another bridge I need to cross.

I'm grateful to Uncle Claude for taking her on a vacation. I need more time to think about how I plan to deal with things. My life might be better for me, but the truth of it is the exact opposite of what my mother wanted for me.

Rico

I haven't been this happy in years. I once put an ice pick through a guy's eye because he joked that I needed to get laid. In all fairness, he sent a stripper to my club for me.

I didn't find it funny. It was the anniversary of when I met Oni, and the stripper favored her too much, as if he was taunting me. That behavior can be a thing of the past—to an extent.

The sun is still out shining as I walk with my arm around my girl. We have our shades on, strolling without a care in the world.

"You know you're going to have to answer that soon," Oni says as my phone rings again and I send it to voicemail.

I shrug. "I'll get to it when I'm ready."

"You're only pissing him off. Is that wise?"

I sigh. "I don't want to talk about him. Knowing what you know has only pissed *me* off more.

"He has swept so much under the rug. I guarantee you, when I start to dig, I'm not going to like what I find. I know he didn't leave it all to go away on its own," I say more harshly than I mean to.

"Maybe we should let it go," she murmurs.

"Nah, not a chance. That beef has been between our families for generations. I need to know what happened so it doesn't come back to blow up in my face."

Releasing a heavy breath, she nods. "You're right. I wouldn't leave it either. I also know your uncle. He's not going to give you the answers you want unless it's something he wants you involved in."

"Who says I'm going to him for answers?"

"Whatever you do, know I'm here when you need me."

"That's why we're here," I croon as I stop in front of my jeweler's storefront.

Oni looks up at me. "You were serious?"

"When have I ever played about you?" I peck her lips. "Come on, I want you to pick it."

"Rico. We … I … how long have we truly known each other?"

"My soul has known you from the moment we were created. I know what it's like to lose you. Now I want to know the feeling of loving you for the rest of my life while you're in my arms."

"You don't feel we need to date?"

"No, it will end the same way no matter what. Like you said, you will be my donna. No matter what I have to do to make that happen."

She stands searching my gaze for a beat. Then a huge smile comes to her face. I love that smile.

"Okay, let's do this."

I kiss her forehead then lead her into the store. It finally feels like my life is moving in the right direction. Nothing can tear us apart.

CHAPTER THIRTY-ONE

Not Your Enemy

Rico

Oni was right, I can't ignore my uncle forever. I also should have known he would use her to get to me. If not for Oni, I wouldn't be here at one of his restaurants, where he's summoned us.

"Stop looking so pissed off," Oni says as she cups my face after I help her from the car.

I look her over and smile. She's wearing a navy-blue tailored pantsuit with a tie around her neck, but no shirt, just a bra under the jacket. She looks good.

Her bangs are blown out of her face and curled back into waves. I love how versatile her haircut is. I've seen it in a number of styles since she's been home.

I chuckled when I first saw her tonight, as I'm wearing a similar suit in the same color. We look like a power couple together. In the last week, we've been just that.

"I can't help if I look how I feel," I mutter.

"Let me ask you something."

I lean in and peck her lips. "Go on."

"Are you happy?"

I wrap my arms around her and pull her in close. Having her in my arms makes everything in the world feel right. As long as she's with me, I'm always happy.

"I am now," I answer.

"Are you any closer to the goals you had when we met?"

"Yeah, I'm a lot closer. You know that."

"I do. That's what I want you to see. You can't be mad at him for making us who we're meant to be."

I purse my lips and frown. "He's made you a traitor. You know that, right?"

"Does that mean I have to give the ring back?"

I chuckle and bring her hand to my lips. I kiss the four-carat engagement ring I placed on her finger. She picked the setting, but I chose the stone.

My baby wasn't about to wear anything less than the rock I put on her precious hand. I've done nothing but spoil Oni in the last week. Sex, gifts, love, I've given it all.

"Never," I croon and wink at her.

"Come on, we should get inside. We don't want to keep the Don waiting."

I scoff and shake my head. Never in a million years did I think Oni would be this loyal to my uncle. What he has done is unforgivable in my eyes.

However, I shove my shit down and head into the restaurant with my arm around her waist. I'm not surprised to find my uncle and all his capos when we get inside.

However, I am surprised when my uncle stands to greet Oni, then introduces her to everyone else like she's a capo herself. I mean, I know the role she's been playing while in Italy, but I didn't know Uncle Emilio truly intended to give her the rightful respect.

Oni is a woman and she's Black. I never thought I'd see the day. I stand with my mouth hanging open.

"Let me see," Uncle Emilio croons when he takes Oni's hand and lifts it. "Ah, fellas, I guess we have one more thing to celebrate tonight.

"My boy here has proposed. My daughter and my nephew, who's like my son. I couldn't be prouder. Come Rico, come."

Still in shock, I walk into my uncle's embrace. When I turn to the table, there are mixed emotions on the faces of the men sitting around it. I don't miss the proud smile on my father's face.

I move behind Oni and kiss the top of her head. I then look each man in his eyes to let them know I'll be the face they see if they ever try to cross my woman.

These motherfuckers have been stubborn against change for as long as I can remember. If Uncle Emilio was any other don, I don't think this shit would fly at all. Oni and I would have to shoot our way out of here.

"Bring the champagne," Uncle Emilio croons as he points for me and Oni to take our seats.

"Oni Raven. You're Jack's kid, ain't you? May he rest in peace," Robby Conti says from across the table.

"That she is. We've come full circle," Uncle Emilio says jovially.

"Jack was a good guy. May God rest his soul," Nicky Rizzo says and gives a sage nod.

"I wanted to talk to you. I have some business I want to do," Tony Grassi says.

"Not tonight, Ton. Make sure youse exchange numbers. Tonight, we celebrate my nephew and my prodigy."

I have to fight not to roll my eyes. I'm still not buying his shit. I want to know what his endgame is.

***

"I'm glad you stuck around to talk to me," Uncle Emilio says.

I grunt and throw back the whiskey in my cup. Glancing across the room, I set my gaze on Oni, Emilia, and the guys at a table. They all arrived about thirty minutes ago.

"Ah, you know that's what my crew looked like back in the day when I started."

I turn my gaze to him slowly. "What are you talking about?"

"We were all close once. Me, your father, Jack, and Brenda, we thought we would take over the world."

"What happened?"

"I did. I got entitled. I thought I could marry your aunt and keep Brenda as my goomah." He chuckles.

He throws his drink back, then licks his bottom lip. "I should have known that shit wasn't going to fly. Oni is as strong-willed as her mother. Brenda left me as soon as I proposed to your aunt.

"I was convinced she would see things my way and come back to me. In my world, we could never be more than what I was offering her, but I could still give her the best in life."

"Looks like that shit didn't work out for you," I snort.

"*Marone*, I was crazy about that woman. Everyone knew it too. That's why I was so furious when a year later she and Jack got together.

"I felt so betrayed. Never once did I stop to think about how Brenda felt. I let my ego and pride get in the way of everything.

"The business, our friendship, my relationship with your father. I made a lot of mistakes. Mistakes I'm trying to keep you from making."

"By taking her away from me?" I seethe.

"By making you a better man than I was. All I have done has been for you and where you want to be," he says.

"Where *you* want me to be," I snap back.

"Ah, so you don't want my seat, is that what you're saying?"

I sit back in my chair and work my jaw. All my life I've wanted to be Don. However, now I have to ask myself if it's something I want or if this has been what he's drilled in my head since I was a baby.

"Nah, that's not what I'm saying, but what are you saying? I'm tired of your games."

"My stupidity caused me to lose my best friend and allowed my enemies to take his life. I will forever regret that. I failed Oni, Brenda, and Jack."

"Still not seeing what that has to do with me."

"Those same enemies almost had Oni raped, tried to kill my only daughter, and sent my nephew to jail. This family isn't done with the Sullivans or Abatos. They think they have evaded me. Finn thinks returning to Ireland for a little while will erase what he has done."

"Why now?"

"There are things that only recently came to light concerning Jack and Finn's involvement. Things I hadn't been willing to see in the beginning because of my stubbornness.

"Once the Sullivans chose to come at me by targeting you, they got my attention. I have been plotting and waiting to get back at Finn. When this was just between us, I had been willing to play these games.

"However, I didn't plan for you to inherit the shit between us. What happened in front of my estate was too much disrespect. Aiming at my children was the final straw.

"Sullivan thinks he has won. That isn't going to work for me. It isn't good enough for him to just take a break and then return to his former glory. Not after what they have done. This will be my wedding gift to you both."

"What will?"

"The Sullivans, Abatos, and my seat. I'm going to teach you and your fiancée the art of slow, vicious, and painful revenge. Then you will be ready to be Don and Donna."

I stare back at him and look him deep in his eyes. He always has an ulterior motive, but in this case, I'm not sure that I care. The Sullivans owe me blood.

"Are you finally listening? I am not your enemy, *capisce*?" he says as I stare at him in silence.

"Understood. I'm listening."

Oni

"That wasn't so bad, was it?" I ask as we enter the apartment.

"He left me with a lot to think about, that's for sure."

"Want to talk about it?"

"Not at the moment. I have other things on my mind."

"Like?"

"Like getting you undressed and in our bed."

I smile up at him. The heated look in his eyes sends my heart racing. He removes his suit jacket first, then begins on the buttons on mine. Pushing the jacket from my shoulders, he roams his heated gaze over my body.

"You have no idea how much I've wanted to do this all night. Especially knowing you only had on this tie and bra."

"Less talking and more undressing, Gallo."

He growls and wraps his hand around my tie, then starts for the bedroom. My heels click across the floor as I follow him. He works on the buttons of his shirt as he goes.

Once in the room, he turns some music on. "Feel Something" by Chris Brown begins to flow through the speakers. He turns to me and locks those hazel-gray eyes on me while still holding on to the tie around my neck.

I bite my lip and lift a brow at him. He flicks his gaze over me. His thoughts are running across his face.

"What's on your mind, babe?" I say breathily.

He shakes his head. "I don't think you're ready."

"How will you know if we don't try? Tell me what you want, Rico."

As I speak the words, I unzip my pants and allow them to fall to the floor. I then kick them aside and stand before him in my bra, panties, and heels.

Keeping my eyes on him, I push my hand into my panties then run my other hand from my hip up the center of my body to my breast. A moan slips from my lips as I squeeze my boob and play with my pussy for him.

Rico's eyes darken and his nostrils flare. I lift my head and push my shoulders back as I stick my tongue out of my mouth and press it to my lip.

"On your knees," he says huskily as he loosens his hold on the tie enough for me to lower.

Keeping my eyes on him, I lower to my knees. I reach for his belt and silently ask for permission to open it. His lips part and he nods.

With a wicked smile on my lips, I unfasten it. Still with my gaze locked on his, I run my palms up his thighs until I get to his zipper and tug it down. Once his pants are open, I peel them down and allow them to fall to the floor.

"What now, Rico? What do you want from me?"

"I want you to suck it. Let me feel your mouth around me," he breathes.

"Will you help me? Can you teach me?"

"Fuck, baby. I've got you. I'll show you just what I like. Take it out and open your mouth for me."

I nod and peel his boxer briefs down his legs. He springs free, looking hard and heavy. Slowly, I open my mouth like he told me to. I then wait for him.

Wrapping his hand around his length, he then begins to stroke himself in time with the music. My mouth begins to water. Rico stops stroking and guides his way into my mouth.

He fills my mouth then pulls back and taps the tip on my tongue. I close my mouth and swallow. Rico gives a gentle tug of the tie around my neck.

"Open and keep it open," he commands.

With a nod, I open my mouth again. This time, he pushes in and goes deep. I choke a little but hold my mouth open for him.

He keeps feeding me his dick then pulling it back out. I'm able to take him deeper with every pass. He brushes his knuckles against my cheek.

I decide to take over and close my mouth. He groans and throws his head back as I start to bob my head and suck on him. He widens his stance and hisses.

"Fuck, Oni. Yeah, baby. That's perfect. Add your hands, stroke me. Don't be shy."

I hum around him as I do as he asks. It seems like the more I suck, the harder he's getting. I didn't think that was possible.

"Fuck, just like that," he growls and places a hand behind my head. "Play with your pussy again for me. Let me see you, beautiful."

He's now fucking my face. My eyes roll back as I reach down to play with myself. I keep stroking with my other hand as I suck on him and allow my mouth to soak him.

"Fuck," he roars as he holds my head in place and comes down my throat.

I look up at him with tears stinging the backs of my eyes. He slips from my mouth and stumbles over to the bed, where he falls onto his back. I grin to myself, happy with my first attempt at giving head.

"Oni. Get your ass over here, baby, and sit on my face."

I lift to my feet and kick my shoes off. I then go to him and climb his body to settle over his face. He clamps his hands over my thighs and locks me into place as he dives in.

I end up riding his face until I'm a shaking mess. His hands are all over my body the entire time. Rico makes me feel like I'm being worshiped.

When he's done bringing me pleasure with his mouth, he spends hours pounding me into the sheets until I'm sobbing his name and not sure if I'm begging for more or for him to give me a break.

"You were made for me," he says in my ear some hours later as I'm drifting off to sleep. "I love you."

CHAPTER THIRTY-TWO

The Crew

Rico

We're all sitting in a chop shop I took over about a year ago. I had it converted into a little bar and lounge. This is where my crew and I meet up the most.

The guys tend to hang out here when not out working. I had a meeting tonight with the fellas, so Oni came along. We've been hanging out with our original crew to catch up since things finished up.

I look Oni over in her jeans, ankle boots, and black T-shirt. She looks right at home as she sips a beer and kicks it with my cousins. A smile comes to my face to know and see she's safe and happy.

"You finally look happy," Mario says as he comes to my side.

"What's that supposed to mean?"

I turn to him as he takes a seat on the stool beside me. He looks back at me with a smile. That scar a reminder of how far he's willing to go to have my back.

"Come on. You have to know it hasn't been easy for anyone to work for you in the last two years. But as your friend, it's been hard to watch you fall apart and not know what to do for you.

"I'm happy she's alive and back. You need her. This feels like it always should have been."

I sigh and pull a hand down my face. I know I was fucked up, but I never thought about how it affected everyone else. To be honest, I didn't have it in me to give a fuck.

"Have I been that bad?"

"Are you fucking kidding?" He laughs and shakes his head. "You've been mean for no reason. I'm talking beyond the ruthless shit. You've become cruel outside of all of that. It wasn't hard to tell you were always angry."

"And yet, you're still here," I murmur.

"Where the fuck else would I be? You're my best friend. I'm here until the end."

Turning to face him, I then grasp the back of his neck and press my forehead to his. I couldn't have asked for a better best friend. If not for Mario, I wouldn't have made it through the last three years.

"You're my brother. This wouldn't be if not for you by my side."

"Now you have us both. She's going to make one hell of a donna."

"I think you're right, but I still want to keep an eye on my uncle. I don't trust him. In fact, I trust no one outside the people in this room. I need you to have her back like you have mine."

"Without question. You already know this."

I watch as Oni throws her head back with her laughter. She's full of so much life. That smile on her face pulls me in every time.

"Yo, Rico, have you heard her Italian? She makes me sound like a stunad," Eduardo calls out as everyone else laughs at him.

"Bro, that's not hard to do," Aldo laughs.

He and Ed begin to tussle, causing me to laugh and shake my head at them. For all their fussing, the two are as tight as ever. I'm grateful to have them around.

My cousins have stood by me as much as Mario has. In this life, it's hard to find true loyalty. However, there is something that's been nagging me. I shrug the thought off, not wanting to ruin the moment.

"She speaks a few languages and several Italian dialects," Emilia says like a proud big sister.

"All tricks of the trade. The more you know, the further you go. I had to learn fast and gain an understanding of the art culture. I didn't have time for language barriers."

"Man, it's good to have you back. I thought I was going to explode before Rico learned the truth," Ed says, bringing my nagging thoughts back.

"About that. Who didn't know?"

As I thought, Mario is the only one who raises his hand. Everyone else drops their heads. I'm not angry with them. I still place all the blame in Uncle Emilio's lap.

"Let's talk about something else. The night is young, and we were having a good time," Al says.

"It's all good. As long as it never happens again," I say. "This is our family. I would die for all of you. Nothing comes before all of you."

"You have my word on that," Emilia says.

"Me too," Ed says.

"You don't even have to say that twice. I wasn't told until they were on their way back," Al adds.

Oni looks up into my eyes, and I can see her promise without needing to hear her words. I give her a nod, letting her know I see her. I know she's still ready to ride for me.

Oni

"I love you too, Mom. I'm glad you're having such a good time."

"This island is beautiful. You and I need to take a vacation like this together. I've missed you so much."

"We'll plan something soon. I promise."

"I'll have to save up first, so it might be a while."

"Mommy, you have nothing to worry about. I'll take care of it. I have a bonus coming in from work," I say and frown into the mirror.

It still sours my stomach when I have to lie to her. She thinks Uncle Claude is paying for the trip she's on. In fact, I'm covering everything for her.

"I don't want you spending all your money. You've been working so hard. Have I told you how proud of you I am?

"Going away was the best thing for you. I'm so happy you were able to turn your life around. You're such a smart girl."

"Thanks, Mom. That means a lot. Listen, I should go," I say as tears burn the backs of my eyes.

She sighs. "I have to run too. I promised Claude I'd go for dinner with him and Monica."

"Have fun. I love you."

"I love you too, baby. Be safe and stay away from those Italian men."

I laugh as she hangs up. She has no idea I've returned to New York and fallen right into the arms of an Italian man. In fact, I melt into Rico's arms as he comes up behind me.

"You all right?" he asks as he kisses the top of my head and looks into my eyes in the mirror.

A smile comes to my lips as I look at our reflection and nod in response. We look good together, me in my bra and panties, him in his sleep pants with his chest bare.

He has way more ink than he had three years ago. I reach behind me to push my hand into his hair. He's watching my eyes in the mirror.

"It's just tough lying to my mom," I choke out.

"You still hiding your involvement in our world from her?"

"What else am I to do?"

"Baby, we're engaged. You're going to have to come clean at some point. She has eyes and if she's as smart as you are, she's going to figure it out."

I sigh. "I know. I'll figure something out before she gets back to the city. For now, I just want her to think I've done something with my life she can be proud of."

"Oni, you have done a ton she can be proud of. No matter how you look at it, you've accomplished a shit ton."

"I know … can you help me get my mind off this?"

He squeezes his arms around me and kisses the side of my neck. "As you wish."

CHAPTER THIRTY-THREE

Time Together

Oni

"I said just do it. I'm not going to ask you again," Rico bites out into his phone.

I can't take my eyes off him as he barks orders at whoever is on the other end while he walks toward me. I still can't get over how much he has changed. For one, he's filling out his clothes with all those muscles.

His back and chest are so much broader than they used to be. Rico at twenty-two is a beautiful thing. I love how his torso tapers into a slim waist.

His powerful thighs and tight ass are something to marvel at. He makes everything he wears look good. Rico with a blowout used to make my heart race.

His thick, dark, curly waves that he keeps combed out of his face match perfectly with his facial hair. I love when his locks start to fall into his eyes as the day goes on. Rico is fine as fuck on any day of the week, twice as much on Sunday.

"No, that's all. Call me when it's done," he says and hangs up his call.

He looks me over and lifts a brow. I'm still taking him in. His black dress shirt is sitting open at the top while tucked into his tailored black slacks.

"You're not dressed and you're staring at me like I'm naked and you're ready to eat me. *Che cosa succede?*"

"I'm just thinking. You've changed in all the right ways," I reply.

He looks down at his watch then back at me. I know I should have gone to get ready, but I've been sitting here lost in my thoughts since I hung up with my uncle. I need to have a conversation with him and my mother.

"Baby, I'm all for every dirty thought you might be having right now, but you need to get ready," he says against my lips as he leans in for a kiss.

I slide my hand around his neck, encouraging him to deepen the kiss. When he begins to pull away, I whimper into his mouth, not wanting him to leave.

"Come on, *bella*. Be a good girl for me and go get ready. I have a surprise for you."

I look at him suspiciously. He's asked me to get ready to go out more than once, but still hasn't told me where we're going. I pout and get up from my seat.

Rico tugs me into him and gives me a searing kiss. I love being in his arms. I feel safe and warm.

"You can throw on sweats or something. You don't need to make a fuss."

I scoff. "You have a lot to learn about me."

"Trust me. It's not going to matter."

"Now I'm supercurious."

He pecks my lips and gives me a squeeze. Reluctantly, I pull away and head to get ready. I've been in one of his T-shirts all morning.

I love the way his scent clings to it. Just like the one I stole before I left for Italy, it makes me feel like he's wrapped around me. I nearly cried when that shirt lost his scent.

The memory causes me to lift the neck of the T-shirt to my nose as I inhale deeply. It's still the same as I remember, one of many things that remain the same about him. His eyes and scent have been familiar and welcoming.

"What should I wear?" I blow out and twist my lips as I stand in my closet.

Rico

Yesterday was a bit intense for Oni. One of her guys fucked some shit up and she was pissed. I thought I lost my shit when my crew made mistakes.

Oni made me look like a saint. I could feel the stress in her body as we fucked last night. I decided I wanted to do something for her today to help her relax.

I know how that shit feels and how hard it can be on the mind and body. Funny, I have to chuckle now as my guys turned around and put me in the same position today. I guess this will be for both of us.

"Don't worry about it. I'll take care of everything. You and Oni have a good time."

"Thanks, Mario. I know she wants to hang with you guys some more. The next few days will be busy, but set something up for the weekend."

"You want to head up to the Hamptons or something?"

"Yeah, that sounds good. Have someone stock the house and have the place ready."

"I'm on it."

"Thanks, bro. I need to go."

We hang up and I place my phone in the locker with the rest of my things. The next few hours will be all about Oni. My girl and I need this.

I want to connect with her on a deeper level. Sex is amazing between us, but I want to fill in all those gaps we never got a chance to plug in. We need to build more of a foundation.

I step into the massage room to find Oni sitting on the edge of one of the beds in a robe. Her hair is brushed flat, leaving it to fall in her face. With not a stitch of makeup on, she looks younger than nineteen and has a glow about her.

"Why are you looking at me like that?"

"You're effortlessly gorgeous. I'm always in awe of how you take my breath away."

"Keep sweet-talking. It will get you everywhere."

I walk over to her and peck her lips. I groan in frustration as our massage therapists walk into the room. When I pull away from Oni's sweet lips, I note that they have given us a masseur and masseuse.

"Didn't I request two females?" I say tightly.

Oni snickers beside me. I look to her and narrow my eyes. The amusement in her gaze only ticks me off more.

I don't find this funny. This dude isn't putting his hand on my girl. Personally, I would have preferred a female.

The guys tend to get too rough as if trying to prove they're masculine. In the end, I never enjoy a massage from a guy. I always feel like it's a waste of time and leaves me more tense than when I started.

"Sorry, but one of the girls called out. Ricki has a range from light to hard touch. We hope he will be a suitable replacement for your couples massage," the chick says.

I grunt, still pissed, but not wanting to fuck up our date. I glare at the dude, daring him to go near Oni. Nodding for him to move to the table waiting for me, I then walk over to the other bed.

They ask us a few questions then excuse themselves from the room so Oni and I can climb on the tables under the sheets. I look to her as she lies on her back laughing. I wish I had something to toss at her.

"What's so funny?"

"Nothing."

"Then why are you laughing your ass off?"

"You're still crazy jealous. I don't know why I thought that would change."

"It wouldn't eat you up that she'd have her hands all over my body?" I tease.

"Nope, because if you so much as moan, I'd slap the shit out of you," she deadpans.

I burst into laughter. However, she's now glaring at me. I shake my head.

"This might have been a bad idea," I chuckle.

"Not at all. Thank you, Rico. This is sweet. Enjoy your massage. I'm just joking … maybe."

"Maybe." I snort. "You would have nothing to worry about, trust me."

"I do."

I grunt and settle in for our massages as the two reenter the room. We fall silent as our session gets started. For the first time in a long time, I find I'm not angry, not thinking of what I need to handle next. I'm in the moment and at peace.

When the massage is over, we make our way to the private sauna room. Oni and I quickly down the lemon water they have waiting for us. We then take our seats inside and settle in.

Feeling totally relaxed, I lean my head back and close my eyes. My mind drifts to Oni's mother. I don't know how she's going to take our engagement. Neither does Oni.

It's something we've talked about a few times. I'd be lying if I said I'm not anxious about her return to New York. I love her daughter and can't see my life without her again.

"What are you thinking about?"

I open my eyes to find Oni settling her naked body over my lap. We lock gazes as I place my hands on her waist. I glide my hands up her sides, savoring her soft skin.

"Our future. I can't wait to meet your mom."

"She's going to have the shock of her life," she laughs.

"I think it will be okay. She'll love me like I'm sure my mother will love you."

I don't mention to her that my mother has seen her around in Italy and has been curious about who she is. However, my mother stays out of business.

Now that she knows Oni is my fiancée, she's dying to meet her. I can't wait until we get all of this out of the way and can start planning our wedding. Emilia has already been calling my phone to gush about the engagement party Uncle Emilio is throwing for us.

Oni looks back at me with a wary expression. "I don't know. I'm dropping you and an engagement into my mother's lap all at once."

"We will handle it. Besides, at the end of the day, nothing can take you away from me. We're getting married no matter who doesn't like it."

"Don't be so sure. My mother will hit you upside your head with a frying pan about me."

I smile and raise a brow at her. Then I nip at her chin as I smooth my hand over her skin to her breasts. Beginning to roll her nipples between my fingertips, I look into her eyes.

I don't break eye contact with my next words. "Like I said. We're getting married no matter what. I will make sure she loves me."

"Rico—"

I cut off her moaned protest as I take her lips. The kiss grows heated and deep within seconds. I pull my towel free from around my waist and guide her to sink down on me.

Her eyes roll back, and she bites her lips as she pulls away to look into my eyes. Reaching for her ass, I used her cheeks to guide her up and down on my length. I'm so fucking hard for her.

Sweat is dripping from both our bodies and faces, but I couldn't care less. I wrap my arms around her body and move to the edge of the seat, planting my feet. I then take over from beneath. She starts to cry out my name, really crying out when I begin to bounce her body with my thrusts.

I groan and take one of her sweaty breasts into my mouth. My baby pushes her hands into my hair and tugs my head back to look down into my eyes. She sticks her tongue out of her mouth and I capture it in mine.

As I suck on her tongue, she starts to rock her hips, taking back control. I smile and take her mouth in a passionate kiss. I groan into her mouth as she squeezes her pussy around me.

"You know that shit drives me fucking crazy," I grunt into her mouth.

"You want me to stop?"

"Fuck no. Keep that pussy popping on me and squeezing my shit. Don't you dare stop."

"Shit, Rico. Please don't stop."

"If you can take it, I'm going to keep fucking this good-ass pussy. Shit, you're wet."

"You see what this hard-ass dick does to me?"

"I see, baby. I feel you about to come. Tell me what you need."

"Ah, mm, Rico. I need you. Your strong arms around me feel so good."

She reaches for my biceps as I run my hands down her back and grab ahold of her ass. I latch my lips onto her sweaty neck and suck while we fuck each other.

Oni reaches back and grabs my wrist as if that can hold me off from fucking this good-ass pussy. I allow her a reprieve as I still and release her. She looks at me like I've lost my mind.

Lifting her to her feet, I then stand and turn her to bend her at the waist. Then I enter her from behind and get all up in her guts. I fuck her deep, alternating between deep and short thrusts.

"*Fuck*, Rico," she keens as I roll my body into hers.

I place my foot on the bench seat and really get into her pussy. As I'm thrusting down into her, her walls are rippling around me as she gushes all over me.

"You like that, baby? Is this what you were looking for?"

"Yes, yes. You feel so good. You're so deep. Don't stop."

I slap her fat ass and watch it ripple around me. Sweat is dripping from my nose onto her back. I turn my face up to try to catch it, but it's useless.

I fuck right through her orgasms. Running my hands up her sweat-slick back, like I'm rubbing lotion into her skin. When I feel my orgasm coming, I grab her shoulder with one hand and wrap the other around her neck.

"Oh my God, Rico," she screams.

I bite my lip as I pound into her. My orgasm hits so hard my eyes cross and my toes curl.

I slump forward, landing on her back. Using the wall to hold my weight off her, I begin to kiss across her skin. When I get to the tat of the pot of butterflies on her exit wound, I lick the flesh, then place soft kisses against it.

"That was amazing," she giggles beneath me.

"Phenomenal. You're perfect. Come on, let's go get cleaned up. Our lunch will be waiting."

"What time is naptime?"

I chuckle. "We'll make that happen after we hydrate and get some fuel."

"Fuel? Are you trying for round two?"

"Um, and three and four," I say and kiss her neck.

"You spoil me, you do," she sighs.

CHAPTER THIRTY-FOUR

A Mother's Love

Rico

"You ready for this?" I ask as I take Oni's hand in mine.

She looks up at me and gives a tight smile. I know what this means to her. Tonight has to go right.

"No, but I have to be."

Oni's mother is finally back in New York. We can't keep putting this off. It's time to face the truth.

My uncle has already set the date for our engagement party. He says he's throwing it to send a message. Romano still wants to have words with me, but I don't need him and don't plan on explaining myself to him.

The conversation about marrying Alyissa had been casual. After all, he brought it up. I didn't know he told her and got her hopes up.

I only started taking her out after meeting Romano to talk about business and him pushing her on me. I thought I'd take her out a few times and get the real deal rolling. One date turned into a few months of me entertaining his brat.

I only stuck with it because once Uncle Emilio got wind of it, I saw how much it pissed him off. Then I started to entertain Romano's ideas of a marriage between me and his daughter because I never intended to find love again. I told him I would think about it, but I never said I was going to marry her for sure.

The fact that this is even a thing is annoying the fuck out of me. I got the docks and connections I wanted without him. Thanks to Oni, I realized I had a way in without Romano.

"We're perfect together, she will see," I say as I lift Oni's hands to my lips.

We are, in life, in business. Each day, we prove how well we fit and how much we belong together. We even finish each other's thoughts.

So much is going on around us, but we ground each other. The engagement party alone has been weighing heavily on our schedules. Thank God it's in the next two months and we'll have it behind us.

I want to meet Oni's mother before that. That's why I've planned this dinner. Oni can meet my mom, and I can meet hers.

I give Oni's hand a squeeze as we walk into the restaurant. We can do this together. Everything we do is possible if we do it together.

As always, she looks gorgeous. She's in a black dress that's cut high across her collarbone and dips low in the back, revealing her soft, silky skin. The top of the dress molds to her body and then fans out into a full skirt that stops just above her knees.

The strappy heels she has on expose her cute little toes and play up her shapely legs. She's wearing the ankle bracelet with the infinity sign that I gave her a few days ago. Her hair is in a softer style, like the first night of her return.

"Mom," Oni squeals as she pulls away from me and rushes toward the woman who stands the moment we come into view.

I had wanted to arrive before our guests, but her mom is early. She had been surprised when Oni told her she was in the States and wanted to meet for dinner. All I see right now is a mother who misses her daughter.

As the two embrace, Oni's mother has a tight hold on her as her eyes are squeezed shut against the tears spilling down her cheeks. She looks so much like her mother.

Oni is darker, but I can see the resemblance around the nose and mouth. They break apart and her mother cups her cheek as she stares into her eyes. She then runs her hand over Oni's hair.

"You cut it all off. Oh my God, you look all grown up. What happened to my baby?"

"It's still me."

Oni chuckles and goes to wipe away her tears. I notice the moment her mother sees her engagement ring. Her expression becomes confused and then she bounces her gaze behind Oni to me.

I give a warm smile and close the distance I had given them to have their moment. Placing a hand on Oni's back, I settle at her side. She looks up at me and smiles.

"Mom, I want you to meet someone. Rico, this is my mother, Brenda Raven. Mom, this is Rico Gallo."

Her mother says my last name at the same time Oni does. I shouldn't be as surprised as I am. I know she dated my uncle.

The men in my family have strong genes. We all look alike. I could pass for Uncle Emilio's son.

The way Brenda is glaring at me, I would think I was my uncle himself. However, it's the venom she says the name with. There's so much hatred in her voice.

"It's nice to meet you, Mrs. Raven," I say and hold my hand out.

"Oni, what's going on? Why are you wearing that ring and where on earth did you meet this … this young man?"

"Rico and I met three years ago when I was in Miami. He proposed when I came home. We asked you here tonight so we all can get acquainted."

"We who?"

"Rico, his mom and dad. Please, Mom, Rico and I love each other."

Brenda places a hand to her forehead and the other on her hip. My stomach sinks. This isn't going how we wanted.

"Are you close with your uncle? Is he involved in your life? What is it you do for a living?"

"I'm not close with my uncle. We don't see eye to eye on some things he has done. However, he is involved in my life. I run a few clubs and manage some properties," I reply.

"Fuck, I need a drink," she gasps.

"What? What's going on, Mom? Rico makes good money, but I don't rely on him for my income. What's the problem?"

"Oni, please shut up. I can't do this right now. I can't sit and pretend you're not lying to my damn face. Not when you're involved with these people."

Oni jerks her head back. People are starting to stare, so I lead them both to have a seat at the table. My thoughts are all over the place.

"Can I have two fingers of whiskey?" Oni's mom says to the waitress she waved over. "Make that three."

"Mom?"

She shakes her head, then places her elbow on the table and palms her forehead in her hand. I look to Oni and she looks like she's about to lose it. I lean in and peck her lips then whisper into her ear.

"It's going to be okay. She's just in shock."

The waitress comes back with Brenda's drink. She downs it in one gulp. For the second time, Oni and I refuse a drink, but Brenda asks for another.

"I've known from the beginning you weren't telling me the whole truth, but Claude was backing you. Never in a million years did I think he would allow you to get mixed up with their family.

"I turned a blind eye because you went away to school. I thought I finally got you away from their world. Engaged?

"How is that even possible? A few clubs and manage some properties." She scoffs. "Do you know that's the same bullshit he and your father told me when I met them?"

"Mom, slow down, my head is spinning."

"Does he know?" She looks to me with her last question.

"Yes, my uncle knows."

"Oni, I can't allow this. Emilio will eat you alive."

"I hate to hear that's how you feel about me, but you're wrong, Brenda. Oni has a special place in my heart. I would never allow any harm to come to her."

Brenda stiffens and slowly turns to look up at my uncle. I glare at him, wondering what the hell he's doing here. I didn't invite him.

"How dare you?" Oni's mom hisses. "What kind of sick game are you playing? Have you done this to pay me back?"

"Believe it or not, they found each other on their own. It was his car she stole. This wasn't my doing."

"But you knew she was mine from the moment you first set eyes on her, didn't you?"

He nods. "I did. She looks so much like you and Jack."

"Oni, we're leaving. Take that ring off and leave it here."

Uncle Emilio unbuttons his suit jacket and takes the seat on the other side of Brenda. Pop and my mother move to sit on the other side of me. I sit watching Oni as she tries to decide what to do next.

"Sit down, Brenda," Uncle Emilio barks.

Brenda jerks her head back and glares at him. However, seeing Oni hasn't left my side, Brenda sighs and reclaims her seat. I reach to grasp the back of Oni's neck and kiss her temple.

"Having my husband killed and taking her father from her wasn't enough? He was her world. Why can't you people just leave us alone?

"First Finn, now you. I wouldn't be what you wanted and you've made my life hell because of it," Brenda says.

"This has nothing to do with us. My nephew is genuinely in love with your daughter. I tried to pull them apart, but I only drove them closer together.

"I've learned that they belong together and pulling them apart will only ruin them both. The two have potential as individuals, but they are magic together. They remind me of what could have been had we stayed together," Uncle Emilio says as he looks at Brenda in a way I've never seen him look at his wife.

"But we didn't stay together. You know why we didn't. How will any of that be different for them?"

"Because I will make it so. I have the power to make it so. I'm doing for them what no one would do for us. I didn't take Jack away from you and Oni. That blood isn't on my hands—"

"It's not? Because I remember your best friend calling you to ask for your help. You did nothing, so how am I supposed to trust you now with my only child?"

"You can trust me because your only child almost gave her own life for my only child right before my eyes. I owe Oni this and so much more. I tried to help Jack, I did, *cara,* but I was too late."

I clear my throat.

"Ma'am, I'm not my uncle. I love your daughter with every fiber of my being. There isn't a person alive who can tell me not to love her or be with her.

"I would die for Oni. She means everything to me. I know what it's like to be without her and I never want to know that feeling again.

"I know you have a history with my family, but I ask you not to judge me by what they have done. I'm my own man and I want to be Oni's man. If that means I have to start over all on my own, so be it.

"Your approval means everything to Oni and me. All we ask is that you get to know me. Understand who I am and how much I love your daughter. Please," I plead.

"I was made so many empty promises before my Italian replacement was brought in and I was dismissed to be nothing more than Emilio's goomah, so forgive me for not wanting that for my baby. I—"

"That's the way you took it. You know you meant more to me than that. Listen to how you say it.

"Like I planned to treat you like a filthy whore. I was in love with you. You ripped my heart out and started sleeping with my best friend," Uncle Emilio says angrily.

"Fuck you, Emilio. I fell in love with your best friend. Who didn't have to hide me and was willing to take me home to his family, where I was welcomed at their dinner table."

"Enough," Oni barks and slams her hand down on the table.

Everyone at the table and those nearby have their gaze on her. She sits like a queen, commanding everything around her. The shock of it all seems to have cleared.

"Stop making my life about you, the both of you. Mom, you should know I work for Emilio.

"He paid for my schooling and has made sure I've wanted for nothing. I know who's behind Daddy's death and it wasn't Emilio. I'm nineteen and I will decide who I plan to marry.

"Rico is right, I would love your approval, but I will not be torn from him again. If you can't get over your lover's quarrel with his uncle, that's on the two of you. I'm engaged and will become Mrs. Rico Gallo," Oni says confidently.

"I only want what's best for you. Nothing good has ever come from being involved with this man," Brenda says.

"Nothing?" Uncle Emilio snorts.

"Eww." Oni scoffs.

"I see why my son has fallen for you. That fire matches his own. It's nice to finally put a name to the face. Hello Oni, I'm Carlotta Gallo, Rico's mother."

"Oni is right, this isn't about us. You and I can talk later. I came to celebrate the two of them," Uncle Emilio says.

"Uninvited," I growl.

"*Marone*, why is it the two people I love most in this world only see me as some monster?"

"Because you promised me I would pay for my betrayal, and you've never broken a promise since I've known you."

"We have suffered enough. I'm not here to hurt you."

"Then why are you here?"

"Because Jack can't be and I thought … never mind."

"Oh my God, that's it. You think you can replace her father?" Brenda chokes out.

"No, she reminds me so much of him. He would be so proud of her. I'm proud of her, but I know I'm not him."

"You two still aren't getting it," Oni huffs. "Whatever this is going on between you, figure it out before the engagement party. As a matter of fact, neither of you are welcome at our wedding if you can't at least be civil. Rico, I need some air."

With that, Oni stands and marches out of the restaurant. I groan and close my eyes. Could this have gone any worse?

"Does your wife know about this?" Brenda hisses at my uncle.

"I've been a widow for seventeen years, Brenda. I raised my daughter on my own. I don't need to take Jack's little girl from you. My princess comes with enough headaches."

"Never stopped you from having your cake and eating it too in the past." Brenda looks at my father as he sighs. Her shoulders slump. "I'm sorry. It's good to see you, Fredrico, Carlotta. I'm sorry for your loss, Emilio. I know just how that can feel."

"Which is why I tried to save you from that hurt. I'm sorry I was too late. Jack was like a brother.

"I let my ego and pride get in the way. Don't punish my nephew for that. He isn't like me. He's a better version of me and Fred."

"Emilio," she says as her voice cracks. "If I allow this … If I choose not to fight it with every ounce of blood in my body, know that I will take down every don, capo, minion and all their crews over my baby girl with that same strength I reserved. Your world doesn't get to steal from me again."

"I would rise from my grave to help you because they will touch her over my dead body. That I promise."

Oni

"Are you all right, *cara?*"

I look up from my phone as I stand outside the restaurant angry texting with Emilia about her dad and my mom. Staring back at me is Rico's mom. She's a gorgeous woman. Tall with dark hair and big gray eyes.

"I'll be okay. I just wasn't prepared for any of that."

She moves closer and points to the little bench in front of the restaurant. I nod and follow her to take a seat. I don't realize how much my feet are aching until I get off them.

I'm too angry to feel anything else. Emilio and my mother made tonight about whatever it is they used to have going on. I know he said he knew my mother, but I didn't realize he *knew* my mother.

I could have lived a happy life never knowing those details. Now I can't help cringing at the thought. Emilio was once in love with my mother. Eww.

"Ah, yes. Emilio blindsided us all. If I had known he was planning to come, I would have advised against it.

"Not that he would have listened. He never does when it comes to your mother. I warned him she wasn't going to go for his plan."

"You knew about them?"

"Oh, yes. Brenda was the love of Emilio's life. He was devastated when his father arranged for him to marry Patrica.

"For months, he tried to figure out a way to get out of it. The man was obsessed with your mom. He treated her like a queen," she answers.

I think I could see that. Emilio has been spoiling me since I saved Emilia's life. Not to mention Emilia wants for nothing.

"What happened? He doesn't seem like the type to fold because his father tells him to."

"Back then, he was a different man, but he hadn't planned to give in. He was going to allow Fred to take it all over. In those days, there was Emilio, Jack, Fredrico, and Gino.

"Gino and Jack were Emilio's right hands. They did everything together. I think you know Mario, yes?"

I nod.

"Emilio was so proud when Gino asked him to be Mario's godfather. Isabella and I were pregnant at the same time with Rico and Mario. We were all happy.

"Then one night, Gino was found slaughtered in the Irish territory. I've never heard or seen Emilio sob like that. The two were made together; they came up through the ranks together.

"Emilio wanted revenge. The only way to get that was to stay in the family. Finn Sullivan became his new obsession.

"I've always believed your father didn't betray Emilio when he went to work for Sullivan; he gave his life for Emilio's same obsession—their revenge for their friend. However, something along the line went wrong."

I work my jaw. Nowadays, when I hear the name Sullivan, I see red. Why does that name keep coming up alongside the pain suffered by the people I love?

"You know a lot, don't you?"

"We women learn to listen and not speak. Your role is unique. Not only are you honoring soldiers like your father, who were loyal and should have been made, but never could be.

"You're honoring us women who have whispered in the shadows to keep our men happy, safe, and rising. My son is a lucky man. This change is good, and I think the two of you are perfect for it."

"I'm the lucky one. I know Rico loves me no matter what. In this world and the next, he will always have my back." I smile.

Carlotta's eyes light up. "And the grandbabies, they're going to be so cute. You were adorable when you were born."

"You knew me as a baby?"

"I did. Brenda and I met up a few times before she fully pulled away. Want to know a secret?"

"Yes."

"Rico was obsessed with you then. He would sit and just stare. 'Pretty baby.' That's what he kept calling you."

"Does he know this?"

She shakes her head sadly. "I had been forbidden from going to see your mother. Emilio was so angry and didn't allow any of us to communicate with her or your father.

"I bribed Rico with ice cream not to tell where we had been," she chortles. "He asked after you maybe once when he was five. I think after that he forgot."

"Oh, wow," I breathe.

"You see it too? You and Rico were destined to be together. Promise me you won't let the past get in the way."

"I won't. Do you mind if I give you a hug?"

"Oh, of course. I wanted to pull you into my arms from the time I saw you."

I laugh and lean in to pull her into my embrace. She smells nice. Giving me a tight squeeze, she then kisses my cheek.

"Now to get your mother to calm down enough for us to plan a wedding. You're going to make such a beautiful bride."

"Good luck with that."

"You leave Brenda to me," she says with a warm smile.

CHAPTER THIRTY-FIVE

Time to Relax

Oni

"She's here."

I nod as the words come over the comm in my ear. I've been waiting for this day. This outlet will help me to deal with all the current stress in my life.

"We're ready," Rico replies.

Emilio and my mother have come to an agreement of sorts. The two can be in a room without breaking into an argument, at least—that's been an improvement. I think my mother finally understands I'm getting married to Rico no matter what.

However, I haven't had time to go back and forth with her over that. I have more important things to handle. Like an entitled Mafia princess who thought it wise to fuck with me and my man.

When Emilio gave the green light to take out Abato and his bitch daughter Juliana, I was happy to accept the job. Rico wanted to play it quick and easy. Get it over with and be done.

Me, not so much. I've spent the last two months making her life hell. I've fucked with Juliana in ways that make me question my own sanity.

Rico can only laugh and call me petty. I have this bitch so paranoid she sleeps with her eyes open. I've broken into her car and moved it from where she parked it so many times, I know she's on the verge of committing herself.

First, I would only move it out of the driveway onto the street. Then I started to change her rows at the mall or her spot on the street. When she set up the cams at her place and in the car, I switched it up.

For two weeks straight, I had nails placed at the base of her driveway. Every single day, she ended up with a flat. That bitch has had so many flats, even if she has tire insurance, I'm sure they didn't cover all those incidents.

With those five-hundred-dollar tires, I'm fucking with her pockets too. Pockets that have been light because while I fuck with her, Rico and Emilio have effectively fucked with her father's business.

Daddy doesn't have it to spoil her ass anymore. Abato is running out of moves. He's going to need to cut loose some dead weight. Juliana or the Sullivans are at the top of my wish list.

"Thank you so much, Anton. You have no idea how much I needed this," Juliana's annoying voice fills the suite Rico and I are waiting in.

Why, after three years, haven't I let this go? She tried to have me raped. I took my first body because of her stupid ass. She had Rico and his family ambushed, then I was shot.

I'd say what I'm about to do to her isn't good enough. I wanted to drag this out for at least four more months. If Rico hadn't said enough, I would have.

"You're welcome. Everything is on me. Make yourself comfortable and relax. You don't have to worry about a thing while you're here."

"I'm so exhausted. When I get my life back on track, I owe you one. Please don't tell anyone about all of this. It's so embarrassing."

"Shit happens. You'll bounce back. Your pop will figure his shit out. Besides, it's nobody's business. Your secret is safe with me."

I have to stifle my laughter. Rico's buddy is laying it on thick. He doesn't give a shit about her. He's doing us a favor by getting her here to one of Emilio's hotels.

"I'm so glad you reached out when you did. I thought I was losing my mind. No one would listen to me.

"You're such a lifesaver. You have to let me pay you back somehow. I mean, in any way I can," Juliana purrs.

I roll my eyes as the sound of her and Anton making out reaches my ears. I guess he better get it while it's hot, she's about to be a cold, dead bitch. I just hope they don't take this too far while we're waiting.

"Listen, I need to go. You'll find a little something-something in the room waiting for you," Anton says.

Relief washes over me when the sound of the heavy door of the suite clicks shut. A few moments go by, and Juliana makes a call. This bitch makes my butt itch.

Her voice is like nails on a chalkboard. I look across the room where Rico is standing in the shadows. It's like I can feel him rolling his eyes too. However, we want this to happen just right and will wait to make sure it does.

"Hey, it's me," Juliana says into the phone.

"I thought you were coming with us to the salon. The girls are looking for you. Are you on the way?" her friend says as she places the phone on speaker.

"No, I'm taking some time to chill."

"Are you still coming to the club?"

"I don't think I'm going to come out tonight."

The friend sighs. "Is this about your car? You can be forgetful sometimes, Juliana. I don't think anyone is moving your car around."

"I don't want to talk about it. Look, I have to go."

"Okay, call me later. Okay?"

"Yeah, I will."

She hangs up and starts mumbling to herself about no one believing her. "Forgetful. I'm not a fucking idiot. This is not all in my head.

"Oh, look, just what I need. Thank you, Anton," she sings to herself.

It looks like she's found our parting gift. Just as we hoped, she enters the bathroom and starts the water for a bath. We continue to wait impatiently.

I know I'm ready for this to be over. My wish is granted as Juliana starts to play music from her phone as she gets undressed. A smile comes to my lips as the scent of off-smelling weed fills the room.

You see, we had Anton bring Juliana here to relax and let her guard down. Then we made sure to leave her a K2 blunt laced with fentanyl. Juliana is about to have the high of her life.

Right on cue, she begins to cough in the bathroom. Rico and I walk out of our hiding places and join hands as we stroll into the bathroom. Juliana's eyes grow wide the moment she sees us.

I give her a bright smile and wink at her. She starts to pound at her chest as her eyes water. Rico kisses my temple as we both start to laugh.

"Wh … what are you doing here?" Juliana manages to choke out.

"Neither of us believes in sending people to do our dirty work. When we want someone touched, we make that shit happen ourselves," Rico says smoothly.

"Ge … get the fuck out," she says in a panic.

"Not yet. We're here to watch you die, bitch," I hiss.

Her coughing fit increases, then she begins to foam at the mouth. It doesn't take long for the life to leave her eyes as she slumps in the bathtub.

I brush my hands together as if wiping off dirt. Then we turn to leave the way we came. Our job here is done.

CHAPTER THIRTY-SIX

Old Friends

Mason

Two years later ...

"Everything all right? You hanging in there?" Da asks on the other end of the phone.

"I'm doing fine," I lie.

Boston sucks, but I guess I should be happy I'm still in America at least. Lorcan didn't get so lucky. After Da made a deal with Abato, Lorcan had to fake his death and go to Ireland with Da.

None of us are welcome back in New York. Emilio Gallo made sure of that. We're lucky we made it out with our lives.

Da has been disgraced because of our fuckups. Lorcan and I shit the bed big time. The only reason our territory wasn't stripped from us is because of Abato's deal with Da.

I still don't know the details. Da said we would give it some time, and we'd be back, but then the boss back home got involved and our cousin Darragh was sent to take over. That was about two years ago, after everything went to shit.

It seems whatever deal they made fell apart after Abato found Juliana dead in a hotel from an overdose. A hotel owned by Emilio Gallo. I don't believe there were any coincidences there.

Now I don't know where any of that leaves us and I can't ask Da because he loses his shit every time I mention it. I've been biding my time here with a small-time crew.

I went from running my own shit to being an errand boy overnight. I can't even tell anyone who I am. The Sullivan name has become shit far beyond New York.

It makes me sick when the guys start talking shit about us. I took pleasure when the boss needed someone to off Maxton. I volunteered right away. He talked the most shit all the time.

"You hold your head up, you hear me? I'm going to make this right if it's the last thing I do. This is my fucking karma for what I did to Jack. You boys don't deserve this," he says, almost like he's speaking to himself.

"Jack Raven? As in Oni's father?"

"Aye."

"What are you talking about, Da?"

"Forget I said anything. I should have kept you out of her life. I knew her being around was going to come back to bite me."

"What does Oni have to do with any of this?"

"Your little friend works for Gallo now. She's the one who killed Christopher on your brother's dummy mission." He pauses and snorts.

"She's engaged to Rico. The two run New York together. They'll be getting married in a month.

"That's what she has to do with it. She's sleeping with the fucking enemies. Just like her father, she is.

"They love those fucking Italian pieces of shit. That's why I had him killed. No matter what Emilio did, he wouldn't go against them. Not even when the motherfucker tried to take his woman," Da bites out.

I pause. Oni is engaged to Rico Gallo? How the fuck did that happen?

She said she didn't want someone like me. She couldn't date someone in the life. Her mother wouldn't allow it.

Well, Rico Gallo and I are cut from the same shit. I used to hold the same position in my family. How the fuck did she even get involved with him?

I close my eyes and groan. This is all my fault. That fucking TrackHawk.

"Your brother has been asking after ya. Make sure ya give him a call."

"Thanks, Da. I will."

"Be safe, son. We'll be back if it's the last thing I do. I have a plan. It might take some time, but I have a plan, I do."

"I'll be waiting, Da."

CHAPTER THIRTY-SEVEN

Crew Time

Rico

I stand on the second level of our newest New York club, looking down on the dance floor. Claw and Ash has been a hit. The club has been packed every single night.

I couldn't have asked for more. In the last two years, I've accomplished more than I ever thought I could, and Oni has been right by my side. Uncle Emilio has been true to his word.

First, we took aim at Abato and his bitch daughter. She was so desperate to hide out and get away from Oni she didn't think twice about the trap she walked into. I still have a good laugh about that one.

I have to say, my uncle is diabolical. The way he had everything stripped from Sullivan and Abato was a thing of beauty. If you ask me, he's enjoying himself way too much. I've been seeing another side of him.

"She's here. Just walked into the front," Ed murmurs into my ear, letting me know Oni has arrived.

I nod and take a sip from the drink in my hand. Ed walks back to our group and Al comes up beside me, throwing his arm around my shoulders. However, my focus isn't on him.

I search the crowd to set eyes on Oni. I find Mario, then Oni comes into view behind him. If I'm not with Oni, Mario is.

My heart stops when I find her moving through the thrashing bodies on the dance floor. She gets more beautiful with each day. I never thought I could love this woman more than I already did.

However, I'm crazy about her and grow more obsessed every day. She's been growing her hair out over the last year. It's now long enough to brush her shoulders.

I love it, although I miss having access to her tat. I can no longer kiss the skin covered with that alluring ink without having to move her hair out of the way.

"Bro, this wedding needs to happen. Look at your face. She's killing that dress, you know," Al says in my ear.

I grunt. She is killing that off-the-shoulder black bodycon dress. I'm growing hard watching her move through the crowd.

We're definitely fucking. I can't wait to have those gold heels wrapped around my neck. Al is right, this month needs to be over.

I can't wait until our wedding. The day I get to call her my wife is going to be the greatest day of my life.

I can't take my eyes off her as she climbs the stairs leading to me and the VIP, where our crew is. I say our crew because our guys have become one. The guys who came over from Italy have blended in with my guys.

Since Oni and I do everything together, it works. We are the definition of a power couple. You fuck with one, you're fucking with us both.

"Hey, handsome," she sings as she gets to me.

I wrap my arms around her and take her lips. A deep groan rises in my chest as I devour her mouth. Pushing my hand into the back of her hair, I tug her head back to kiss her deeper.

"Get a room," Ed taunts.

I break the kiss as I smile down at her. Her eyes are sparkling as she looks back at me. I flex my fingers against her ass in a promise for later tonight.

"It's not our fault you can't find anyone willing to sleep with you," Oni tosses back at my cousin.

"*Oh*," the rest of us croon.

"If I didn't love you like a sister … never mind," he snorts when I glare at him.

"Come on, these shots aren't going to drink themselves. We have a ton to celebrate. Our crew is killing it," Al calls out.

He's right, we do have a lot to celebrate. We're the top earners for the past year. We've opened several new ventures, and they've all been successful.

On top of all that, our wedding is coming. I couldn't be happier with my life. My uncle and I have even been cordial with one another. I haven't forgiven him, but I'm not as pissed as I used to be.

He even offered to walk Oni down the aisle. I know my father would have if he hadn't. In fact, Oni refused Uncle Emilio and asked Pop instead.

She told him it was to keep the peace with her mom. I think she was being honest, but I saw the flicker of hurt in my uncle's eyes. It was then that I realized how much he cares about Oni.

"Where's Emilia?" Oni asks, cutting into my thoughts.

"She took a walk with Fredo. By the way, who invited him?" Al says.

"I did," Oni says. "You guys need to stop excluding him. He's not as bad as you all try to make him out to be."

The fellas groan. "Yet, he had to step out to take a break from all this," Ed grumbles.

"He's trying to adjust and he's doing it because he wants to be a part of things," Oni bites out.

She has a soft spot for Fredo. I love that about her. In the last year and a half, she's been trying to help him. His crew has grown and he's finally getting the hang of things.

Oni's patience is rubbing off on him. That's all he needs, the patience to deal with people and his own emotions. Uncle Emilio is happy not to have to reprimand him all the damn time.

Fredo is known to fly off the handle and implode. That's the reason I've never feared him being my competition. Uncle Emilio would never trust him with the family. He's lucky he got a crew.

"Just last month, you shot a guy in the kneecap for not answering your question fast enough, but you have patience for Fredo? I don't get it," Al says.

"I didn't do that because he didn't answer me fast enough. It happened because he was lying to me. Two very different things."

I pop Al upside the back of his head and narrow my eyes at him. He looks back at me as he holds the back of his head.

"What's wrong with you? Why would you bring that shit up here?" I bite out.

"You're right. Fuck, I'm sorry."

"Bro, just shut the fuck up for the next hour," Ed says.

"Hey, Oni," Fredo says, causing me to turn.

My cousin has his gaze fixed on my fiancée as he smiles at her. Oni returns his smile and pulls him in for a hug. Emilia is next to embrace Oni.

Soon, we're all throwing back shots and having a good time, including Fredo. The night is just what we all need. We work hard, so it's only right we play harder.

"Come dance with me," Oni leans to whisper in my ear.

I turn to her and nod. I take her hand and stand to follow her to the dance floor. When we get to the lower level, we move through the crowd until we find a spot just for us.

"Too Sweet" by Trinix and The Macaroon Project begins to play. Oni places her arms around my neck, and we begin to sway to the beat together. I slide my hands down to her hips as I look her in the eyes.

She moves her body in front of me, causing me to bite my lip. Then she turns her back to my front, I step up behind her and get into the music. Moving her hair from her neck, I then place a kiss against her tat.

When I once asked her why the butterflies and pot, she told me she felt like she had become one. She said she left me to transform into my donna and then take flight to come back to me. I have loved this tat more after hearing that.

"You smell good enough to eat," I whisper in her ear.

"Good, I know I'm hungry for you and plan to have my fill; it's only right you're in the same boat."

I growl and nip at her shoulder. She lifts her arms and locks her hands behind my neck. Reaching for her chin, I turn her face up and take her plush lips.

As I devour her, the club and the music are forgotten. I get lost in my girl as she pulls me into her orbit. Gliding my hand down her front, I make my way to the hem of her dress.

When I feel her exposed skin beneath my palm, I wrap my hand around her thigh and squeeze. She moans into my mouth as I begin to claw my fingers against her soft flesh. I grow harder as she grinds her ass back into me.

"We're leaving," I growl into her ear.

She looks up at me with a smile on her face as she shakes her head. I frown. This night needs to end so I can get her home.

"We can't leave. Everyone came out for us." She lifts on her tiptoes to say in my ear.

"And?" I lift a brow at her.

She laughs and turns to face me then cups my face. I wrap my arms around her and press my forehead to hers. Taking a moment, I simply breathe her in.

"You can wait a little longer. It will be worth it, I promise."

I peck her lips. "I'm holding you to that."

Oni

"Did you have a good time?" I ask Fredo.

His cheeks and nose are red from drinking, and his hair is a tussled mess. He looks back at me and smiles. Fredo is as handsome as his cousins.

"Yeah, I did. Thanks, Oni."

"Thanks for what?"

"For inviting me. You got them to see me. I mean, Rico has always been cool, but he has kept his distance too.

"Since you've been around, it's been different. He has more patience with me. Uncle Emilio doesn't treat me like a stunad."

"You're a genius, Fredo. It took me one summer to see that. I'm glad things are better for you."

"Can I ask you something?"

"Sure, you know you can," I say and smile.

"Have you ever wanted to do something else?"

"Something else? What do you mean?"

"You're smart. I've seen you draw. Are you only here for Rico?

"If you are, you can do better. You weren't born into this. You can leave."

I give a small chuckle. "I don't know how to explain it, but I was born into this. I was born to be by his side.

"If he walked away today, I would walk with him. If he stays and has to go to war, I would be with him. Being smart is what makes me perfect for him.

"Besides, art will always have a special place in my heart. Being with him gives me that too. I might be able to do better, but this is where my heart is," I explain.

"Then I feel like the others." He nods.

"How's that?"

"I'll protect his queen with my life. You're special, Oni. So is Rico.

"He was always meant to be Don. Uncle Emilio never thought of me for the spot. He only made Rico think that when we were little to drive him. I never stood a chance."

I tug him into a hug. I don't know where this is coming from, but I can see it's important to him. He's wrong though. Emilio sees him.

I don't think he would make him Don in Rico's place, but he's still grooming Fredo for something else. For now, I keep my mouth shut. Rico and the others come over all drunk and smiling.

"You trying to steal my girl, Fredo? Don't make me fuck you up," Rico teases.

"She's in love with someone else. I can't get her to leave with me," Fredo says.

I knit my brows because something in his words doesn't sound like he's joking. He won't look at me either. Rico pats him on the cheek, then tugs him into a hug and whispers something to him.

Fredo pulls away with his eyes lit up. I don't know what Rico just said, but it sure has made his cousin happy. Our cars begin to pull up and everyone fills into their respective rides.

When Rico and I settle into the back of our SUV, he leans his head back and groans. He ditched his jacket and rolled up the sleeves of his shirt to his elbows. Almost all the buttons in his shirt are now loose.

That chiseled chest is peeking out to taunt me. You can tell he had a time tonight. This is not my put-together, not-a-stitch-out-of-place Rico, but he still looks as sexy as he did when I arrived.

I reach over and push his longer locks out of his face. These days, he still wears the top long, but the sides are in a close taper. Yes, my man has a Black barber.

It's not hard to tell. His cut is always sharp, bringing attention to his handsome face. Allowing my gaze to dance over his features, I drink him in.

"What did you whisper to Fredo?"

He chuckles but doesn't open his eyes. "I told him to come out with us anytime he wants. I also told him to come by like he asked me if he could."

"To learn from our crew? Really? I wasn't sure you were going to do it."

He opens his eyes and looks into mine. "I've never been scared that he'll take my spot. To be honest. His mother held on so tight he became a brat.

"Anytime he wouldn't get his way, he would throw a tantrum. He had no control over his emotions. After thirteen, that shit was a red flag.

"Since his dad was killed when he was little, no one checked that shit. He's not a bad guy. What you have done for him by being kind has made him grow up.

"I can see him thinking about others before reacting. Everyone else isolated him and tried to label him when all he needed was some fucking people skills outside of the coddling his mother forced on him," he says tiredly.

"You know it's not just me. He looks up to you. I met Fredo in Italy. However, I noticed the change in him when I came home, when you started to acknowledge him."

"Nope, it's you. We all want to be better when we get around you."

I pull a face and scoff. "I don't know about that, but thanks for trying to make me feel special."

He reaches for me and pulls me from my seat to straddle his lap. "You are special. To me, you are everything. I couldn't live this life without you."

In the next breath, he takes my lips in a searing kiss. I moan into his mouth and lace my fingers in the top of his hair. Rico pushes my dress up to my waist and palms my ass as he devours my mouth.

I stick my hands into his shirt and run them over his warm skin. Rico groans into my mouth as he fists my thong and snaps it in his hand. He starts a trail of hot kisses down my neck while starting to finger me from behind.

Locking my fingers in his hair, I tug his head back. We lock eyes and he looks back at me with fire in his hazel grays. I grasp his face and kiss him.

I'm in control for about two seconds before he takes over the kiss. He nips at my lower lip and tugs it. I whimper and grind into his lap.

"I've wanted you all night. I can't wait any longer," he says huskily.

"Then don't. Rico, I'm yours."

He grunts and makes quick work of unfastening his belt and pants to free himself. When he tugs me down onto his length, my eyes roll back. This will never get old.

I place my palms against the roof of the SUV and begin to ride him. He tugs the zipper of my dress down, then peels the front away from my body so he can have access to my breasts. Palming my mounds, he goes back and forth between them as I gush all over him.

"That's it, baby. Keep riding me just like that. This tight-ass pussy drives me crazy."

"Oh God, Rico. How are you so fucking hard?"

"Have you looked in a mirror? How could I not get this hard for you?"

He tilts my body back and takes over from beneath me. He's so deep. I'm dripping all over him.

I'm so wet, I knit my brows trying to figure out if he came or if that's all me. Knowing what it feels like when he comes, I realize that's all me.

"*Fuck*," Rico growls then maneuvers our bodies so I'm on my back with my legs pinned to his shoulders.

"Rico, yes," I cry out.

He leans into my ear and begins to talk dirty to me. He's growing harder with each thrust. My heart is pounding, and my pussy is singing his praises.

"You feel that? This is the only dick you'll have for life. Am I making it worth it?"

"Yes, Rico. So worth it."

"I can't wait until the wedding. I'm going to come all inside you. Then I'm going to watch you swell with my baby.

"Do you want that, gorgeous? Me coming all in this tight pussy for you to carry my baby? Tell me how much you want this shit, Oni."

"Yes, that's what I want. I want it so bad, Rico. You're the only one who can fuck me like this," I whimper-sob.

"I'm not ready to come," he says and pulls out.

Moving his big body until he's between my legs with his face buried in my core, he then eats me like a man on a mission. I rock my hips against his face, greedy for more. Our drivers have become used to this.

I've ridden his brains out plenty of times in the back of one of our cars. Rico customized all our vehicles with partitions just because of that fact. Not caring about any of that, I begin to shake and come all over his face.

Rico hums in satisfaction. He then gently rolls me off the seat and onto all fours. He kisses all over my back, then thrusts back into me from behind. I reach to shove my hands in the seats to hold on.

He begins to fuck me like I owe him something. My next orgasm is already starting a fire in my belly. Rico leans over me into my ear.

"Who's is this? Tell me who this pussy belongs to."

"It's yours. It will always be yours."

"Say my fucking name, baby."

"Rico, it's yours. Rico, fuck."

"That's my girl. Take this dick for me. You know I'd never touch anyone else, don't you, baby? You're it for me.

"If I can't have you, I don't want anyone else. You make me crazy for you. I wouldn't want it any other way," he groans.

CHAPTER THIRTY-EIGHT

Wedding Bells

Rico

The day is finally here. Oni will be my wife in less than an hour. We made it.

"Are you ready?" Mario asks at my side.

"Yeah, bro. I don't deserve her, but she's willing to marry me after all the shit I've brought into her life."

"You two were made for each other. I don't think she would have it any other way."

"Yeah, I hear you."

I swallow hard. What if she does think about it all and changes her mind? Suddenly, standing here at the altar, our lives play in my head.

When I found my truck missing. The footage we pulled of her taking that truck. Me becoming obsessed with watching that video over and over.

The moment I caught her trying to take the Lambo. Pushing back her hoodie and seeing her face for the first time. When I looked into her eyes, I felt connected to her right then and there.

That night at the club when she pulled a gun to protect me. The day she took her first life. Waking up in the hospital, then being told she was gone.

The night she walked back into my life. Slipping that ring on her finger. All the shit we've been through and done together in the last two years.

Those are all reasons why she can and should turn and walk away from me. My heart races as I don't know if she's thinking the same things. She could be bolting right now.

Then the music cues. I stand unseeing until Oni and my father appear. My breath whooshes from my lips.

She looks gorgeous. Her dress is classic but elegant in a modern Oni way. All the sheer lace and intricate details make her look like a living doll.

My throat gets tight. I didn't know I would feel like this. My heart swells, knowing she did choose me.

When Pop hands her off to me, I feel like a kid on Christmas. She stands before me, looking up at me through her veil. With shaking hands, I lift the veil.

It's like I'm sucker punched. The wind is knocked out of me. It takes everything in me to keep standing.

That smile is like life to me. I brush the back of my fingers against my cheek. As her big brown eyes search my face, I swallow hard as it's all I can do to keep the tears from falling.

"You look … I can't find the right words. I love you so much," I say as I cup the side of her face.

"You look amazing. I love you too."

I press my forehead to hers. "Are you ready?"

"Yes, I'm ready."

"You sure? There's no turning back after this."

"I have nowhere else I want to be. I'm ready, Mr. Gallo. Let's do this and get you the world."

I grin and nod. "Let's go, baby."

Everything moves in a blur as we make our way through the ceremony. I half hear everything as I get lost in Oni's eyes. When I'm told I can kiss the bride, I capture her lips and nearly eat her face.

"Hello, Mrs. Gallo," I croon as I rub my nose against the tip of hers.

"Hello, my husband."

"Say it again."

"My husband."

"Fuck, I must be crazy. I married a car thief," I tease.

"I married the future don. So who's really crazy here?"

I growl and take her lips. "It's too late to change your mind now."

"Who said anything about changing my mind? You're stuck with me."

"Wouldn't want it any other way." I nip at her lips.

"Okay, youse two. We have a reception to get to," my father croons.

Oni and I laugh and turn to face the crowd. I glance around at all the people here for us. It's insane how much support we're being shown.

They have all accepted Oni into our world. Nothing can ruin this day for me. Nothing.

Oni

I stand at the top of the church stairs with my mom. My face hurts from smiling so much. Today has been perfect.

I'm finally married to Rico. Someone needs to pinch me because I still can't believe it. I look down the stairs to where the guys dragged Rico for pictures. He looks as happy as I feel.

"My baby is married. Look at you. You're so beautiful," Mom chokes out as she squeezes my shoulders.

She kisses my cheek and continues. "I don't think I've ever seen a prettier bride. You're glowing. Are you happy, baby?"

"Yes, Mom. I am. This is where I belong."

"I just want to make sure," my mother says as she tears up.

I glance to my left and the sun bounces off something that's pushed out of the window of a passing car, grabbing my attention. Everything begins to move in slow motion.

My mouth falls open as I realize what I'm looking at. I shove my mother out of the way without thinking. My heart is racing as I realize I'm in my wedding gown. I don't have any guns on me.

"Oni, get down," Fredo calls out.

I look toward where Rico is standing. I can't make it to him. Before I can decide my next move, gunfire explodes around us. Fredo makes it up the stairs and wraps around me.

"Oni," Rico bellows.

He has pulled his guns and is starting to fire back, as he tries to move up the stairs toward me instead of taking cover. Suddenly, Fredo's back bucks and he falls into me.

My mother reaches for me, pulling me toward her. Emilio comes out of nowhere and covers the three of us as Fredo bleeds out all over me. I scream as Emilio's body begins to jerk as he's hit while covering my mother and me.

"No," I roar.

I pull Fredo's gun and begin to fire. I hit one of the guys in the second car and blow the back window out of the other. The three cars speed off. The last one swerving as if the driver in it was hit as well.

"Oni, baby. Are you okay?" Rico says as he races to me.

"Yes, this isn't my blood. I'm fine."

"We need an ambulance. Someone help me," my mother screams. She's trying to help Emilio while looking frantically at Fredo, who's face down, bleeding out.

"No, no, no," I say as I rush to turn Fredo on his back.

"Come on, buddy. You're not going to do this to me," Rico says as he moves to sit and place Fredo's head in his lap.

"Oni is safe. That's all that matters," Fredo strains to say.

"Emilio, you stay with me, you hear me. Don't you leave me," my mother sobs.

"*Fuck*," Rico roars.

CHAPTER THIRTY-NINE

Who's Left

Rico

"I'm looking for Rico and Oni Gallo," the nurse calls into the waiting room where we've been waiting for news.

I've barely been containing my rage. Instead of dancing with my wife at our wedding reception, we're here in a hospital. Of all the days to pick to do this shit, they would pick today.

I stand and look down at Oni. She's still in her blood-stained wedding gown. I took off my tux jacket and wrapped it around her shoulders hours ago.

She looks up at me and blinks a few times. I give her a tight smile and hold my hand out for hers. Oni stands as if on autopilot and places her hand in mine, then we walk over to the nurse who called our names.

"That's us," I say.

"Mr. Gallo would like to see the two of you, but you can't stay long. He needs his rest."

I close my eyes and nod. My uncle nearly gave his life for Fredo, Oni, and her mother. I still can't believe what he did.

He should have taken cover and stayed close to his men. The interesting thing is, I'm not sure who he was trying to cover. His nephew, my wife, or her mother.

Whoever it was, he earned a new respect from me. I prayed the old bastard would pull through. We're not ready to lose him.

Oni gasps as we walk into my uncle's room. I don't blame her. I've never seen him look so fragile in my life. Tubes and machines are everywhere.

We move to the side of his bed and Oni takes his hand in hers. Uncle Emilio opens his eyes. It takes a moment for his gaze to focus on us.

With his other hand, he reaches to pull the oxygen mask down. He swallows thickly and frowns. I squeeze Oni's waist as she begins to tremble.

"Fredo?" he says, barely above a whisper.

I shake my head. "Still in surgery. They said the bullet hit his spine on the way in, then nicked his lung on the way out. We're still waiting to hear if he'll pull through."

"He might not be able to walk again," Oni sniffles.

Uncle Emilio gasps in a breath of air. "Find out who did this and you kill them and their entire family," he wheezes out then places his mask back on.

"Already on it," Oni replies before I can.

Uncle Emilio nods firmly then closes his eyes. There's nothing else to be said. I kiss Oni's temple and lead her out of the room.

When we get back to the waiting room, Mario is waiting with a somber look on his face. He comes to my side and leans to whisper in my ear.

"This was a play by Sullivan. He's hiding behind old connections, but it's him, no doubt," he whispers.

"I want a meet with McFarlan. He should know what his boy has done."

McFarlan is the Irish boss in Ireland. He's the one Sullivan has to answer to. We went to McFarlan to have Sullivan stripped of everything here in New York.

He was reluctant until he learned how fucked up things were in my city. Sullivan and his boys weren't reporting back like they should have been. There are more parties that haven't been happy with Sullivan and his dealings for a while now.

They just didn't have the balls to speak up. Once Abato was out of the way and Sullivan didn't have a way to cover up his shit, McFarlan was more than happy to strip it all away.

"So we're changing our honeymoon to a trip to Ireland?" Oni says.

"That we are. I have an old dog I want to put down. We'll need his owner's signature on a few things."

Oni

We're finally home from the hospital. I think I'm still in shock. This was the last outcome I expected for my wedding day.

"Let me get you out of this dress and into the shower," Rico murmurs.

I have to admire how strong he's being for the both of us. This is his uncle and cousin, who risked their lives for me. I will never forgive myself if Fredo doesn't pull through.

My mother is a wreck. She refused to leave the hospital. Once they got Emilio to his private suite, Emilia and Mom settled in and stayed for the night. I almost laughed at how happy Emilio looked as we walked out to head home.

My mother better be careful. Once Emilio is healthy again, she might be in trouble. In a matter of hours, so much has changed.

"Talk to me, baby. What's going on in your head?" Rico asks as he places me in the shower and turns the spray on.

I turn to him and wrap my arms around him. I could have lost him today. Hearing his heart next to my ear goes a long way to calm me.

He wraps his arms around me and holds on tight as the water cascades down around us. A single tear falls before I can stop it.

"I'm here. Whatever you need, I'm here. You don't have to be strong for me, Oni."

"They don't deserve my tears. They took one of the most important days of my life from me. The only thing they will receive from me is my rage."

"I promise you, we will find a way to make this day right. All that matters right now is that you're here in my arms, still breathing."

"They have to be okay. Fredo doesn't deserve this."

"He's going to pull through. Uncle Emilio is too stubborn to die. Besides, now that he knows your mom still cares, he's going to be back with a vengeance.

"We all know how he can be about her. My mother-in-law might be my step-aunt soon," he chuckles.

"Ew, please don't."

He pulls back and looks down at me, lifting my chin with his fingertips. Searching my face with his gaze, he then drops a kiss on my lips. I sigh into the kiss as my body melts against his.

"I just wanted to get you to smile."

"Thanks, Rico. I love you."

"Anytime, I love you too."

CHAPTER FORTY

Here to See a Man

Rico

I pull off my shades as Oni and I step into the dark, dank-looking pub in Ireland run by the man we came to see. Mario, Al, and Ed follow us in. We're patted down, then waved to the back, where some men are sitting at a table.

I notice the strawberry blond we came to see sitting in the middle of the table. He signals for the other men around him to get up and they all leave.

"Ach, I didn't think I would see ye again so soon. What about ye?" Tim McFarlan says as we walk up to the table.

I shrug my shoulders and unfasten my suit jacket as he points for us to take a seat. Oni does the same to her suit jacket and sits gracefully. I don't miss the appreciative looks she receives from the men around us.

"It seems you're not receiving information from the States again," I say as I take a seat after Oni.

"Aye, I think I did hear something about a wedding, but that had nothing to do with me. No one under my nose would be that fucking stupid."

I frown. He doesn't have the control he thinks he does. That's going to be a big problem for him, but who am I to tell him how to run his business? He's about to learn the consequences on his own.

"I'm afraid you need to wipe your nose. My wedding was shot up because of the same scumbag who had my father killed in prison," Oni bites out.

I release a heavy breath. "As far as I'm concerned, you now have two options. One, go to war with me, and you and your people won't make it out of the week. You know this.

"Or two, cough up Finn Sullivan. We kill him for his crimes, and we'll leave Ireland and all that's yours intact. So what will it be?"

Tim sits back in his chair and starts to laugh like we've told him a joke. I haven't come here for jokes or to play games. I haven't said a thing that's funny.

When his laughter dies down, he frowns and glares at me. "Ach, you have balls of steel, you do. Who the fuck are ya to come in here and threaten me? What's to keep me from blowing both your heads off and sending the rest of your bodies back as a wedding gift?"

Oni pulls her tablet, turns it on, places it on the table, then sits back in her seat. I place a hand on the back of her neck and massage it. McFarlan looks back at us and snorts.

"What's this?"

"Take a look. Anything look familiar?"

I watch as he homes in on the tablet, and his face goes pale. He then looks up at us and swallows hard. I'm not fucking around.

He's looking at live footage of my men's current points of view. Red dots trained on each of their targets. Even those McFarlan prides himself on keeping a secret.

"Like I said. You'll be finished before week's end. I know where all your family is right at this moment. If we don't walk out of here at the designated time, if anything shifts in a single one of those locations before my wife or I call, if my guys so much as think you're up to some bullshit …

"You're going to lose your family here in Ireland and each one of them in the States. I told you to keep that dog on a leash. He clearly has no respect for you, so here we are. Your choice. Him or everything you love," I hiss.

Oni sits up in her seat and crosses her legs then leans forward. "And before you even think about growing a pair and testing us … I will freeze every asset you and your men own. It doesn't have to be today, and I don't even have to be breathing.

"Any move against me, my husband, or our family will trigger the implosion of everything you own. If you don't believe me, log into your bank account right now and see what I mean."

He swallows hard and pulls his phone to log into his account. His face grows white as a sheet. Oni sits beside me, smiling from ear to ear.

"Jesus, Mary, Joesph. What have ya done? Where the fuck is all my money?"

"Do we have a deal?" I say.

"Ye can have him. Travis, get them the address for Sullivan's hideout."

"Good. You can refresh your screen," Oni purrs.

"Ach, this is a load of bullshit. How did ya end up working for the Italians? Didn't Finn have ya running with one of his crews?" McFarlan asks bitterly.

"I guess finding out my best friend set me up and his family had my father killed was unforgivable to me. Might have even compromised my sanity. Loyalty goes both ways," Oni replies then stands to walk out.

Oni

"Are you ready?" Rico asks as we turn onto the road to the house Sullivan is held up in.

"Yes," is all I can manage to push out.

Apparently, Finn isn't wanted here in Ireland either. He's been hiding away from some people he owes answers. McFarlan has been keeping him safe for some reason I couldn't care less about.

That time is over. I have something special just for Finn Sullivan. This kill will mean more to me than any of my others.

This is the man who had my father killed. He set in motion my losses. I don't care that I used to spend all my time in his home with his son.

Fuck breaking bread with them at their table. A rat will eat the food from your hand, then bite you. The Sullivans are no better than a bunch of rats.

The sooner I put Finn down, the better. We pull up to the house and hop out of the SUV. I gently grab my bag to bring with me.

The front door opens before we can get to it. Finn sees me and his eyes light with recognition. My stomach turns in disgust as he smiles at me.

"Oni Raven. I didn't think I would ever see your face again," he croons.

Rico rushes forward and wraps his hand around Finn's neck, shoving him back inside the cabin-like house. I take my time following them inside. Mario, Ed, and Al bring up the rear.

"Why didn't you think you would see her, you smug prick?"

"Because I thought I'd be on my way back to the States for your funerals. I had much more success with having her da set up and murdered, the traitor bastard."

I pull my gun and cock it. "What did you just say?"

"Aye, I did it. I had Jack locked up and then made sure he never got out. I treated him like family, only to find out he was trying to infiltrate my crew to help that Italian scum take me down.

"Gallo all but left him for dead and he decided to go against me. Aye, but you were a little gem. I made sure Mason kept you around so I could mold you.

"Too bad those Italian fucks got ahold of you first. I should have let Lorcan pull you in. He's the one who would have kept an eye on you and made sure you didn't get anywhere near this son of a bitch," he snarls.

Rico punches him in the face to shut him up. I'm numb. It was one thing for others to tell me he was involved, but hearing him say the words with his own mouth, confirming what Carlotta thought all along, aches something fierce.

"You had to bring your little boyfriend with you to handle a grown man's job. Why don't you go back to the States and find Mason, let him take care of you and bring your real family back? Stop playing with filth," he snarls.

I snort and begin to laugh. "You know, I was going to have mercy on you because you were like a father to me at one time. I couldn't reconcile the monster with the sweet old man I thought you were.

"Now you're going to die screaming like the filthy pig you are. And as you die, it can play in the back of your head that I'm going to find Mason and Lorcan's dead-playing asses. And when I do, they're going to die screaming just like you," I hiss.

He laughs like I just told a joke. However, I'm the one who will have the last laugh. Mario and Ed rush forward to help Rico secure him to a chair while I set up.

I open my bag and pull on a pair of chemical-resistant gloves. Then I unzip the pouch with the borosilicate glass syringes. Rico ties his arm off for me and steps away.

This is going to get messy. I carefully pull one of the fat syringes from the case and pluck it with my finger. The bubbles inside the glass bring a smile to my lips.

"They said my father was stabbed a hundred times before he bled out on that prison floor. That had to burn and sting, don't you think?" I say as I walk over to him.

"I hope like fuck it did," he bites out.

"I'm so happy you feel that way," I sing.

I then plunge the syringe into his vein and push the liquid into his arm. He screams like his veins are on fire because they are. I just filled them with acid.

I grab another syringe as his veins pop in his neck while his arm melts at his side. I plunge the needle into his neck and sigh with satisfaction as blood and foam spill from his mouth.

I pat his dead cheek and snort. "What was that? I can't hear you."

Rico scoffs. "Let's go. Someone will come find this sludge later. We have a plane to catch."

"Damn, that shit was vicious. Remind me not to piss you off," Eduardo says.

"Don't fuck with my family and you'll never have to see this side of me for yourself." I shrug and collect my things.

"Keep that bag away from me, please," Al says.

"Wimps," I snort.

"Psycho," Ed and Al murmur in unison.

Rico and I laugh and walk out. Sullivan is as good as forgotten. My father can rest in peace knowing I took care of the man who took him from me. Ireland owes me nothing.

I came, I saw, I conquered. The world will think twice about fucking with Rico or Oni Gallo from here on out. To think we're just getting started.

CHAPTER FORTY-ONE

Out of Hiding

Mason

"Little Brother," Lorcan croons as he opens his arms for me.

Numbly, I walk into his arms. I can't believe Da is gone. We don't even have a body to bury.

He was killed like an animal. No, his death was crueler than that. Da could be cruel, but he still didn't deserve that.

"Welcome home. You look good," Lorcan croons.

This doesn't feel like home. I haven't felt welcomed since landing in Ireland. I get the feeling we need to settle our affairs and get the hell out of here as fast as we can.

"How are you holding up? This shit is crazy, ain't it?" Lorcan says.

"Bro, what happened? How did they get to him? I thought he was in hiding. Who did this?"

"You don't know?"

"No, how would I? I've been in Boston keeping my head down. All I know is what you told me about how they found him."

"It was that scumbag Rico Gallo and that bitch Oni."

"Oni? How could she have been involved?"

"She and that motherfucker went to McFarlan for permission to take Da out. He gave Da up and they killed him."

I pull a hand down my face. This all sounds crazy. Oni is a sweetheart.

She wouldn't hurt a fly. If she did, maybe Da brought this on himself. We've done nothing but hurt her and her family.

"I'm sure she's only doing what he wants from her. She loved Da. He had a soft spot for her too."

"Bro, you're not this stupid. Da didn't give a fuck about Oni. She was a means to an end.

"She was as expendable as the rest of us. The man didn't care about any of us. If you weren't useful, you were no better than shit under his shoe," he says.

"Fuck, man, he was still our da and knowing Oni was involved … I just can't wrap my head around this shit."

"Well, you're here now. We'll do right by Da and then we can get the fuck out of here and get our city back. I can't wait to get the fuck out of here."

I knit my brows. "What are you talking about? We're still banned from New York. Nothing has changed."

"The fuck it hasn't. Da was too scared of McFarlan to push back. He's here, we're there.

"We run shit and bring the paper in. Why the fuck do we even answer to that asshole? It was his ass who gave Da up. Fuck him."

I rub at my temples. This is the kind of shit that used to make Da kick his ass. Lorcan doesn't think.

I groan. "It's shit like that that's going to have you right with Da."

"I wish that pussy-ass bastard and his bitch would. I'm going to make them pay. You can either stand with me or fuck around until you're next."

“Why would I be next?”

“Because once I start, all this shit is going to come full circle. I’m not going to stop until they all pay for this. McFarlan, Gallo, Oni, and our bitch-ass cousin,” he growls.

“Darragh? He’s only doing what he was told. Fuck, man, you can’t go waging war with no resources, no support, no fucking money.”

“Our crew back home is still loyal. With you by my side, they’ll all ride with us. New York is our home. Why the fuck are you in Boston while I’m stuck here?”

“Because it’s the smart thing to do. So what if we have the old crew? That’s not enough to go up against the Gallos and McFarlan,” I drop my voice as I hiss the end.

“Right now. It’s not enough right now. We get back home, and we put our heads down. Then we make our move when we have all our shit lined up.”

“Lorcan, man, let’s just take care of our da.”

“Fine, but this isn’t over. I’m not letting this go. If you had found Oni like I told you to, this wouldn’t be happening,” he bites out.

A cold chill runs through me. This isn’t going to end well. I’ll have to keep an eye on him.

“Fuck,” I mutter under my breath.

CHAPTER FORTY-TWO

Life of the Gallos

Rico

Ten years later …

"Why won't any of you tell me where we're heading?" Oni grumbles from her seat on the private jet.

Emilia is seated beside her, looking like she's about to burst with the truth. I shake my head as Mario looks at her, ready to laugh. He knows his wife as well as I do.

Emilia would have told Oni everything if Mario hadn't waited until this morning to tell her. I still can't believe the two are married. So much has happened in the last ten years.

"Be patient and you will know everything soon enough," I murmur.

Oni rolls her eyes at me, causing me to chuckle. My wife hates secrets, yet here we are because I know she's keeping a huge one from me. Something is going on with Oni.

I keep asking her what it is, but every time I ask, she tells me it's nothing. I know my wife. Something is off.

That's why I thought some time away would be good for us. I planned this trip for us to relax and get back to basics. Business has been taking over our lives lately. Uncle Emilio relies on us both heavily.

For ten years, we've given our all to the family. At thirty-four, I want to start a family and focus more on that. It's time we create balance.

It was Fredo's idea for this retreat. When I told all the guys how I'm feeling about slowing down and wanting to be a father, Fredo was quick to offer up ideas.

He and Oni have become closer than ever. Oni saw him through his recovery and made sure to research all the best resources to get him as close to his old self as possible.

"Well, I'm here so you know we're not going anywhere that involves hiking, rock climbing, or taking long walks," Fredo says and laughs at his own joke.

Everyone groans as I chuckle, understanding my cousin and his dry humor. Fredo doesn't always need his wheelchair. However, he gets exhausted when walking long distances and he's not back to being able to rock climb like he used to.

"What? You guys are not allowed to be offended on my behalf. If I'm not offended by a joke I told, you all need to get over it," Fredo scoffs.

"This guy," Al says, and shakes his head.

Fredo winks at me. I give him a nod. His antics have officially changed the subject.

I glance at Oni. She has her head back and her eyes closed. Just like that, she's fallen asleep.

I stand from my seat and nod for Emilia to switch with me. She gets up and I slip into the seat next to Oni. Tugging her into me, I allow her to rest against me and kiss the top of her head.

I hope this trip to the island is just what we all need, blowing off some steam and getting back to being able to trust each other with the truth. No business, no family, nothing to keep us from connecting the way we should.

Oni

"Oni, you ready?" Rico calls as I stand in the bathroom trying to calm down.

"Give me a minute."

I sigh as I look at my reflection. I shouldn't be this annoyed. Rico means well.

I can't believe he planned this trip without me knowing. I mean, this place is amazing and I'm happy the gang came along, but how did I miss that he's been planning this behind my back?

To be honest, I'm not angry. Frustrated, yes. Blindsided? Definitely, but not angry. I'm frustrated because he didn't think to bring any of our men along.

We are never without armed men. I always have at least three of my guys with me. With the deals we're in the middle of, I don't think now is the time to go lax.

Then there's the secret I've been keeping from him. A few weeks ago, Emory reached out to me. She may have been my best friend when I was younger, but it's been years.

I know nothing about her. In all honesty, she and Mason were my closest friends and look where that got me. I just don't have that same trust anymore.

I almost didn't agree to meet her for lunch. When I did, she told me Mason and Lorcan have been pulling their old crew together. She thinks they're going to make a move against me.

I don't see how they plan to pull that off, but in case she is right, I prefer having our men around. I didn't tell Rico because he has enough on his plate and I plan to handle it myself.

In fact, I would have been in motion today if my husband hadn't whisked me away for this surprise vacation. We're in a whole other country, so for now, I plan to brush it off until I get back.

Rico is right, we do need some time to relax. I can get back to business when we get home. The Sullivan brothers don't have the means or the balls to come at me.

For all I know, Emory could have been their only play to get me off my game. Instead of being so frustrated, I should probably talk to Rico. However, if I say something now, he's going to end this much-needed vacation.

Nope, I'm going to enjoy my husband. We can go off when we get home. Whatever the Sullivan brothers think they're up to, we'll shut that shit right down.

"Oni, baby, come on," Rico groans with impatience.

Mind made up, I give myself a nod in the mirror. It's been so long since Rico and I have kicked back and pretended to be ordinary people.

I turn and head out of the bathroom, ready to enjoy this thoughtful surprise. Rico is standing by the sliding glass doors of the bedroom, shirtless and in a pair of board shorts.

I walk up behind him and wrap my arms around him then kiss his back. He turns to face me and cups my face. Searching my gaze, he sighs in relief when he sees I'm no longer annoyed.

"I'm sorry. I shouldn't have gotten mad at you. This was a great surprise."

"You're right. You do have responsibilities I should have thought about. Next time, I will ask what's on your plate and if you have the time to take a break."

"Next time?" I tease.

"Baby, we've been consumed with business. When was the last time we took a real vacation?"

"Last … oh wait, we had to cancel that. Okay, I see your point."

He pecks my forehead, then the tip of my nose. I can tell this has been on his mind a lot. I can't help but wonder why now.

"From now on, spending time with you comes first. I want to start taking trips at least once a month for pleasure, not business."

"Really? Your promotion is coming soon—when we finish what Emilio has asked of us.

"You're done. You will be Don. Can you really promise me this?"

He rolls his eyes. "Okay, every other month at least."

"That sounds fair. Can I ask what brought this on?"

"I want a baby. In the beginning, we said we would wait to let our connection grow. We are stronger than ever. I think it's time," he says as he rubs my back.

"You want a baby?" I say with a goofy smile on my face.

"Do you?"

I reach to palm him over his shorts. "You know you didn't have to bring me all the way here for that. If a baby is what you want, you know how to get one."

He takes my lips in a heated kiss before I can finish purring the words. I lift on my toes to wrap my arms around his neck. He bends his knees and lifts me into his arms.

I wrap my legs around his waist and hold on tight. Rico slips his hands into my bikini bottoms and palms my ass. We were supposed to be meeting the others at the pool, but I don't think that's going to happen.

When Rico climbs onto the bed and places me down in the center of it, I know it's not. He kisses his way down my body, taking his time as he sucks and licks at my skin.

"Rico," I moan.

"I will never get tired of hearing you call my name," he groans.

I squirm when he pauses over the tat on my hip and just breathes against it, causing goose bumps to rise across my skin. It's the gold-and-black crew tat. It took months for me to find an artist who could get the coloring right on my dark skin. I wanted mine to be as vibrant as everyone else's.

Rico traces the tat with his tongue as he peels off my bikini bottoms and tosses them over his shoulder. He licks his way from my belly button up to the center of my breasts.

He then moves to my lips and kisses me passionately. I grasp his shoulders and kiss him back with just as much passion. Gasping, I buck up from the bed as he sinks into me.

Wrapping my legs around the back of his, I can feel he hasn't even taken his shorts all the way off. I try to push them down with my feet, but he reaches for my legs and pins them to my chest.

"Oh," I breathe.

"We're making a baby before we go back home. I'm going to come so deep inside you, there won't be any doubt that you're carrying my baby."

"Yes, Rico, yes."

He's fucking me so hard my scalp is tingling. I can feel him growing harder and harder as he thrusts in and out of me. I can only grab the sheets and cling to them when he sits back on his heels and grabs my waist as he continues to rock into me.

My eyes roll back and my toes curl. I can feel my juices flooding my core. When he reaches for my nub and starts to rub it, my body begins to convulse. I scream so loud, I know everyone in the villa can hear me.

"Fuck, I love it when you come like that. You're so fucking beautiful. Come on, Oni. Give me one more, baby."

I want to tell him I don't think I have it in me as my lids grow heavy and I feel like I'm going to pass out, but he traps my nipple between his lips and keeps pumping into me. Soon, he gets exactly what he's asking for.

"Rico," I cry out as I come again.

His hot seed fills me seconds later. Rico pulls out and drags my body on top of his. This time I do fall out.

He wants a baby. I think I'm ready too. I might need to see a doctor for some vitamins. I've been tired a lot lately.

CHAPTER FORTY-THREE

Past Faces

Oni

Rico thinks he's slick. He sent me out shopping with Mario and Emilia. I would be fine with that if this wasn't meant to be a vacation for the both of us.

However, my dear husband is up to something, and I don't think it has anything to do with our vacation. I get the feeling he's working.

Which would be fine if he hadn't made such a big deal about us needing to take some time to relax. Truth be told, I would have been fine staying at the villa to get some more sleep. I don't know why I'm so tired.

"You okay? You don't look so good," Mario says as he places a hand on my back.

I look up at him and smile. "I'm fine. Just a little tired."

"You want to head back?"

"No, not yet. I want to go into that shop across the street when Emilia is done in here."

Mario groans. "They might be closed by the time she gets done fucking around in here."

I snicker. "Spoken like a true husband."

"Tell me I'm wrong."

I roll my eyes. "You love waiting around to see what she tries on. Stop complaining like you don't."

"Only when I get to help her out of it in the dressing room before we leave. Can't do that with you here." He winks at me.

"Oh no. You stay here with your wife. I'm going to that shop."

"Rico would want us with you. Just hold on a sec."

I give him a pointed look. "Mario, this is me. I'll be fine. I'm just going right across the street."

"Nope. Not happening."

"Mario, can you come help me real quick?" Emilia calls.

"Hang on, babe." He looks at me. "Don't move. We'll be right back, and we'll all go together."

I laugh and shake my head. Knowing Rico would lose his shit on Mario if anything happened to me, I stay put. If I have as much as a paper cut, Rico would threaten to shoot Mario if not act on it.

I begin to look through the racks. Nothing has caught my attention. The things in this place aren't my style.

I'm surprised Emilia found anything in here she likes. A strange aroma hits my nostrils, my stomach begins to feel queasy, and I feel lightheaded for a second. I knit my brows.

What's going on with me? I shake my head to clear it, but that makes me feel like I'm going to pass out. I stumble to the nearest shelf and reach out to hold myself up.

That's when my brain begins to kick into overdrive. I pull my phone and open my calendar. My mouth pops open when I see my cycle is late.

Oh my God, Rico might already have his wish. Excitement fills me. I can't wait to get back to the villa to tell him.

Maybe we can find a test before we head back. That same scent hits me again. I need some fresh air.

I step out of the shop to gulp down some fresh air. I'm only going to stand out here until Mario and Emilia are done. My stomach settles as I wait and scroll through my phone.

Going to my contacts, I think to text Rico the news. I decide against that and close my phone to head back inside.

Feeling like I'm being watched, I glance across the street. Mason Sullivan is standing there with his eyes on me. My blood boils.

I reach into my bag as he starts across the street toward me. We lock eyes and he has the nerve to smile at me like we're still old friends. I wrap my hand around the handle of my gun.

"Hey, Oni. You look great."

"Are you fucking kidding me?"

I go to put my gun to his belly and give him a new hole to leak from. However, something stabs me in the neck, and my vision starts to fade as my body grows heavy. Next thing I know, I'm falling forward face-first.

Rico

My chest heaves as my cousins hold me back. I look at the marks around Mario's neck and growl. He had one job.

One fucking job. I flop onto my ass on the floor. I can't believe this is happening.

"We're sorry, Rico. We're so sorry. We're going to get her back," Emilia sobs.

"We don't have time for this. I was lucky enough to get into the only working cam on that street, but I lost them from there.

"I called in a favor to see what else I could find. They left the island. We need to head home where I can dig and find some answers," Fredo says.

"Who the fuck are they?" I seethe.

"The Sullivan brothers," Fredo replies.

"I want everyone on this. Find her in the next twenty-four hours, or I'm going to start killing people. Starting with those who failed me."

"Rico, is that necessary?" Emilia whispers.

I don't answer. I get up and go to pack my and my wife's things. When I get to our room, I see the dress I laid out for her for our surprise evening.

I only sent her shopping so I could get things ready for a romantic evening. She thought I was trying to slip in some work, but I needed to meet with the coordinator about the chef, flowers, and the decor. I wanted everything to be perfect.

I'm holding on by a thread, knowing those bastards have my wife. Something has to be wrong for them to have been able to take her. Oni is no damsel.

She wouldn't have gone down without a fight. This fact worries me the most. I grab her head wrap and bring it to my nose.

Inhaling deep. I close my eyes and picture her face. Just this morning, we were making love.

I took my time with her to remind her how precious she is to me. Even though I didn't think it possible, I love her more than I did when she said I do.

"What have they done to you, baby? Where are you?"

Determination fills me; I'm going to find her and get her back. Then I'm going to destroy everyone involved. There will be no mercy.

CHAPTER FORTY-FOUR

Not the Plan

Mason

"You did good, bro," Lorcan croons.

I don't reply. This wasn't the plan. Not the plan I was a part of.

I didn't know Lorcan had followed me to the marketplace where Oni was shopping. I had gone to talk to her. I hadn't decided whether or not I would warn her about Lorcan's plans for Rico.

I wanted to know if she's happy. It seems like she is. If she told me to my face that she is truly happy, I would have warned her about my brother and his plans.

However, Lorcan followed me and knocked Oni unconscious before snatching her. The asshole didn't even give me time to think. He rushed right to the airport, where Romano's plane was waiting to bring us back to New York.

"This was a mistake. We need to drop her back where she belongs and get the fuck out of here," I hiss.

"Shut the fuck up, you pussy. Romano is paying us top dollar for her to be out of the picture."

"What?"

This can't be his fucking plan. My head is about to explode. I should have known not to trust him.

"Do you see this place? We're in the big leagues now. All we have to do is hold her here until they tell us what they want done with her."

"Lorcan, this is crazy. You just kidnapped her from another country. How long do you think we'll be able to hide out here before he comes for her? Why hasn't she woken up yet? Fuck, how did I get involved in this?"

"Why the fuck do you care whether she's awake or not? Are you forgetting what this is all about?"

"I've never understood what any of this is about. For ten years, you've been ranting about getting back at everyone. How the fuck does this help you do that?"

"Boys, boys, boys."

I freeze and look to the doorway. I think I'm going to be sick. This crazy bitch is as off as Lorcan is.

I figured that out from the first time I met her. She has it out for Oni as much as Lorcan does. If you ask me, Lorcan is pissed because he can't have Oni, and this crazy bitch is out of her mind because she can't have Rico Gallo.

"You should look happier to see me. After all, I talked my father into bankrolling all of this for you. Did you get her?"

I look to Lorcan in confusion. Rico was supposed to be our target. What's she talking about?

"We have her. She's upstairs."

"I want to see her."

Lorcan frowns. I get the feeling he wasn't planning on handing over Oni this soon. I need to figure something out fast.

My brother storms from the room with Alyissa Romano following behind him. I rush to catch up before the two do something I can't fix.

When we enter the room, Oni is wide awake. Lorcan restrained her arms and legs. I think that's a good thing. The look in her eyes says she would try to kill us all with her bare hands.

Alyissa grabs Oni by the hair and tugs her head back. This is a mistake. They are only fueling the fire.

"I've found you, bitch. This time, nothing will save you. You have nowhere else to run. With you out of the way, I will finally get what I deserve."

"You're delusional. Where have I been running? You weren't looking too hard to find me. I'm never hard to find.

"Don't you mean you've been running from me? Daddy sent you away as soon as your big mouth got my attention. I'm still going to kill you, just like I promised these two assholes' father I would take care of them. You're all going to die."

"Ugh, knock her out. Fucking nuisance. What does he see in her?" Alyissa huffs. "When you're done, come downstairs. I want to talk about what's next."

I groan. This is ridiculous. Alyissa had a husband of her own; she's just pissed he went bankrupt and they divorced.

Rico, meanwhile, has only gotten wealthier and is still married to Oni. It's all she talked about when I first met her.

Her father holds a grudge because he couldn't use the Gallos the way he wanted, so he entertains his spoiled daughter's hatred and desire for revenge.

"I'll be there in a bit," Lorcan says.

Alyissa walks out. I don't take my eyes off Lorcan. He's looking at Oni with his eyes full of lust.

"Shouldn't we know what's next? We can come back and check on her after," I say nervously.

He looks to me as if just remembering I'm standing here. Running a hand through his hair and readjusting himself, he nods. I don't think I start breathing again until he starts to walk out of the room.

I sigh and pull my phone to text Emory. I need her here. Someone needs to watch over Oni.

Me: *It's going south. Get here now.*

White-hot pain shoots through my skull. I've been having these headaches for two years now. The last thing I need is to deal with my brother's shit.

Fuck.

Oni

My knees are hurting from sitting on this floor like this and my back has a dull ache. I don't feel good. Whatever they did has my head thumping and my stomach cramping.

My baby.

"Please hold on," I whimper.

I didn't get to confirm the pregnancy or tell Rico. After realizing I might have missed more than one cycle, I just know. I want to break down and sob, but I have to be strong to get out of here.

I've never trusted Lorcan. It's the way he always looked at me. Mason would never leave me alone with him.

However, Mason distracted me so they could take me. He's the reason I'm here and the reason why my baby is in danger. When I get out of here, I'm killing them all. That bitch Alyissa is a fucking nut.

This isn't the first run-in I've had with her, but it will be the last. I should have killed her father when she first crossed me. Just to leave an example.

Her disrespect was unacceptable. Her father hiding her away after showed even more disrespect if you ask me. He knew she owed in blood after the stunt she pulled.

Pain rockets across my back. "Oh God, please no."

I double over and press my forehead to the cool floor. I need to get out of here and get to a doctor. This can't be happening.

I try not to panic. Picturing Rico's face and feeling his arms around me helps me to calm down some. I just need to hold on.

Please, baby, hang in there. Daddy's coming for us. He'll be here.

CHAPTER FORTY-FIVE

Awakening

Oni

Back to the present . . .
He's back. The one with the scent I recognize. Every time I try to wake up, he's here.

I know he's not Rico. I established that the last few times I tried to become fully conscious. What I have managed to figure out is that Rico is hurt.

He's not with me because he's hurt. I still feel like I have something important to tell him. I want to wake up so I can remember what.

"Still nothing?" One of the other males who keeps coming in and out says.

"*Oogatz,*" my watcher says.

"*Marone,* Mario is sick about it. Emilia can't stop crying. Rico is going to be pissed when he finds out Romano and the Sullivans got away."

The other guy sighs. "They may have gotten out of the fire, but they're not getting out of the city. Alyissa Romano's luck has run out when it comes to her great escapes.

"Her father wasn't as lucky. He didn't see me coming. All he saw was a guy in a wheelchair.

"I blew a hole right through his chest. Clearing the rest of the room was light work for Mario and Emilia. Emilia might be in tears now, but Oni and Rico would be damn proud of her," he scoffs.

"Your idea was brilliant. To hit both places at once. Rico and Ed may have taken hits, but it worked out for the best.

"Romano wanted a war; he got one. He needed to go down. He's been a problem for years if you ask me."

"Yeah, we should have done him regardless of the green light. Made or not, he was a piece of shit."

Fredo. That's Fredo and his scent. He's the one keeping watch.

Alyissa Romano, Lorcan and Mason Sullivan, that's who took me. Suddenly, I'm hit with another fragment of a memory.

My stomach is cramping again as I wake. I'm on an old mattress in the same room as before. I'm still restrained, but my hands are now secured above my head.

I try to focus and look around as I hear a clinking sound and something rustling. Not able to focus my eyes, I begin to take a mental note of my body.

My ankles are no longer bound. However, my legs and lower half feel cooler than the rest of my body. The mattress dips under the weight of something other than me.

"I've waited so fucking long for this."

Panic shoots through me and I start to kick and buck like crazy. My foot connects with something, causing a howl to fill the air. I keep kicking in that direction to see if I can make a connection again.

"Fucking bitch."

The sound of a door crashing open fills the air and the lights come on. The light stings my eyes, and I have to snap them shut as pain blasts through my head.

"What the fuck do you think you're doing?"

"Emory," I murmur, still not able to open my eyes.

"Get the fuck out and mind your damn business."

The sound of a gun cocking catches my ears. "The only one leaving this room is you. I'm not allowing you to rape her, Lorcan. Get out, you sick bastard."

"Is that why he called you here? To watch over this slut while I keep him busy. She's a whore.

"Those Italians probably passed her around. Now it's my turn. Go mind your business."

"When he comes for her, I hope he blows your head off. Things were peaceful while you were away. The last two years have been hell since you've been trying to lift your head.

"Romano is using you and you're too stupid to see what's coming. I said get the fuck away from her before I break your brother's heart by making him have to bury you."

I smiled to myself. That's the Emory I know and love. I give her a silent thanks as the drugs they've been filling me with take me under once again.

Fire? Did Emory make it out? Rage fills me; I need to wake up.

I have fish to gut. Rico needs me. I need to make sure Emory made it out.

I push harder to open my eyes. Blinding pain rocks through my skull. I have to keep fighting.

"Any word on Rico?" Fredo asks.

"He's finally stable, Doc says now we wait, same as here."

"They're going to be devastated. Rico wants to be a father. When he finds out Oni was pregnant and lost the baby, no one will be safe."

Fredo sighs. "I wish that Emory chick had called with the location sooner. We lost a week trying to find her."

"Bro, did you see that?"

"See what?"

"I think her finger twitched."

"Wait, her eyes are moving under her lids," Fredo says. "Oni, hey, sweetheart, can you hear me?"

"Oni, it's me, Al. If you can hear me, give my finger a squeeze," he coaxes as light pressure settles in the center of my palm.

"Where's my gun? They killed my baby, and he tried to rape me."

They both chuckle.

"That's my girl," Fredo croons.

"Welcome back, baby girl. We're going to get them. You and Rico need to recover first," Al says.

Rico

"Where is she?"

"Rico, hold on. You're recovering. You need to rest," Uncle Emilio says as he tries to stop me from getting out of bed.

"I can recover when I know she's alive and well. Forgive me for not being able to trust you where she's concerned. I need to set eyes on her."

"*Marone*, when are you going to forgive me for that? I thought we got past all that."

"This isn't about us. My wife was taken. I should have killed Romano when I wanted to.

"I would have kept the blowback from your door. Out of respect for you, I let him live," I snap.

"Oni, wait. You should be in bed. Please," my mother-in-law says on the other side of the door.

In the next moment, the door bursts open, and my wife comes into view. I go to stand to get to her, but pain sears through my leg. I stumble forward and have to pause.

Oni rushes to me and wraps her arms around me. I wrap her in my embrace and hold her tightly to me. She breaks down sobbing, which is so unlike my wife.

I tighten my embrace and move back toward the bed to sit and bring her into my lap. With her in my arms, I'm able to ignore the pain firing through my body.

"I'm here now. It's okay, baby. I'm here," I murmur into the top of her hair.

She takes a calming breath. "The baby is gone. The drugs and lack of nutrition … I lost the baby," she sobs.

"What? What are you talking about?"

"I stepped out of the shop because I was feeling nauseous. I realized once I stepped out that I was already pregnant. That's why I've been so tired and cranky lately.

"When I woke, the doctor told me I miscarried once you saved me and got me home. I'm sorry. I did everything I could."

"Shh, baby, shh. This is my fault. I took too long to find you.

"If not for Emory reaching out, I'd still be looking for you. She said they only brought her in a few days ago. She had been somewhere else when the call first came in.

"She called me as soon as she was able to get a number for me. You were at one of Romano's properties. We hadn't known to look there; the Sullivans were the ones who took you," I say as my thoughts race.

I still haven't processed what she said. She was already pregnant? Our baby is gone?

"I knew you would come for me. I was waiting," she whispers.

I can only nod. The pain in my body no longer registers as the pain in my chest takes over. It feels like I've been stabbed through the heart by a hot knife.

"The city is on lockdown. They won't get away, youse two do whatever you need to.

"I have no objections. Burn the fucking city down if you want," Uncle Emilio says, then walks out.

"Rico?"

"Yeah, baby?"

"About Emory. Is she okay? I owe her. Lorcan was going to rape me. She stopped him."

"What did you say?"

"I woke to Lorcan trying to rape me. I fought as best I could with my hands tied, but then Emory came and pulled a gun on him. I want to thank her."

"Mario has …" I pause to swallow hard. "She's been in one of our safe houses. Lorcan knows she led us to you. He wants her dead."

"That's not going to happen."

"No, it's not. I'm going to kill him with my bare hands as soon as I get out of here."

"I'm not going to rest until they all pay for our baby."

"Me either, baby. This is far from over."

CHAPTER FORTY-SIX

Recovery

Rico

Six months later ...

"Human" by Rag'n'Bone Man blasts through the speakers in our home gym as I push my body to its max. However, I don't feel like I'm only human. I've crossed over into a different zone.

My one goal is to fully recover so I can avenge my wife and child. I haven't stopped seeing red since Oni told me we lost our baby and that bastard tried to violate her.

I know exactly where the brothers and Alyissa are. We've trapped them in New York City. All the families know the deal.

If anyone aids Alyissa or those two assholes, their entire family will be wiped off the map with them. They can't move outside the five boroughs without running into my men, one of the crews, or one of the other families.

Everyone has been ordered to bring them to me on sight. I have a torture room ready. They bring them in; I'm going to put them through all nine circles of hell.

"Rico," Oni calls as she enters the gym and turns down the music.

I rack the bar and sit up. Sweat is dripping down my face and chest. Oni walks over and hands me a towel.

"Babe, you're pushing too hard. Come chill with me."

"Not yet. I still have a few more sets and I want to hit the treadmill."

"Rico, come on. You can't keep pushing yourself like this."

"I love you, Oni, but I'm not going to stop pushing until I make this right."

She cups my face in both hands and straddles my lap. I settle my arms around her waist and look into her eyes. This woman is so fucking strong.

"I love you too," she says. "Believe me, I want them dead as much as you do. It's going to happen. We're going to make that happen together, like we do everything else."

"We should have been together when they took you. I'm never going to forgive myself. I need to do this. I need to get back to a hundred percent so this can be handled."

"Rico, this isn't your fault. You have to forgive yourself. There's something I should have told you before we even left for that trip. You might be angry with me when you find out, but you should know."

"Tell me. I'm not going to be angry. Just talk to me."

"You know how you kept asking me what was going on?"

"Yeah, something was off. I knew something was bothering you. That's why I planned the trip."

"Well, Emory had reached out and asked me to meet up with her. When I did, she told me Lorcan and Mason were coming after me."

I groan. I can't believe she's just telling me this. I asked her if someone was fucking with her. She told me it was nothing.

"Listen, I hadn't brushed it off. I told you I was fine because I had it under control. At first, I didn't know if it was a credible threat.

"Then, I didn't care either way. I planned to put them down the day you surprised me with the trip—"

"Why didn't you tell me then?"

She gives me a pointed look. "If I would have told you once we arrived at the island, you would have canceled our trip and come back here to put them down yourself.

"I was going to tell you when we got back. Who knew Romano was funding their operation? I wouldn't have thought that in a million years.

"They didn't have the money to follow us, so I wasn't pressed about it. My mistake. It will never happen again."

"Underestimating our enemies or not telling me what the heck is going on?"

"Both. I'm so sorry."

"I'm still not blaming you for this. They took something from us. I should have protected you, and I didn't. That's still on me, no matter what."

"Yeah, but Rico—"

"When this is over, maybe I'll be able to forgive myself."

"Fine, but can I ask you for something?"

"Anything."

"Instead of burning your legs out on the treadmill, will you use them to give back what they took?"

I nip her chin and palm her ass in my hands. "Are you asking me to fuck you and give you a baby?"

"Yeah, handsome, you're looking hot from all the working out. I need a little attention from my husband. Do you think your body is up for a good fuck? I miss you."

I take her lips and devour her. Palming the back of her head, I keep her close. She wants a baby, and so do I. I'm not about to deny her.

So for the next two hours, I take my wife all over this gym. I keep her calling my name and coming all over me. When I'm done, we end up on a mat panting for air with smiles on our faces.

I can't help praying that she's pregnant again. I'll protect them with my life this time.

Oni

"There she is," Emory says.

It looks like Alyissa couldn't take being in hiding for a minute longer. Two of my guys caught her trying to leave the city. Wrong move.

I got the call during dinner that she was on the move. I decided to go get the bitch myself. Emilia and Emory asked to come with me after finding out what I was up to.

Emory has been staying with Mario and Emilia, so she overheard when the call came in. Rico agreed to allow me this as long as he and the guys followed to keep an eye on me. A part of me had hoped the other two would try to run with her.

I want this to be over. Rico is obsessed with making them pay. His recovery is the only reason the three are still breathing. Rico wants to handle this himself. However, taking those hits to the leg and his back is taking longer to heal than he would like.

"I'll make this quick. Open the hatch for me, will you?" I say and hop out of the SUV.

My guys have Alyissa's car surrounded. She's in a blacked-out BMW. The bitch was too stupid to try to escape in something inconspicuous.

I pull the door open and drag her ass out by the back of her hair. She's kicking and screaming as I drag her to the SUV. Rico stands with his arms folded over his chest in front of the SUV he, Mario, Ed, Al, and Fredo rode in.

I stumble from all her thrashing and get pissed off. I turn and punch her in the face. Her nose gushes blood and she stops flailing to cover it.

"Now shut the fuck up," I snarl.

I drag her the rest of the way to the SUV and toss her ass into the cargo area. The guys are all laughing behind me as they watch on. Rico shakes his head at me, then winks.

Emilia places tape over Alyissa's mouth as Emory zip-ties her hands and feet. I slam the door closed on her whimpers then roll my eyes. She has some fucking nerve.

"Let's go. It's going to be a long night," I say as I go to get back into the car.

I smile to myself as I climb back into my seat. Once everyone is in the truck, I peel off. I have plans for Alyissa.

***

"It's all ready when you are," Rico says as he pops his head into the room I've been waiting in.

I nod as I finish my bag of chips and crumble it in my hands as I stand. Lazily, I saunter toward him. He dips his head and pecks my lips.

"Don't get lost in there," he murmurs and taps my ass.

"Never."

I pat his cheek and head for my mission. When I step into the room we're holding Alyissa in, I find her curled up in the corner, trembling. She looks like shit.

I beat the shit out of her when she got bold and tried to attack me. Emory had cut the ties, not thinking much of it, but Alyissa took that as an invitation to lunge at me. I whipped her ass like she stole something.

I have never rag-dolled someone with so much force. I'm surprised I didn't break her neck. She'll think twice about trying that shit again.

I scoff and go to grab her. Grabbing her by the back of her long-ass hair once again, I drag her behind me. She starts kicking and screaming again.

"No, no, no. Please, I'm sorry. I only gave them money. Lorcan came to me with his plan.

"I don't deserve this. You took my fiancé from me. How am I paying for this? Rico was going to marry me," she sobs.

"He was never your fiancé, you crazy bitch. And if you don't shut the fuck up, I'm going to hack you up into little pieces until you stop all the fucking screaming."

"What are you going to do to me? I just want to go home."

"Oh, honey. You're going home all right," I scoff.

Emory opens the door that leads outside to my little surprise. I already have on my boots, I'm ready. Not missing a step, I drag her ass out the door.

Alyissa's screams are music to my ears as I slowly pull this bitch over a bed of hot coals. When I get to the end, I step off the coals and turn to step on her face, pressing down with all my weight as she hollers.

The smell of burned flesh fills the air. One of her eyes looks like it fell out along the way as I dragged her. Blisters are forming all over her front.

"Please stop. I don't deserve this," she gasps out.

"Excuse me? Say that again." I seethe.

"I don't deserve this. Please."

"My baby didn't deserve what you motherfuckers did to me. Did that stop any of you?"

I kick the shit out of her, right in the face. She flips over on her back and screams some more. I put my foot on her face and press her head down into the coals. Her screams are muffled by my boot.

I keep pressing until she stops moving. Fuck, I didn't want to kill her so soon. I lift my foot and look down at her. Her chest isn't moving.

"Oops," I sing and step back.

Rico stands against the side of the house, laughing. He straightens and opens his arms. I saunter over to him and melt into his embrace.

"One down, two to go," he croons.

CHAPTER FORTY-SEVEN

Squealing Pigs

Rico

Two months later …

Today is the day. I will finally wipe these two bastards from the face of the earth. Emory has told me that Mason was trying to help Oni, but we're beyond that.

Oni and I don't give a fuck. He lured Oni into Lorcan's clutches. He didn't come to me right away with Oni's location. Losing our baby was as much on him as it was on Lorcan.

If he wants forgiveness for that, he's barking up the wrong tree. I'm glad Oni hasn't tried to save him. He doesn't deserve her forgiveness or mine.

"They're bringing them up," Mario says as Oni and I wait on top of this skyscraper for them.

I've already spent a day with Lorcan after Ed and Mario collected the brothers and brought them to me. I beat the shit out of the bastard for twelve hours straight. If you ask me, Alyissa got it easy.

My thoughts are confirmed as Ed shoves Lorcan onto the rooftop. Ed wanted to go collect them from the shithole apartment in Queens where they've been hiding right on the outskirts of Brooklyn.

He took a bullet for me and Oni, so I was happy to grant his wish. When he asked again to bring them here, I shrugged and agreed once more. I see a few new bruises on Lorcan and Mason is holding his ribs.

I guess my cousin didn't like the job I did. I snort as I look Lorcan's fucked-up face over. One of his eyes is shut and he's sporting a permanent smile from my hot blade.

He's lucky I didn't feed him his dick. I had planned to, but Mario stopped me before I did, claiming the asshole would bleed out before tonight. I promised Oni we would do this together, so I stopped before it was too late.

That's the only mercy these motherfuckers will get from me. I have no more patience for this or them. Finding out Lorcan's supposed plan only pissed me off more.

Mario and Ed lead the brothers to the edge of the roof and stand them there as if lining them up for the firing squad. I pull my gun and check it. Oni does the same.

"What's she doing here?" Lorcan snarls as he looks at Oni with his good eye.

"I made your father a promise. I'm going to make good on my word," Oni says like she's talking about the weather.

"Oh yeah, what was the promise?"

"I told him when I found you two, I would make sure you both die screaming like he did."

"So it's true? You had something to do with his death?" Mason says as if he's shocked.

"Oh no, Mason. I didn't have *something* to do with it; I did it. He squealed like the pig he was." Oni tilts her head to the side.

"Just like your brother here. You know, I might have spared you if my baby hadn't been taken from me. However, you're going to scream for me too."

Mason looks at Oni with wide eyes. I laugh. I guess he doesn't see the best friend he used to know.

Lorcan scoffs. "I'd like to see that."

"Is that right?" Oni says and nods toward me.

"Yeah, bitch. I wish you would—"

He doesn't get to finish the words as Oni plants her foot in his chest and kicks him over the edge. At the same time, I kick Mason over with his brother.

Just as promised, they both scream as their bodies fall sixty stories to the ground. Oni walks into my side and I wrap an arm around her.

This didn't bring our baby back, which leaves a bitter taste in my mouth, but my chest loosens just a bit. If nothing else, it feels like I can finally forgive my uncle. What he did brought this version of Oni to me.

The version that I need by my side. I will never regret that. I turn to face her and squeeze my arms around her.

"I have to tell you something," she says as she looks up into my eyes.

"What's up, gorgeous?"

"I'm pregnant."

EPILOGUE

Second Time Around

Oni

Five years later …

Rico has done it again. He has pulled off a surprise I didn't see coming. Don Gallo has whisked me off to Italy for our second wedding.

He planned the whole thing without me. I think this wedding is better than our last one would have been. Fifteen years of marriage and I still love this man more than life itself.

"Mama, Mama," our two boys call as they come running toward us as we dance on the dance floor for our first dance.

Rico's eyes light up as he grins down at me. I return the smile then turn to face our twins. My smile broadens when I see their sister trying to toddle after them. She's two years younger than her brothers.

I will never not have what-ifs about our first baby, but I love these three to life. They are my world. There is never a dull moment with them around.

Rico lifts both our boys into his arms and I pick up our princess. This moment is perfect as our little family sways together. I look around the room at all the love we have around us.

I spot my mom and Uncle Emilio. A smile comes to my face. I have to laugh.

"And that was his endgame. He made everything right for her," I say.

Rico looks over my head and snorts. "He paid the price and we elevated."

"But we all learned a lesson," I finish.

"Yup. Sounds about right."

"I wouldn't change a thing," I say out loud.

"Neither would I. Who knew that little car thief would be the love of my life?"

"Don Gallo, I'm so much more than a car thief, I'll have you know."

"That you are, baby. That you are."

ABOUT THE AUTHOR

Blue Saffire, award-winning, bestselling author of over eighty contemporary romance novels and novellas, writes with the intention to touch the heart and the mind. Blue hooks, weaves, and loops multiple series, keeping you engaged in her worlds. Blue writes for her own publishing company, Perceptive Illusions, as Blue Saffire, as well as Royal Blue.

Blue and her husband live in a house filled with laughter and creativity in Long Island, NY. Both working hard to build the Blue brand and cultivate their love for the arts. Creative is their family affair.

Blue holds an MBA in Marketing and Project Management, as well as an MED in Instructional Technology and Curriculum Design. She is also an NLP Master Practitioner.

ACKNOWLEDGMENTS

That's it for the Vella stories. I've completed Touchdown and Unforgivable. These were cool detours. This one took a few turns I wasn't expecting. I was trying to go sweet, but this one didn't want any such thing. LOL.

Oni and Rico will always hold a special place in my heart. It started out on Vella, moved to Patreon, and has finished here. I hope you enjoyed them.

My dear reader friends, thank you so much for your continued support and patience. I want you to always know how much I appreciate you. I'm working extra hard to bring you the goods this year. Thank you for allowing me to bring you an escape.

Thank you for the encouraging emails, videos, posts, shares, comments, and DMs. Y'all are ah-mazing. Remember, sharing is caring. If you have a friend who reads, let them know about me, please.

Boo, thank you for listening. I know it's been interesting this year with all the books talking in my head. Thank you for supporting my dream.

Much praises to be God. This couldn't be done without my source. Thank you for allowing me to tap in. I continue to walk by faith and not by sight. Thank you for your presence and your blessings. Always unapologetically blessed and highly favored.

Next!

Wait, there is more to come! You can stay updated with my latest releases, learn more about me, the author, and be a part of contests by subscribing to my newsletter at

www.BlueSaffire.com

If you enjoyed *Unforgivable*, I'd love to hear

your thoughts and please feel free to leave a

review on my website. And when you do, please let me

know by emailing me TheBlueSaffire@gmail.com

or leave a comment on Facebook https://www.facebook.com/BlueSaffireDiaries or Twitter @TheBlueSaffire

Other books by Blue Saffire

Placed in Best Reading Order

Also available …

Legally Bound

Legally Bound 2: Against the Law

Legally Bound 3: His Law

Perfect for Me

Hush 1: Family Secrets

Ballers: His Game

Brothers Black 1: Wyatt the Heartbreaker

Legally Bound 4: Allegations of Love

Hush 2: Slow Burn

Legally Bound 5.0: Sam

Yours 1: Losing My Innocence

Yours 2: Experience Gained

Yours 3: Life Mastered

Ballers 2: His Final Play

Legally Bound 5.1: Tasha Illegal Dealings

Brothers Black 2: Noah

Legally Bound 5.2: Camille

Legally Bound 5.3 & 5.4 Special Edition

Where the Pieces Fall

Legally Bound 5.5: Legally Unbound

Brothers Black 4: Braxton the Charmer

Broken Soldier

Brothers Black 5: Felix the Watcher

A Home for Christmas

Doctor Feel Good

Brothers Black 6: Ryan the Joker

Brothers Black 7: Johnathan the Fixer

Wild Hearts

Pieces of Trevor's Heart

Ballers 3: His Team

Ronan Book 1: Kings of New York

Dylan Book 2: Kings of New York

Brooklyn Book 3: Kings of New York

Coming Soon…

King of Gods Book 4: Immortal Iron Brothers Series
King of Past Book 5: Immortal Iron Brothers Series
Jamie: Book 4: Kings of New York

Other Blue Saffire Series

Hold On To Me Series
My Funny Valentine
Be My Valentine

Hitter Squad Series
Remember Me

Work Husband Series
Unexpected Lovers
My Best Friend's Wish
The Ones Left Behind
The Last Ones Standing

The Lost Souls MC Series
Forever
Never
Always

The Moran Brothers Series
Love Notes
Stay With Me

The Ahole Club Series**
Pit Book 1: The A**hole Club
Ox Book 5: The A**hole Club
Kelex Book 6: The A**hole Club

Immortal Iron Brothers Series
King of Knights Book 1
King of Inferno Book 2
King of Tides Book 3

Touchdown (standalone)

Check out Blue Saffire exclusives on the
BlueSaffire.com website
The Fixer
His Miracle Baby

Dark Disciples Series
Razor
Dane
Trip
Bay Breeze Series
Professor Jones
Room 112

Other books from Evei Lattimore Collection Books by Blue Saffire
Black Bella 1

Destiny Series
Destiny 1: Life Decisions
Destiny 2: Decisions of the Next Generation
Destiny 3 coming soon …

Star

Other books from Royal Blue Gay Romance Collection written by Blue Saffire
Kyle's Reveal
Beau's Redemption